"WOULD YOU LIKE ME TO STOP?"

"Maybe in about forty years, but I doubt it," Dane said in a ragged voice.

Tildie smiled. He held a breath while her fingertips edged along the waistband of his slacks.

"Are you sure you want to do this?"

"I only want to think about the two of us in this room now," she pleaded. "I don't want to think about tomorrow." Her round blue eyes were wide.

"What if I want more?" He put his arms around her and gently lowered her onto the divan.

"Only tonight," she whispered. "Agreed?"

"You know we never agree on anything," he said, bending to tug on her vulnerable lower lip with his teeth. His eyes glittered in the lamplight as he slowly unfastened the buttons of her blouse one at a time....

ABOUT THE AUTHOR

Avid romance fans will no doubt recognize Joanne Bremer's name. Joanne, who makes her home in Deshler, Ohio, is a successful romance writer, though this is her first book for Harlequin. Between books, Joanne is kept busy running a local newspaper, *The Leipsic Messenger*, with her husband. Yet she still manages to keep her life romantic. Like Micki, the heroine's little girl in *It's All in the Game*, Joanne makes a habit of wishing on stars!

Joanne Bremer

IT'S ALL IN THE GAME

Harlequin Books

TORONTO • NEW YORK • LONDON
AMSTERDAM • PARIS • SYDNEY • HAMBURG
STOCKHOLM • ATHENS • TOKYO • MILAN

Published April 1988

First printing February 1988
Second printing April 1988

ISBN 0-373-70302-3

CHAPTER ONE

Dear Captain Starblazer,

I have watched your cartoon show *Star Power* every day since I was a little kid, so I want to warn you. On Monday morning my mom, Matilda Moore, is coming to Fun Design to stop your show. She has an important job and people listen when she talks, so be careful. Sometimes she does things that no one wants her o do, like sell her car to get enough money for classes at Ohio State, or yell at my brother Jeremy because he broke a window with his baseball.

Please don't let her take *Star Power* off the air. She doesn't understand anything about space exploration or Cyclon or the royal court of the Sercerian moon or anything like that.

P.S. I like Spinner too. I think he's cute.

Respectfully,
Michelle Moore
age 8 almost 9

Dear Michelle,

Thank you for the warning. I'll keep an eye out for Matilda and make sure the planet stays safe. Thanks for caring about us. Be a good girl and always do what your mom says. Spinner and I will see you at the space station for more galactic adventures.

Your Friend Always,
Captain Starblazer
Defender of the Planet

Matilda Moore hauled her new attaché case across the worn seat of the cab and stepped out onto the curb. The June breeze caused her linen bolero and the tie of her print blouse to flutter. The outfit was borrowed; only a couple of accessories she wore belonged to her—the no-nonsense taupe shoulder bag and the matching size-nine pumps. Unfortunately her sister Sally's wardrobe for her work in real estate wasn't quite buttoned down or tailored enough for a promising attorney on her first solo law case. But it would have to do until Tildie got on her feet. Tildie tugged at the taupe dirndl skirt one last time; the skirt accommodated her sister's average height, but revealed too much knee on Tildie.

She felt like a green recruit with the new briefcase her father had given her as a graduation present clutched in her hand, but there was no reason for anyone to know that. She would use all her talents, including her wit and her keen ability to think on her feet, to argue her case, and with high-heeled shoes she could look most anyone square in the eye. Somewhat cautiously she looked up at the clown logo of the Fun Design Toy Company, Inc. Today, at age 35, with two children and a defaulted marriage behind her, she was starting her first career.

She had already met tough resistance about pursuing this case—at home—so there was no reason an executive at Fun Design should deter her—or so she tried to tell herself. Contrary to her daughter Micki's opinion, Matilda did not carry Kryptonite in her briefcase. She had no intention of destroying the eight-year-old's favorite cartoon superhero, Captain Starblazer; however she did have a bone to pick with the Captain and his creators. That's what she'd told Micki, the staunch cartoon fanatic, at breakfast this morning. Micki was determined to protect her cartoon hero, and had told her mother as much in a sophisticated tone:

"I don't want you to persecute Captain Starblazer. It's un-American. Really, mom, it's embarrassing. No one else's mother tries to destroy institutions and great American heroes that millions of children watch every day."

"Not everyone's mother is a children's advocate."

"Why couldn't you have gone into corporate law like everyone else? I won't be able to hold my head up at school," Micki grumbled. "And what will Captain Starblazer say when my mother—"

"You know that I won't really see Captain Starblazer," Tildie reasoned with the child, who sounded as if she were eight going on twenty-one. "Captain Starblazer is a cartoon character. He's not real."

Micki sighed and rolled her blue eyes, as if she couldn't believe her own mother's naïveté. "I know he's real, mom, and he'll be very upset with you."

"Better watch out. He'll blast you with his laser gun, mom," Tildie's thirteen-year-old son, Jer, warned with a laugh, tormenting his younger sister.

"That's not funny!" a hurt Micki responded. "Besides, he's chivalrous. He wouldn't hurt a woman."

"He's what?" Jer inquired, amused.

"He's kind to women and admires them from afar," the brainy, righteous-sounding eight-year-old intoned. "Women like that. They think it's sexy, don't they, mom?"

"I wouldn't know. I'm only a mother." Tildie's serious blue eyes met and matched her daughter's.

"He likes mothers—he told me so!" Micki said to redeem herself.

"How could he tell you? He's not real!" Jer argued.

"He is! I can prove it!"

"Go ahead!"

"I...I...don't want to!" Micki clamped her lips tight and swung her wheat-colored pigtails as she turned away from her brother.

"Honey, I like Captain Starblazer, too," Tildie said reassuringly.

"See, I told you. Women do like him!" Micki finished her argument with her brother.

"Don't humor her, mom," Jer said with a groan on his way out the door.

"Do you think he's handsome, too?" Micki asked her mother in a dreamy tone.

Tildie ignored the question and began to list the Captain's saving graces. "He protects his planet from destruction and he fights evil," she said firmly, looking into Micki's large eyes. Sometimes, she thought, it seemed as if the kid had skipped childhood entirely. "I don't always agree with the way he fights it, but that's another argument. Our main complaint is that Fun Design, not the Captain, makes a lot of money by packaging the cartoon show with the toys they sell—"

"You really do like him, don't you?" Micki flashed the wide smile guaranteed to win her mother over. "It's hard to watch the show so many times and not like him." Micki stood up and put her arm around her mother's shoulders. "I know he would like you too."

"That would be very big of him," Tildie said with a straight face. "Micki, we only want people who sell Captain Starblazer toys to change some of their advertising practices, and the Captain to do a little less laser blasting, okay?"

"But if the Captain doesn't blast Cyclon, he wouldn't win."

"I want the children who watch the program to be winners. Kids just like you."

"But if he stops blasting, the bad guys would win!"

"Bad guys never win," Tildie assured her daughter as she gave her a hug.

"Not with Duke Starblazer around!" Micki began to sing: "'Ta-ta-ta-da-Tah! Defender of the Planet! He is always there . . .'"

Tildie Moore found herself humming the silly tune now as she pushed open the glass doors of the home office and manufacturing plant of Star Power toys.

"Welcome to Fun Design, home of the Captain Starblazer doll. Our business is putting fun in your life," the receptionist said in a lilting voice as she looked up from her work. There was a ceramic clown holding pencils on her desk, and smiling faces on her stationery. "May I help you?"

"Yes." Tildie wondered how many people the toy company had interviewed before they'd found someone with a voice that was somewhere between Big Bird's and Lamb Chop's. "I'm Matilda Moore. I have an appointment with Mr. Tundry in advertising." Tildie spoke clearly and succinctly. This was the chance for which she'd worked and studied for many, many hours until her blue eyes had turned red. She vowed to remember this day, this minute, this case, as the beginning of her new and better life. She had started with Nigel and Associates six months ago, and this was the first case the senior partners had allowed her to tackle on her own.

"My appointment is for ten o'clock with Mr. Tundry." Tildie answered before the question. "I'm an attorney with Nigel and Associates." Matilda enjoyed the inherent weight of the firm's name. "I'm here to discuss the *Star Power* cartoon show."

"Yes. We're very proud of our Captain." The woman spoke of him as though he were a real person, and Tildie had to hold back a smile.

She had studied hours of cartoon footage, and by this time, she could see the blond space-age hero in her sleep. "I'm here to discuss the advertising practices for the Defender of the Planet products—including the Captain Starblazer doll—with Mr. Tundry. I spoke with him yesterday by telephone," she said with confidence, telling herself that after working two jobs and going to night school for six years, she could do anything from slinging hash browns to arguing legal precedents to intimidating advertising executives from million-dollar corporations. The brunette receptionist pored over the schedule again, read the notes near the phone, and then cricked her neck to look up at Tildie's dramatic, finely sculpted features.

"I'm sorry, Ms Moore, you're not on Mr. Tundry's appointment schedule."

"This is the second of June, and it is ten o'clock. Mr. Tundry is expecting me, I'm sure." She refused to allow anyone at Fun Design to give her the runaround. She'd been warned about this very possibility by the group who'd engaged her services.

Members of Better Television for Children had come to Nigel and Associates wanting someone to present their complaint regarding Fun Design's advertising policies on "Star Power." Tildie was perfect for the job since her youngest child watched the cartoon program every day at the same time, on the same station. The case was a public-service project for the firm with no retaining fee being paid by the client—that was how it happened to filter down to the lowest associate on the totem pole—but it was still a plum, since she would be making a presentation on children's programing at a special hearing of the Federal Communications Commission.

The case wasn't of great importance to the firm, except for publicity purposes. Nigel and Associates spared no expense investigating cases that filled the coffers of the senior partners, but for this *gratis* service case, Tildie had been allowed only a few dollars for postage. Even the cab fare today had come out of Tildie's own pocket; she had already mentally altered the Moore weekly menu to include plenty of hamburgers. The case could result in an important precedent for the welfare of children, and that was a cause Tildie believed in strongly.

"Would you wait a moment, please?" the receptionist requested in a cool tone, motioning toward a nearby grouping of chairs. After Tildie reluctantly left the desk and chose a chair, the receptionist picked up the phone and made several hurried calls between answering incoming ones. "Fun Design. Putting fun in your life is our business."

The temporarily sidetracked attorney tried not to appear agitated while she waited, and forced herself to stare at the grinning clown on the wall that held the company name. She could only think of the mountain of paper on her desk that she needed to go through in preparation for the SynTech Incorporated case. Tildie listened to bits of the next phone conversation. "…Ms Moore is waiting now…he's tied up in conference too…" From the receptionist's tiny apologetic smile Tildie guessed she was being shifted from one company executive to the next.

Bits and pieces of the *Star Power* theme song continued to intrude on Tildie's brainwaves as she sat there—Micki's fault since she'd sung, hummed and whistled it on the way to school this morning. "No matter what the odds, your friend is always there…Defender of the Planet!" The song marched through Tildie's brain unrelentingly. She smiled as she remembered Micki's enthusiastic expression when she slid out of the car on her way to school. "You know, mom, while you and Captain Starblazer are working together, you could fall in love with him. It's perfect!" Tildie nearly laughed thinking that despite Micki's attempts at sophistication, the childlike qualities in her usually won out. What a kid! And what an imagination, thinking that her on-the-ground mother would be working with—and falling for—a space-age cartoon super hero!

"Ms Moore . . . ?" The song and accompanying thoughts faded as Tildie looked over at the receptionist. "Mr. Tundry is tied up right now . . . ."

"Then perhaps I could speak with Mr. Carson in finance."

"He's in a conference."

"Or Mr.—?"

"Dane Scott, our celebrity Fun Design spokesman, will be right with you as soon as he can be found." The Lamb Chop voice tittered. "His secretary says he's gone fishing, but sometimes Mr. Scott leaves funny messages like that when he's just stepping out."

"I don't find that amusing." Tildie figured that she had filtered down through the higher echelon of Fun Design executives until she had bottomed out with the company's spokesman, who probably knew nothing about Fun Design's advertising practices.

"Yes, of course." The receptionist coughed discreetly. "I'll buzz Mr. Scott again."

Matilda had heard of Dane Scott, of course. Ohio regularly celebrated its wealth of astronauts: John Glenn, the first man in orbit, now a popular senator and presidential hopeful; Neil Armstrong, the first man to have set foot on the moon, currently a professor at Chicago University; Amy Noroff, who was involved in the current shuttle program and was scheduled to go up late next year; and Dane Scott. She actually didn't remember much about him. His Sky Lab flight was years ago, when she'd been preoccupied with her first baby. He'd dropped out of sight after that—until eighteen months ago, when Columbus, Ohio's favorite son returned as a part-time race driver and part-time after-dinner speaker. What could he know about the advanced advertising strategies of *Star Power*?

Bert Tundry, of advertising, was in office 105 according to the information board that Tildie had glanced at a dozen times while she'd been waiting in reception. The man was only five doors away, but it was apparent that no one had any intention of allowing her to see him. When the petite receptionist escorted a businessman into office 103, Tildie slipped through another door marked Employees Only, and walked down a corridor that eventually turned and followed a parallel course to the executive offices. She heard voices as she got close to one of the doors, and it opened.

"Certainly you can handle this one. How dangerous can a Matilda be?"

More than you could ever imagine, Tildie thought. The fellow speaking so casually obviously didn't recall the hurricane of the same name.

"She's an attorney from Nigel and Associates, not the president of a mothers' club."

"We more than meet all the federal safety standards," the calm, slightly bored voice reasoned. "How bad can her news be?"

"We shouldn't take any chances. I think we're going to need your golden touch on this one. After all, you're the celebrity spokesman for Fun Design, Dane."

The smooth, playful tenor laughed again. "I told you before, Bert, the Fun Design spokesman gives speeches and writes the occasional letter. He doesn't entertain hostile attorneys like Matilda Moore.'' He hesitated. ''Why does that name sound familiar?''

''Because she's at reception waiting to speak with you.''

''I don't have time to play tour guide, Bert.'' The door knob rattled again. ''As you can see, I've got my jogging shoes on and I'm late. Watch me walk out the door.''

''It better be the back door,'' a woman's voice warned him.

''Maggie, what would I do without a secretary like you?'' The voice bubbled into pleasant laughter. ''Relax, Bert, you can handle it. The Moore woman is all yours. And Maggie, would you have those prints ready for me later? I'm on my way.''

So, Dane Scott was trying to duck out of meeting with her, Matilda thought in annoyance. She would certainly mention that when—and if—she spoke to him. She straightened her bolero jacket and smoothed the slim skirt to prepare herself before surprising Tundry, but when she looked up she was startled to a halt.

''Whoa! Collision course.'' Dane Scott laughed and protected her from contact with guiding hands at her waist. ''Are you all right?'' His voice held genuine concern.

''I didn't know you were at star speed yet,'' she murmured. Her first instinct had been to fend off his broad chest with the palm of her hand. Her long graceful fingers and tapered pink nails provided a contrast to his sporty orange shirt.

''I'm sorry I ran into you. But…ah…there's usually not anyone in this hall.'' His smile was apologetic. ''However—'' he searched her face as though he were collecting vital fragments of information from her pointed chin and the smooth blond hair that turned under slightly to meet her delicate jaw line— ''you may be exactly the person I wanted to meet.''

"That's unlikely." Tildie stared relentlessly into a pair of sparkling eyes framed by full, expressive brows. She had hoped that she had heard her last line when she'd stopped waiting tables six months ago. She certainly recognized one when she heard it. Then why did his clear eyes look so Scout's-honor sincere? "I had the distinct impression that you were avoiding me."

"Never."

Tildie ignored the stir she felt at the nearly whispered word and the warm circling motion of his sure hand on her back, a motion gradually increasing in pressure.

"Believe me, it's my pleasure." His shy, boyish expression knocked her off-balance for a moment, until it grew into a smile that former astronaut-heroes undoubtedly used to drop women in their tracks. Suddenly things seemed too familiar.

Tildie stepped away from him and lifted her chin. "Perhaps you'll change your mind when you discover why I'm here."

His expression was curious and he seemed to be studying her carefully, especially the way her mouth moved and the manner in which her round eyes avoided his interested gaze.

"We're both busy people, Mr. Scott," she said impatiently. "So let's save time. I represent a group of parents and concerned citizens who wish to register a complaint about the advertising policies on *Star Power*."

"I see." His appraising eyes acknowledged that she was very serious. "I believe Mr. Tundry would be much better—"

"I agree. But it appears that he's made his escape." She gestured to the now-empty office. "So it seems it's up to you." Without warning the *Star Power* theme song clicked into her mind again— "He is always there...Defender of the Planet...he'll never let you down..."

"I always do my best, Miss . . . ?" His raised brows and twinkling eyes drew her attention to sun-burnished hair that was combed easily back off his smooth forehead. Similarly, his All American Hero smile attracted her eye to the long, easy laugh lines beside his mouth, and to the deep cleft in his sturdy chin. He looked like . . .

"You're Captain Starblazer," she said, verbalizing the absurd thought. But it was true! She was standing face-to-face with the imaginary hero, just as her eight-year-old daughter had insisted she would. It was impossible! Yet after having researched *Star Power* and Captain Starblazer for dozens of hours, she'd recognize the crusader anywhere. "You're a lot shorter—"

"Painfully honest, are we?" Dane Scott said, the deep laugh lines creasing his tanned cheeks. Tildie couldn't help thinking that the whisper of gray at his temples couldn't make him a day younger than forty years. Yet the pale orange polo shirt that gently hugged his biceps and the trim khaki slacks around his lean waist argued that assumption.

"And older—"

He laughed at her candor. "That's not the way to win interviews and influence captains." Dane Scott seemed an expert at using his unassuming nature and sincere manner to camouflage his own analysis of her. She sensed that he didn't miss a trick.

"I've studied the Captain thoroughly," she explained.

"How very flattering."

Bert Tundry was right, Tildie said to herself. *He does have a golden touch.*

He smiled. "I'm sorry I'll have to miss our interview." His piercing glance took in her borrowed suit that unfortunately hugged her curved frame when it should have declared that business was foremost. "But I'm on my way to an appointment. If you follow this hallway around the corner, you will be back at—"

"You aren't going to get out of our meeting that easily, Mr. Scott," she said, sensing a brush-off.

"Well, it certainly hasn't been easy so far," he replied dryly. "Not only was my ego shot down in flames, there was also this!" He held up a piece of white drawing paper creased from their unexpected meeting. His voice suddenly acquired mock severity, but his eyes were jovial. "Your briefcase could be registered as a lethal weapon, Miss...?"

"I'm Matilda Fitzsimmons-Moore."

"So you've met at last," a woman said as she came to the open door.

"Maggie, this is—"

"Ms Moore," Tildie said. "I'm an attorney with Nigel and Associates—"

"Heavy-duty firm," Dane Scott informed his secretary, his gaze never leaving Tildie.

"I represent a grass-roots organization called Better Television for Children."

"The BTC, of course. Make a note of that, Maggie. Would you also contact Roy Baker to let him know I'll be delayed a few minutes, and locate Charlie Patrick, please?" The latter request reflected an organized mind behind his easy style, and Tildie couldn't help but admire it.

"Right, boss. See what you get for sneaking out the back door?" Maggie winked and her laughter was teasing as she disappeared back into the office. Dane turned his attention back to Tildie, and she mentally postured her argument before she met his frightfully honest eyes again. They were the kind that looked back from recruiting posters, representing honor and duty. A Few Good Men. His face lacked the fierceness of a marine's, but she suspected that his pleasant features hid a steely intelligence that didn't overlook a detail.

As professionally as she could, she said, "I'd like to formally request your cooperation in setting up interviews with the Fun Design executive body in charge of advertising, and the people responsible for the content of *Star Power*, so I can express the BTC's concerns and points of contention before the case is presented at the children's programming hearings in Washington."

"Do you ever smile, Ms Moore?" He shifted the crumpled drawing paper to his other hand and studied the subtle change in her expression.

"I realize everyone has a busy schedule." She ignored his personal question and wondered if he'd heard a word she'd said. "I could see everyone concerned at his or her convenience."

His raised brow conceded a point to her all-business style.

"I figure I could speak to all concerned in a week or two," she said at last. "It wouldn't take long."

"See Mr. Tundry. He can help you." Before she could speak, he turned and walked up the hall. Her only contact at Fun Design was taking jaunty strides away from her on well-worn tennis shoes. He was quick and compact, just about her own height. He looked more like a golfer or tennis pro than a company spokesman. A surge of anger washed over her. She'd waited half an hour to speak with someone and now he was taking off!

"Mr. Scott, you can help me." She hurried to catch up with him.

"I'm booked up today."

"A serious date at the race course, I suppose. I think our discussion may be more pressing than the long straightaway." The barbed remark designed to crush him into submission didn't even slow his gait.

"Obviously you've never seen me race."

"This isn't a game, Mr. Scott."

"Could you at least call me Dane or is that against some code of legal ethics?"

"You are *supposed* to confer with me. It's your job as Fun Design's spokesman. Or have you forgotten your responsibilities?" She meant for the statement to sting.

"They keep me awake nights," he said with more than a touch of sarcasm.

"What else could I expect from a man who skips out on his appointments and plays with toys for a living?"

"Not just any toys," he intoned as he kept walking, "Star Power toys! When in Rome . . . Show a little respect for the Captain."

"I don't play games, Mr. Scott, especially when the welfare of children is concerned. *Star Power* molds young minds."

"I like the sound of that—mind molder." He seemed incapable of a serious thought as his eyes glittered and his lips played impishly. "I'll suggest it for a new Fun Design game." He continued down the hall.

"Mr. Scott!" She dogged his steps until he stopped and pivoted. Surprised blue eyes met curious gray ones.

"Don't you ever lighten up, Ms Fitzsimmons-hyphen-Moore?" he said, breathing deeply.

"I'm here for the welfare of all the children who watch *Star Power*." She straightened her jacket and forced a courtroom edge into her voice. "I care about children. And it's time that someone stood up for them as consumers."

"A noble cause. And what's your law firm's cut of this action?" A skeptical smile bent one corner of his mouth.

She had footed the bill for this case and had a stack of denied requisitions on her desk to prove it. But something in his gray eyes told her he wouldn't believe that.

"Nigel and Associates is handling the case *gratis*."

"And praying for a lawsuit?"

She swallowed a retort before she spoke.

"The commercial advertisements played during *Star Power* leave a lot to be desired." She longed to wipe the crooked smile off his handsome face. "The audience is too young to recognize bullish sales techniques. And there's too much violence in the cartoon. So many explosions numb the sensitivity of young minds. Please, I need your help, Mr. Scott." For an instant his eyes mellowed, then the gray cooled to the color of smooth metal. Had there really been a vulnerable moment when he'd nearly volunteered to join her cause?

"I have another appointment."

"I feel a responsibility toward young children, as should the creators of a cartoon that thousands of kids watch every day. Don't you feel a responsibility, Mr. Scott?" He looked down slightly at her, but essentially they were locked eye to eye. She didn't know where all the anger she was feeling was coming from; the frustrations she had had to deal with thus far today were par for the course. To her relief, he blinked first.

"It's been a very enlightening discussion, Ms Moore. But you know how it is when the straightaway calls." He took her by the arm and marched her toward the red exit sign at the end of the hall, where she'd come in. "You're in a part of the building that is restricted from the public, by the way."

"I need to interview people connected with the cartoon series: the originator, the—" She could barely maintain her balance on her high heels as he quickly escorted her along.

"The studio that writes and animates the cartoon is Chicago-based. I suggest that you—"

"I've corresponded with them. I'd hoped I would get more results at the head office." *More and cheaper results,* she amended silently.

"Well, I'm afraid that *this* part of the head office is done fighting windmills, Ms Moore," he pronounced firmly as he continued to lead her quickly down the hall. "So if you'll excuse me—"

"The Federal Communications Commission will frown on this casual attitude toward children's advocates—"

"Casual? I think it's safe to say that it's impossible to have a casual conversation with you, Ms Moore. Someone will get back to you in a few weeks."

"The Commission will have met by then, and believe me, they'll have heard about your lack of cooperation."

"I heard we have a nine-eleven!" An aging bull of a man stepped around the corner and swaggered toward them with a smile that announced he welcomed trouble.

"Ms Moore, meet Charlie Patrick, our chief of security," Dane said curtly.

The old centurion hiked his belt over his intimidating paunch as if on cue, squinting his left eye slightly as he spoke. "How did you get into this restricted area, miss?"

"I had an appointment... I didn't know that I was in a restricted area..." She remembered the sign on the door that had said Employees Only. "It's really very complicated—"

"No. It's really very simple. We have rules here and everyone is to follow them. That's how we all get along so well," Charlie Patrick said as he held her other elbow, taking one stride for every two steps of hers.

"Charlie means that all visitors are to be registered and approved by our security chief—" Dane Scott bent forward to acknowledge the older man "—each properly identified and escorted at all times and restricted from certain areas of the plant."

"But you know I made an appointment and—"

"Not with me, you didn't." Amused, he watched the storm clouds gather in her eyes. "Don't protest too much in front of our security chief," Dane cautioned. "Like you, he takes his work very seriously. He likes people to follow procedures. Right, Charlie?"

"Strictly by the book, Scottie," Charlie responded, nodding his neatly trimmed white head. "When someone doesn't follow the rules, it makes an old retired cop like me suspicious, ya know what I mean? Makes a guy leery of people being where they ain't supposed to be. Even a pretty perpetrator like you."

She couldn't believe the barrel-chested ex-cop saw her as a threat. It was flattering in a way, but ridiculous.

"I'm an attorney—an officer of the court," she told him huffily.

"You sound like you're fresh out of law school," Charlie came back with a gravelly laugh.

"That's not the point," Tildie said, trying to hide her flushed cheeks. "It's not as though you're guarding the Hope Diamond here," she insisted in a softer tone, one that she hoped would get her farther. "The only things made here are toys."

"And I'm here to protect every one of 'em, and you are trespassing."

"We'll see if you can wangle your way out of this one, Ms Moore." Dane Scott was clearly enjoying the irony of the moment. "Try to avoid the old rubber hose, okay, Charlie?" He nudged the white-haired giant.

"Sure, Scottie." Tildie remembered the media had referred to Dane Scott as Scottie when he'd made his space flight. She also recalled a photograph of him climbing out of his spacecraft, helmet in hand, looking for all the world like a boy wonder with his infectious grin. It was broader, but not unlike the sly, confident smile that slanted across his fresh-scrubbed face now.

"I've seen tougher nuts to crack," the old cop teased.

Tildie glanced from the security officer to the former hero. She knew her only hope lay in that vulnerable light she had seen in Dane Scott's eyes earlier. She pulled away from their grasp and caught his arm to search his eyes once more.

"You could help me, Mr. Scott. You could help thousands of children who watch *Star Power*. The violence in the cartoon isn't necessary. The timing of the ads could be modified." She took a breath and met his curious eyes. "Captain Starblazer is a wonderful hero, but he could be better, if..." *Gold.* Pure gold flecks warmed his gray eyes, and she suddenly sensed that his attention wasn't due only to curiosity or politeness. She quickly averted her gaze and the gold light was gone.

"I do believe the counselor is trying to get out of a trespassing charge." The former astronaut laughed. "What do you think, chief?"

"Please, I—"

"Aha, the magic word!" Dane Scott exclaimed as he walked backward a few paces up the hall. "*Please.* It can open a lot of doors for you, Ms Moore." He stopped for a moment and studied her carefully. "Be gentle with her, Charlie," he said cheerfully, abandoning her to the chief of security. "The Captain would want it that way." His mirthful eyes mellowed for an instant. "Don't worry Ms Moore, you're in expert hands. It should only take a couple of hours to go through procedures, right, chief?" The men exchanged glances.

"Sure, Scottie. Give or take a minute."

"Not another hour! Not another minute!"

"In that case you can escort her out of the plant now, Charlie."

"The commission will hear about this! I've never been thrown out of any place in my life!" she called after the astronaut as he sauntered up the hall.

"Fun Design may open up a whole world of experiences for you, then, Ms Moore!"

CHAPTER TWO

Dear Captain Starblazer,

Matilda Moore is not a bad person. She is really quite smart and pretty and she's my mom. But she doesn't understand that kids know the difference between fantasy and everyday. We know that there really couldn't be any spaceship with weapons on it like Cyclon has.

She's spent too many years going to law school and working in a restaurant to make ends meet for Jeremy and me. My dad doesn't live here anymore, so mom has to work all the time.

Jer is my big brother, who only knows about baseball. I think my mom likes him best, because she used to play baseball with him at the park. But she hardly ever plays *Star Power* with me.

Mom says she likes you, but she doesn't believe you're real. Maybe if you'd talk to her while she's at Fun Design, she'd believe.

A loyal friend,
Micki Moore

Dane glimpsed Matilda Moore at the far end of the assembly line. It had been two days since their first uncomfortable meeting. He wondered if he should talk to her about "believing." He certainly wanted to be a believer again, wanted to have faith in people. Sweet Micki had so much faith in adults, thinking they wouldn't place weapons on spaceships. Her childlike trust made Dane feel hopeful and guilty at the same time. But he didn't want to think about the consequences of weapons in space just now, not when he was looking at someone as beautiful as Micki's mom.

He enjoyed studying the distinctive yet fragile planes of her cheekbones, the twin peaks of her upper lip and the precise corners of her mouth. He tried to picture the sophisticated attorney playing baseball in the park, burning them over home plate or snagging a grounder at short. But her pale lavender blouse, skirt, and fitted linen jacket only promoted a "dress for success" image.

The crusading attorney didn't seem the type to fight windmills. Yet he remembered how her blue eyes had pleaded for his help in the cause. What made her think he hadn't already protested the violence in the cartoon? he wondered, irritated. But maybe she already had guessed and that was why she'd needled him so much. The screenwriters, bent on a commercial success, hadn't listened to him any more than had the officials he'd worked with at NASA. The screenwriters had wanted a hit and NASA had needed to bolster a sagging budget.

Of course he disapproved, just as he had when the military had first approached the agency about carrying payloads. It was contrary to the original purpose and premise of the agency and against his own philosophy. So when he eventually discovered that a project he had worked on was to be used for military purposes, the good-natured boy genius, who had been handpicked out of the Massachusetts Institute of Technology to design some of NASA's most successful projects, had finally walked.

After that he had promised himself he wouldn't care, wouldn't believe in anyone or anything again. That was his only guarantee that he wouldn't be disappointed in people.

Then why did Matilda Moore's eyes haunt him? Why did she get under his skin?

The attorney was getting the public tour of the Fun Design plant because Charlie Patrick had wanted to keep her out of trouble until he could run a make on her. Dane watched her walk gracefully by thousands of Captain Starblazer dolls jiggling along the conveyor, each of them smiling at her. What the plastic heroes didn't know was that the lovely princess before them had the personality of a prickly pear. Maybe that was what had driven away Micki's father, who apparently didn't live with them anymore.

Dane knew instinctively that if he were so lucky to have a daughter, he'd never abandon her; he'd always be there. He had no idea that such a conviction had lain dormant in him all these years. Nor was he sure what or who had prompted the awakening: the little girl or the uptight attorney.

"I heard she was here to get information on *Star Power*," Roy Baker, the production supervisor, shouted above the noise in the factory, his eyes following her.

"She says she's a children's advocate," Dane answered.

"Is that some new kind of lawyer?" Roy questioned as he unconsciously straightened his tie. Without waiting for an answer, he asked, "So if she's interested in the cartoon, doesn't that mean she should be talking to you, since you thought up Captain Starblazer?"

"Take my word for it, in this case our meeting is better later than sooner," Dane said, knowing his priority was to start production on the new toys he'd recently designed. "We don't quite see eye to eye." Actually, when the leggy attorney with the interesting curves and marvelous shoulders wore her high-heeled shoes, he had to look up slightly to meet her eye to eye. It was just as well; he didn't want to look directly into the clear, cobalt eyes that warmed to inky Mediterranean the harder she held to the tough line.

"I think she's out to prove that Captain Starblazer is a fraud." Dane bit the inside of his cheek. Had this female crusader's righteous prodding begun to needle him out of his complacence since his long months away from NASA? Had he, in fact, done all he could to stop the agency from carrying military payloads? What else could he have done after he'd delivered all his protests and ultimatums? The only course left had been to resign.

When he'd walked out of the Unmanned Space Center in Maryland, he had lost not only his job, but a way of life that had started years earlier, when he'd shot off homemade rockets in his backyard. There had always been plenty of adventure in the Scott home between Dane's launchings and his little sister's creatures. Annette had loved animals, and there had always been lots of stray dogs and cats, as well as injured squirrels and birds around.

Micki Moore, with her candor and openness, reminded him of his sister, Annette. Annie had trusted him so much, she had even offered some of her beloved critters to ride in his rockets. When he had accepted the job at Fun Design drawing toy spaceships, it had seemed his life had gone full circle. When he'd called Annie to tell her about his job, she had commented teasingly that he was back in the model-rocket business and should feel at home. Nevertheless, he sensed she had guessed he wasn't as content as he had tried to sound. But he'd found a quiet niche and had been doing fine until Matilda Moore had rousted him, needled him, bothered him.

"We need the mock-ups of the new line of toys to cast the molds if we're ever going to stay on the production schedule for Christmas. People are getting antsy. Are you listening to me?" Roy Baker tried again. "Or is there a *living* doll on your mind?"

"Her?" He was watching Matilda Moore blink blue diamond eyes and toss her smart, chin-length mane of shimmering white gold hair. "She's much too serious for me." Still, he couldn't deny the spontaneous scenarios that had flickered through his mind since he'd met the sophisticated beauty. In each hazy vision, she had slipped willingly into his arms, breathed fire against his bare skin, and had kissed him as if she had wanted much more from him. He forced the visions away. "You know me; I want to regain my misspent youth," Dane told Roy with a laugh. The year at MIT, the few months at the think tank in Philadelphia, and the two decades cloistered in the Space Center had taken their toll. These hadn't exactly been ideal places to find women. The few encounters he'd had over the last twenty-odd years had been full of logic and reason and completely devoid of passion. Maybe that was why he'd speculated about how Matilda Moore's body would fit perfectly against his ever since he'd bumped into her that first day. There had been no logic in his reaction to her.

"She looks like the dangerous type to me, Scottie," Roy teased as he watched his friend.

Dane just laughed.

Friendships that had grown during Dane's twenty-two-year tenure with NASA suffered after his abrupt departure from the agency, so he appreciated Roy's camaraderie. Roy went on to explain what he and his family had done over the Memorial Day weekend. Dane had driven in a race, and for a few hours he had thought of nothing other than getting the best line through the curves, but no one had been there to greet him at the finish line, and his exhilaration at winning had quickly faded. Moonlighting for Corwin Racing Limited absorbed any leftover creative energy. He designed Indy-type race cars for Larry Corwin with the stipulation that he got to race now and then—just as he had insisted that NASA place him on one of the manned flights years ago. The rush of adrenaline that came with racing soothed the risk-taking urges that would otherwise remain in limbo.

"Okay, what's the hold-up?" Bert Tundry approached the two men, interrupting Roy's tale about his little girl and their new puppy. "Why can't I get my hands on those models?" Bert said.

"Are you behind schedule, too?" Roy asked.

"I can't be as relaxed and creative as some people I know—" Bert directed his comment at Dane "—because I've got people giving me flack from every direction: execs, artists, animators. We've got orders coming in for toys I haven't even seen yet." Bert took a deep breath as he pulled an antacid tablet from his vest pocket. "Look at me. I'm forty-nine years old, should be at my executive peak and enjoying it, and I'm falling apart." Bert was the frenetic workhorse of the company who knew toys from the ground up.

"Easy, fella, you know this company couldn't run without you." Wasn't that what Dane had mistakenly supposed about himself when he'd been at NASA? "Relax," Dane soothed the advertising man who was long on tenure, short on patience, and anemic in stature. Obviously everything the man ate was burned up by nervous energy.

"That's easy for you to say. You put the company on the map. I'm just the schlep who greases the wheels. Eighteen years with the company and I'm stuck in advertising, under an idiot."

"Auggie can't have that many more nephews," Roy said cheerfully, referring to Auggie Klopperman, the company's elderly founder and president.

The three men formed a small circle and shouted at each other over the incessant rhythmic stamp of the presses.

"You can laugh. I lost my sense of humor three promotions ago," Bert said. "I feel like I'm going nowhere fast." He turned to Dane. "Then there's this skyrocketing supergenius."

"I just draw pictures," Dane protested, laughing. "You guys turn them into toys."

"You could write your ticket with any company. Maybe all my chances have been used up," Bert said morosely.

"What can we say, Bert? You're Mr. Company," Roy chided.

"Maybe." Bert gave a wry laugh. "All I know is you're speaking to a man who's had his behind chewed one too many times and covered for too many of Auggie's nephews and fourth cousins—"

"You wouldn't leave a fun place like this?"

"I have ulcers to prove that toys aren't all fun and games, gentlemen. So where are the designs that are going to make me forget all my troubles? I need them in my hot little hands."

"Get in line, big guy," Roy said with a grimace. "It seems there's a snag."

"Security," Dane elaborated. "Charlie doesn't want the models unveiled yet, in light of new developments."

"I heard he found listening devices in the offices," Roy said incredulously. "Bugs! Can you believe it?"

"Where did you hear that?" Bert asked, as though this snag would be the straw to break the camel's back.

"From my people on the line," Roy answered. "So much for secrets. I figure that's why we're meeting in the noisiest room of the plant today. Am I wrong? It's a regular James Bond movie."

"Charlie and Auggie are worried about industrial espionage," Dane admitted. "They think it's better to hold up production a few days rather than risk letting the competition beat us to our own punch.''

"You think they'd steal the designs?"

"So the rumors are true...these new designs *are* special." Bert angled for answers. "You invented a toy that's going to rock the market, didn't you?"

"I don't know." Dane shrugged. "That's your area of expertise. I only know they're fun and if I were a kid—"

"Let's see them!"

Dane raised both hands to indicate they were tied.

"I'm trying to do business," Bert complained.

"Does Charlie suspect anyone in particular? If it's Bert we can watch the beads of sweat form on his shiny head," Roy said with a chuckle, clapping the unhappy executive on the back. It was true that things never went quite right for Bert, and he took a lot of teasing because of it.

"Charlie thinks we're being infiltrated by industrial spies. And Auggie is paranoid about Tech Toys. That goes way back, I've heard, long before SynTech Incorporated bought out the old Tots Toys line."

"What!" Bert's long face took on a crinkled hound-dog expression.

"It's not so much a what as a who. Charlie suspects a visitor to the company." Dane motioned to the blond attorney and watched her hips sway lightly as she walked along the line.

"No kidding?" Bert studied the lawyer with an unusual degree of interest.

"They think she's been hired by another company."

"Tech Toys?"

"I've heard they're really beating the bushes for talent. She gives the word a whole new meaning," Roy joked.

"It seems she and the bugs showed up the same day."

"I know the lady bugs someone," Roy kidded Dane.

"So Charlie thinks he's got a regular Mata Hari on his hands?" Bert looked at the woman again.

Dane let his gaze drift toward Tildie and remembered again how her eyes had looked when she'd asked for his help. But he also recalled how vague her explanation had become when Charlie had asked her what she was doing in the hallway. Dane hated to admit that she would have had the time and access to plant a bug or two.

"Industrial spies or not—" Roy nudged Dane's arm to turn his attention back to business "—we aren't going to have a Christmas line if we don't get those molds cast. We rushed and stockpiled production on all the other toys so we'd be ready to go full steam on these new ones. If we don't get the molds done soon, the whole plant will have to shut down. We'll lose time and money. No one has convinced me yet that we really have had an information leak. Bugs and spies." Roy shook his head. "Maybe our new security chief is looking for some robbers to play cops with?"

"Charlie Patrick takes his job seriously," Dane responded, smiling. "That can spell trouble." Dane glanced once more at the blond attorney. Why would he be disappointed if Matilda Moore turned out to be an industrial spy instead of a crusading windmill fighter? He'd be better off if she *were* a hard-hearted spy, he thought. At least then she wouldn't turn his brain to jelly and make him care again. "Even if she is a spy," he said, "she doesn't look too hard to handle."

"Famous last words?" Roy teased.

"We'll make the production deadline," Dane promised. "I know a kid who deserves a new toy in her stocking. I don't want to disappoint her." He conjured up a picture of Micki Moore, a miniature attorney with serious blue eyes and wheat-colored hair. Or did she look like her father? He reminded himself again not to care, but who would the kid turn to and depend on if her mother really were involved in espionage?

"Not to mention Bert Tundry, who's dying of a heart attack here," the advertising man said as he checked his notebook. "Just what I need, a Mata Hari," he scoffed as he walked away.

"I'll see what I can do to speed production along," Dane shouted to Roy before he turned and met the lovely eyes of Matilda Moore. *Speak of the devil,* he thought, *even if she looks more like an angel.* Steam from the presses surrounded her like a cloud while the fluorescent lights above her lit her shimmering hair.

He embraced the challenge. "Hello," he said.

Her fingers absently whisked a lock of ribbon-smooth hair away from her creamy cheek, and her lips parted, but the hiss and stamp of the press drowned out her voice. For a glorious moment he lost himself in hypnotic, round eyes. To break the trance that raised the short hairs on the back of his neck, he smiled. She coolly lifted her chin, pursed her lips and averted her aloof gaze to the assembly line. Why should he even be mildly curious about whether she was a spy or a passionate crusader? he wondered. Why should he allow her to get to him at all? She was a woman who convicted him with her haughty expression and reminded him with every glance that his hairline receded each year and he was undeniably short. His eyes traveled over her briefly and he realized that he wouldn't change a curve or an angle on her. Why would someone so soft try so hard to be so stiff, he mused as he beat a path toward the design room.

"Mr. Scott!" She shouted at him, but he didn't hear her. "Mr. Scott!" She hated herself for chasing after him. The faster she hurried on her narrow-heeled shoes the angrier she became. Why did she need to talk to him of all people? She was still smarting from having been evicted from the plant the first day they'd met, not to mention having gotten no-where on the case since. Dane Scott might have looked like Starblazer, she thought, taking in his cocksure smile and his muscular arms that were several shades darker than his honey-colored, deliciously sun-streaked hair, but he was no hero to her. He was too cavalier, as haphazard as the gol-den hair on his arms that curled carelessly over his leather watchband. Except for the thoughtful lines around his eyes, he appeared as if he didn't have a care in the world. He ex-uded confidence to the point of arrogance, yet at times he appeared incapable of a serious thought.

Still, Tildie, who vowed two short days ago never to speak with the man again, ran to catch up with his quick strides. "Mr. Scott!" She was breathless by the time she grabbed his arm. "I need to speak with you."

"Don't crash into me again, Ms Moore!" He held both hands up in surrender. "My bio-rhythms are low. I couldn't take it today," he shouted above the whir of machines. "You aren't following the orange tour line." He stretched his arm to show her the error of her path. As her glance turned in the direction he indicated, Dane Scott tried to slip away.

"Wait a minute!" She pursued him again. "Stop!"

"You aren't following procedure."

"You aren't playing fair," she called.

"Playing? Do you think this is a game? You're in a re-stricted area again. I could and should have you evicted."

"Why didn't you tell me that you created the whole con-cept for *Star Power* and designed the toys?"

"What—and spoil your fun?" He whirled suddenly and walked backward a few steps to avoid contact as she hur-ried to keep up with him. "I wouldn't want to deprive you of the pleasure of digging down and scraping up every last detail."

"You mean you wouldn't want to cooperate!"

"It's your fight, counselor. I don't want to be caught in the crossfire." His eyes narrowed as he turned and picked up speed.

"Even reducing the level of violence in the cartoon from explosive to moderate would help," she persisted, keeping up with him. "But you have your mind—and heart—closed."

"I agree." He looked at her from the corner of his eye. "There *is* too much violence in the cartoon. I've always thought so."

"Then why didn't you protest? You were the creator; why didn't you—?"

He pulled up short and faced her, stopping her in her tracks.

"Why didn't I ask the writers to take out the laser guns and put in more space exploration, or even add creatures from other galaxies instead of more and more battles?"

"Yes! Why didn't you?"

He rolled his light gray eyes, which were growing stormy. "Because I didn't have a fancy lawyer to point that out. And maybe you're just throwing up smokescreens, counselor. What's in this fight for Nigel and Associates? Who's chasing ambulances and sniffing out lawsuits? You, maybe? Pretending it's for kids, while you're just plain helping yourself?"

His words stung and set her back a few steps. "You're bordering on slander, Mr. Scott and—oohh!" Without warning her body lurched backward and her hands flew up in surprise, the yellow hard hat she'd been carrying banged to the floor. A sure arm wrapped around her waist to steady her.

"Are you all right?" He searched her face for signs of pain and found only confusion.

Tildie couldn't move; his magnetic gaze locked her in place. Beyond the dancing flecks in his eyes she saw a light, easygoing nature, a wry view of life and an obviously keen intelligence, which kept him one step ahead of her. He was an enigma. Still dazed, she asked, "What happened?" and glanced away from the strong arm that held her.

"It's your left shoe."

"What?" As she leaned forward to look down, her forehead bumped into the bill of his hard hat. He laughed so kindly at her startled expression that she couldn't help but smile back.

"Nice smile." His eyes searched hers.

Her expression cooled immediately to fight the unexpected warmth in his face and her own feelings that fluctuated somewhere between pleasure and agitation. She hated it when she couldn't analyze her opponent, when she couldn't calculate and pre-suppose every move. What made Dane Scott so unpredictable?

"The way I see it, we have a couple of possibilities. Either you caught your heel in the drain grate, or you're falling for me." His words held a sober note, but the tilt of his head teased.

"Hardly." It was a laughable situation. They were opponents, all right. For the sake of her family, she had strived for months to avoid men in any situation that could be even remotely construed as close, and now she found herself only a few warm inches away from a sleek, tanned body and a pair of haunting eyes.

"You didn't have to go to all this trouble to get me to rescue you," he said. Then in answer to her outraged expression, he added, "Just say you'd follow me to the ends of the galaxy and the job's yours."

"When pigs fly," she said dryly as she pushed herself away from his strong arm and hopped on her free foot. She tried to twist her captured heel from the crude metal grate.

"Careful, you'll get your other shoe stuck," he warned as he steadied her with one hand and pushed up the bill of his hard hat with his index finger, his expression all knowing.

"I don't need your help, thank you. Anyway, if you hadn't been ducking your responsibilities again, I wouldn't have had to chase you."

"It could be dangerous, you know." His eyes gleamed as he spoke. "A woman wearing high-heeled shoes and not wearing a hard hat on the loose in a factory. That's another very good reason for keeping to the tour, staying where you're supposed to be." He picked up the yellow hat she'd dropped and handed it to her. She ignored it, and he sat the hat back on the floor beside her.

She felt like a fool as she teetered on one foot. She knelt down to unbuckle the narrow strap at her ankle, but Dane Scott beat her to it.

"Stay away from me!" she ordered emphatically.

"You're following me, remember? I'm the desperado who deals in violent cartoons for little kids. Wouldn't it be intolerable if you found out I was a nice guy?" His tawny brows lifted questioningly before his soothing hands went to work on her ankle. "There's apparently no damage."

"I could have told you that."

"Can't be too careful in this lawsuit-happy society." His warm fingers brushed her shapely calf and continued to test her slender ankle for injury.

Tildie rolled her eyes and counted to ten as she watched the workers smiling at them and nudging each other along the assembly line.

"While I've got a captive audience, tell me one thing, Ms Moore—maybe two things?" he asked while he worked on the buckle. "First, do you always wear perfume behind your knees?"

She gritted her teeth.

"Too personal?" He looked up at her innocently, as though he didn't realize that he was still holding her ankle. "Tell me this then, why are you after Fun Design? Why not go after the big boys? There's Kryder Toys. Or you could go after the Snooty Suzie Doll people at Larensen. Or why not our biggest competitors at Tech Toys? Why pick on a little fish like Fun Design in Columbus, Ohio? We're small fry compared to them."

"You *were* small." When the buckle was undone, she stepped out of her shoe and stood on her stockinged foot. She enjoyed the luxury of sure balance, even though she had given up a few critical inches in height. He stood, too, and she lifted her chin to look him square in the eye. "Fun Design has become very successful since the introduction of the *Star Power* cartoon show." She knelt down, pushed his helping hands aside and struggled to free her shoe. "More children watch Captain Starblazer save the world from the villain Cyclon every day than any other cartoon," she said, looking up into his fascinated eyes.

"Why not? He's a good guy." He tilted his head. "At least for an hour a day the planet's safe from evil."

"And the *Star Power* sponsor can rake in a cool $75 million in toy sales during its first three quarters alone."

"That's a lot of dolls." He shrugged, unconcerned, and let his interested eyes slip lazily over her.

"Captain Starblazer enjoyed the most successful launch of a new toy in the history of toy manufacturing." She sat on her heels and tugged with both hands on the stubborn shoe.

"You've done your homework."

"Yes, I have. I'm very thorough." She knit her brows. "I've watched twenty different episodes of *Star Power*, and have counted the number of commercials and timed their length. I've also counted and logged the number of laser blastings, explosions, encounters between human beings, and confrontations with Cyclon."

"Did you see the one—?"

"I've counted the moral or ethical dilemmas, even the number of times Captain Starblazer's name was shown or verbalized." She took stock of his beguiled expression. "I've also gathered from the bits and pieces of information that everyone was told to keep from me," she said with a haughty expression, "that *you*, although I find it very difficult to believe, are primarily responsible for the creation of the Captain, the cartoon, the line of toys and Fun Design's newfound success. What do you say about that?"

"Very interesting," he said, his distracted gaze moving to meet her narrowed, accusing eyes. "Maybe the climate's right to ask for a raise." His mouth lifted in a smile. "What do you think? Shall we discuss it over dinner?"

"You won't be able to sway my conclusions about you or your company, Mr. Scott." Still crouched, she pounded on the shoe in an attempt to loosen it.

"Heaven forbid."

She glanced up to see that his eyes were fixed on the open V of her blouse, which revealed a creamy curve of cleavage, particularly when viewed from above. She straightened immediately and stood, aware of a hot flush rising up from between her breasts.

"Believe me, I wouldn't want to change a thing about you," he went on.

"You are supposed to be an example to children." The embarrassed flush reached her cheeks and angry sparks darted from her eyes. "Captain Starblazer is a hero to thousands!"

Now he bent down and tugged at the shoe.

"You have an opportunity to guide, to teach..."

"I think you're confusing me with the Captain," he said through gritted teeth. "I'm no hero. It's not my job to save the world, lady. I only rescue shoes." Just then the shoe broke loose from the raw force he applied to it. He clapped the sole and dangly straps in one of her hands and the now-separated heel in the other.

"You're a former astronaut—a national hero. People would listen to you." He didn't stay long enough to reply, but turned and headed for a green metal door nearby.

"How am I supposed to walk on this?" she demanded.

"It suits your half-cocked ideas," he called back to her.

"Wait a minute!" She marched behind him like a peg-legged pirate, stepping high on her heel, then low on her stockinged foot, never slowing her pace.

He paused and turned to look at her.

"Are you always all business?" he asked.

"Are you ever serious?"

"Not if I can help it. Being serious dulls the imagination, kills the spirit." He walked on and tossed another comment over his shoulder. "Anyway, I discovered it doesn't pay to take yourself or your work too seriously. You should try it sometime."

"I think the welfare of children is something that cannot be taken too seriously. And so do the people I represent."

He stopped again. "Look. Granted the show could be better, but the kids like it; they love the Captain. Deep down maybe even you have a small place in your cold, tiny heart for the Defender of the Planet."

Tildie hated it when a man assumed she was cold and aloof simply because she didn't swoon from his flirtations.

Didn't he know there were more important issues at stake here? "Well," she said, "if it makes you feel any better, the other major toy manufacturers are being brought to the committee's attention too, not just Fun Design." She despised his indifferent attitude and resented the flush still high on her cheeks and down her neck. "The big four toy companies have their own cartoon shows and consequently, their own advertising machines to sell their products to innocent consumers. If this trend continues, the Saturday morning funnies will be reduced to nothing but dollars and cents. The complaints about the other toy companies will be brought before the FCC by attorneys from other cities."

"Oh, I see. We're just lucky enough to have you as the thorn in our side, is that it?" Dane swung the heavy metal door open and she slipped through it behind him.

"Yes, you are lucky to have me." Her brash declaration brought an amused look to his face. "If it weren't me, it would be another attorney," she said more calmly. "Someone has to stand up for children."

"So I've heard. Suppose you tell me something?" He stopped before he opened another door. "If you're only concerned about the welfare of children, why are you so interested in design?" He pointed to a sign on the door he was about to open. It read Drafting Room. "Why are you always somewhere in the factory where you don't belong?"

Tildie glanced around, surprised by the new surroundings. She really hadn't been paying attention to where they were going.

"You're not talking. That's very unusual for you, Ms Moore."

Her mouth started to form some words, but the realization that she could look almost directly into his eyes when she was standing on her one good heel was a heady sensation.

"Cat got your tongue, counselor? You haven't been shy up until now."

Did she see something in his eyes that no one else could see? Something secret, something caring?

"What are you really after, Ms Fitzsimmons-hyphen-Moore?"

At that instant she wasn't at all sure. "I want..." She wanted to know what lay deep in his gray eyes. She blinked long lashes in disbelief at the startling discovery.

"I heard Mrs. Moore got separated from her tour," Charlie Patrick announced from the end of the hall. He walked toward them carrying her abandoned hard hat. "You're in a restricted area again," he said, putting the hat in her hands.

"Yes." She was close enough to Dane Scott to smell his clean, spicy after-shave—definitely a danger zone, she decided. She'd met and handled just about every type of man during her years of waiting on tables. What made Dane Scott so hard to read? How could he rile her with a word or a smile? "I apologize," she said to the security man, feeling foolish about her breathless voice. Tildie retreated from Dane's compact body and his analytical eyes. She blamed her shaky knees on exhaustion resulting from shouting over the machines. Yet Dane's clear, convicting gaze and the tilt of his sturdy chin with its intriguing cleft told her there was another reason.

"We're in kind of a ticklish situation here," Charlie said, looking from Dane to Tildie. "We want to keep a lid on things since we'll be introducing a new line of toys here soon. But I don't suppose you knew that?"

"New toys?" Tildie met Dane's searching eyes. "No. Why would I...?" She meant to say more, but stopped when the retired cop placed a firm hand on her elbow.

"That's what we've been wondering," Charlie grunted.

"Counselor," said Dane, "Try to keep your hat on your hard head. We wouldn't want any of our machines to get damaged." Dane guided the hand holding the hat to her head and gave the plastic a dismissing tap as though he were saying farewell to an old buddy. "Charlie, introduce her to Mrs. Tuttle. She can show her how a grandmother of ten runs quality control—as if every toy will go to one of her grandbabies." Dane tilted his head and smiled widely, showing her that their temporary closeness hadn't ruffled him in the least.

Tildie shook her head vigorously as Charlie led her away and shouted after Dane, "I'm sure it's heartwarming, Mr. Scott, but I refuse to spend another second learning how many dolls per minute go down that conveyor. I refuse!" But the door swung shut, the sound of her voice was drowned out by the busy clatter and clanging of the assembly line.

"DINNER TONIGHT? No, I really can't, Arthur. But it's nice of you to think of your struggling associate," she joked to defuse the potential problem. Now Tildie understood why senior partner Arthur Hillenbrand had called her at home about the research she'd done for him on the SynTech case instead of conferring with her at the office earlier. He described an elegant evening, his voice smooth, oozing with wealth and savvy.

"I don't want to complicate things," she insisted gracefully, shuffling the research notes that were scattered on the round patio table near the swimming pool. "We have a very good working relationship. I wouldn't want to endanger that." She shifted the cordless phone to her other ear. "But all work and no play makes me an excellent research assistant." It was the upcoming custody suit over her son, Jer, that determined her social life. It made seeing any man for any occasion a foolish move, a risk not worth taking. Tildie wanted to keep both of her children. They'd always made it together; they always would. So she had no intention of going out with Arthur Hillenbrand or any man. She'd spent months avoiding tempting situations—until today. She had let her guard slip earlier when the former astronaut had been so close to her, but that wouldn't happen again.

"...discuss the case over dinner?" Arthur pitched once more. It sounded professional enough. But there would be wine before, during and after dinner, wouldn't there? She held her hand over the receiver a moment.

The high-handed lawyer her ex-husband, Paul Moore, had hired, would jump at any chance to discredit her as a parent. Moral grounds, real or construed, would make his case.

"I really can't, thank you, Arthur. I have all these notes to go over."

She explained in several well-chosen sentences what she had learned in Cleveland the day before in her interviews with SynTech management and the physicians of the plaintiffs. It was her job to do the legwork that would enable Arthur Hillenbrand to find a hole in the $20 million classaction suit that had been brought on by two workers. Yet what she had gathered from the personal physicians and specialists, as well as from company and state safety officials, indicated that the two workers with the debilitating respiratory condition had a tenable case. The physicians linked the condition directly to the chemicals and dust at the SynTech chemical plant in Parma.

"It's our responsibility to serve our client the best way we can," Arthur had told his junior associate, who had balked at the idea of protecting a large corporation when the lives of two men and their families would never be the same again. Now she felt even worse.

"I'll expect the SynTech notes first thing in the morning." Arthur's voice had stiffened, and it seemed to prove her idealism was one of the smaller obstacles she had to overcome.

"I have interviews at Fun Design in the morning." Her voice didn't hint at her dubious feelings about talking with Dane Scott again.

"Remember that case is *gratis*, counselor. Don't waste valuable time on it."

"I promise that it won't affect the quality of my work on the SynTech case." She watched Micki splashing in the pool. "I'll get these notes together and bring them in early."

Tildie's sister, Sally, waved at her as she walked across the yard. It was a relief to see a friendly face. There was obviously good news behind Sally's smile. Tildie had to smile, too, thinking that, thanks to Sally and her neighbor Eloise Caruthers—who happened to be a friend of Tildie's—Tildie and the kids now lived in the lap of luxury. Sally and Eloise had arranged for Tildie and the kids to house-sit while Eloise visited family in Europe for an indefinite period of time. The large elegant Tudor in Upper Arlington wasn't anything like the ovenlike apartment near the university campus that had been home to Tildie, Jer and Micki for nearly six years. Paul's attorney had planned to use the argument that a crowded apartment near a college campus was not a fit environment for children, but no judge in the land could fault this neighborhood. And as an added bonus, the house was on the same block as Sally's home, which gave the sisters the chance to become close again.

Tildie finished her conversation with Arthur with promises of dropping the research notes on his desk at 8:00 a.m. the next day and pledging to make another exhausting trip to Cleveland to search the Cuyahoga County Courthouse records. "Trace their family roots back to Adam, if you must, to prove a medical history of respiratory disease in the family," Arthur had insisted. It miffed her to admit that Dane Scott had been right; Nigel and Associates was sniffing for money. They didn't seem to care about justice; it all boiled down to the bottom line. She hated the SynTech case. She had become an attorney to help people, not to keep a law firm in business by representing the bad guys, or by dragging out cases.

"Thanks to you," Sally said, "I closed the Cramer farm deal today. Now the Halltree Halfway House will have a farm for the kids to work on." She slipped into a chair across the table from Tildie and poured herself a glass of iced tea from a pitcher.

"I only gave you a few names," Tildie said, shrugging, glad that the troubled teens in the Columbus area would finally have a pleasant place to live and work.

"I struck the best possible terms for both parties. Not bad for a lady who dabbles in real estate." Sally grinned proudly.

It was just the type of news that Tildie needed to momentarily forget custody battles and corporate lawsuits. Several years ago, Tildie had convinced her older sister to get involved in a career. Now she was extremely proud of the intelligent, independent woman sitting across from her.

"How did your day go?" Sally asked after a toast with iced tea.

"I don't want to talk about it," Tildie said with a sigh.

"You're wearing yourself out with that *gratis* case in addition to your normal workload."

"I already got one lecture today." She laughed. "Besides, I have a personal stake in this case, remember." She motioned to Micki, who was paddling silently on her back, her wide eyes open to the sky above, her ears below the surface. "I'm being ordered to turn against all that is compassionate on one case, and colliding with an executive who wears tennis shoes on another." Tildie exhaled in frustration, brushing a smooth lock of golden hair from her cheek. She still couldn't completely identify and label her reaction to Dane Scott. "This man is so—impossible. He's obviously talented in his own way and I suspect quite intelligent beneath his veneer of nonchalance. He could do so much to help the children, but it's like he doesn't care."

"Who is this reluctant hero who has stymied the woman of steel?"

"He's the Fun Design spokesman and—"

"Aunt Sally!" Micki popped her head above the surface, swam a few strokes, hiked her body out of the pool and hotfooted it across the sunny patio. "Would you please tell mom that kids really do know the difference between reality and fantasy?"

"This," Tildie said dryly to Sally, "coming from a daughter who shamelessly begs her family for expensive toys she can't possibly live without—like a life-support system for the planet Serceria."

"It's not a planet. It's the Sercerian moon, mother. The oxygen level there is just five percent. Only the princess can magically bestow the power to breathe without a life-support system. She also has a spell that puts people into a slower-metabolism trance. She did that to Captain Starblazer once, I think so she could have her way with him," Micki said, wiggling her wet brows mischievously.

"I think you may have just blown your case, kiddo." Sally smiled at her eight-year-old niece. "How can you keep track of all that stuff?"

Tildie sighed dramatically. "What do you expect? The kid hasn't had anyone less than a graduate student baby-sit her since she can remember."

"I used to play Dungeons and Dragons with Phoebe, remember? And backgammon with Eloise," Micki piped up. "I miss them."

Graduation had disrupted and scattered their support group. At least Eloise would return in the fall.

"We'll do some fun things this summer."

"Who with? Roxanne is in Toledo, Carla went to Western Reserve for her doctorate and Mimi moved to Colorado. Jer used to play chess with her."

"Not a father figure in the lot," Sally said, which reminded Tildie of one of the statements of the custody suit.

"We could invite Captain Starblazer over," Micki suggested. "Mimi always liked him. She could see a higher order to *Star Power*."

"Honey, Mimi had a masters degree in popular culture. It was her job to see higher orders."

"At least she got married. That's the way it should be," Micki grumbled.

Tildie shrugged in answer to her sister's inquiring expression, "She's still angry with me for taking the complaint to Fun Design."

"She didn't even talk to the Captain! Can you believe it?"

"That *is* hard to believe," Micki's aunt marveled.

"I won't talk to the Captain, but I will speak with Dane Scott again tomorrow. He's the company spokesman and the cartoon's creator." Tildie wasn't looking forward to facing him again. Was it because his eyes were too clear and magnetic?

"The astronaut? He's the one who has you frustrated?" Sally asked. "What's he like?"

"Frustrated? Does that have something to do with sexual tension?" Micki asked with an honest, curious expression.

"Nothing at all to do with that," Tildie insisted boldly, trying to drown out Sally's titter. "Just swim, would you please?"

"I'm just a kid! How else am I going to know things unless I ask?" she wailed. "I have an inquiring mind," she whispered to her Aunt Sally, who held her sides to keep from cracking up.

"Back to the pool!" Tildie shouted at the scurrying urchin.

When she was gone, Sally asked, "So what's the astronaut like?"

Tildie tried to dismiss images of sun-streaked hair and a winning smile. "Not exactly your typical American hero. He looks like the boy next door and wears sneakers without socks to the office. He certainly doesn't fit the corporate image of a vice-president."

"What's the world coming to?!"

"Arthur Hillenbrand asked mom out for dinner but she said no," Micki related as she paddled around in the pool.

"Got any more fast-breaking bulletins?" Tildie said sarcastically.

"You turned down Arthur Hillenbrand?" asked Sally, incredulous.

"You know I can't take any chances with Paul's custody suit pending. Besides I'm too busy with the kids and with these notes!" Tildie shuffled through the pages. "I don't have the time or energy to see anyone and I certainly don't need another complication in my life."

"You're here in the morning, in Cleveland in the afternoon, at Jer's ball games on Tuesdays..." Sally worried aloud.

"Just my point. There's no room in my schedule for romance."

"Schedule? My, how romantic." Sally frowned, then added, "Love can't be analyzed, predicted, scheduled, or, or..."

"Denied," Micki supplied from the pool. "It's wonderful, spontaneous and sexy."

"That's it exactly," Sally said, nodding.

"What do you know about sexy, young lady? I told you to stop reading Eloise's magazines," Tildie called to Micki as she made a surface dive for the bottom. "The kid has radar instead of ears."

"She also has a point," Sally said. "At least admit you're outnumbered."

"Agreed." Tildie laughed. Her older sister had a good sense of humor, in addition to luminous green eyes, lovely brown hair and finely sculpted features.

"It's nice of you both to be so concerned. But I don't have time for romance. I'll be up most of the night working to save SynTech's tail and in the morning I'll be talking with Dane Scott, who sees himself as the boy wonder of the toy world. Would you believe he stalled me with a tour of the factory today? As if I have the time," she added.

"The nerve of the man." Sally issued a curious smile, as if to ask if that was all that was bothering her sister.

"His real mistake came after I broke the heel of my shoe—a pair I can't afford to replace right now, I might add. He had the nerve to ask me out for dinner—no doubt to talk me out of bringing Fun Design before the commission. Did he really believe I'd fall for anything so transparent? He didn't even bother to deny it."

"So? Did you say yes to dinner?"

"Of course not! This is a *case*. And you know I can't afford even a hint of an entanglement right now with this custody suit pending." Tildie heaved a sigh. "As it is, the judge will hear how curbed Jer's growth has been by an all-female support group." She shook her head, depressed at the thought.

"Call Captain Starblazer. He can help you," Micki yelled. "He helped the Princess of the Sercerian moon."

"He's good at rescuing ladies, is he?" Tildie teased. A warm memory of Dane Scott's strong arm wrapped around her rushed over her like an unexpected summer breeze.

"Duke could laser blast anybody out of the sky. Zzzzt! Zzzzt!" Micki demolished the brightly striped umbrella over the table with an imaginary laser gun.

"No blasting, please," Tildie ordered. "That cartoon is much too violent," she said to her sister.

"I think I'm in trouble now." Micki scrambled out of the pool, turned her dark blue eyes up to her aunt, then said, "I think I'll go and write another letter."

"This'll be her third letter this week!"

"Are you still trying to convince Prince Charles to marry your mother instead of Di?" Sally teased.

"Please. I was a kid then." Micki rolled her eyes in a pseudo-sophisticated manner. "This is much better."

"No matchmaking, please."

"I'll let it be a surprise for my birthday. I'm inviting someone for dinner," Micki said with a grin. "Don't worry. You know him."

Tildie didn't press the matter. She guessed Micki was trying to improve her relationship with her father, who lived 350 miles away in Chicago. Jer had gone through the same phase when he'd been about her age. He had written letter after letter until he had gotten discouraged by responses from Paul's secretary.

"Well, what about your birthday?" Tildie tried to change the subject. "It's the day after tomorrow. Shall we celebrate with a backyard barbecue, just the three of us?" She smiled widely.

"Do you think dad might come this year, since he wants to make a good impression for the judge?" The question struck Tildie as a bit cynical for a primary schooler.

"I don't know. You know how busy fathers are." She gave her daughter a hug.

"Yeah, like last year," Micki grumbled. "I'd like burgers and chocolate cake for the barbecue. Okay?"

Tildie smiled sympathetically. "Fair enough."

"Where's Jer?" Aunt Sally asked the little girl. "As if I didn't suspect."

"Baseball practice!" All three of them said together.

"Why doesn't that surprise me?" Aunt Sally quipped, then listened to Micki's monologue that didn't miss a beat.

"Jer wants new baseball spikes, but mom says he needs a new suit for his eighth-grade graduation and dance, and Robbie's graduation party. We're going to help with the punch at the party and I'm going to wear my pink dress and pearls. Well, fake pearls," she called as she ran for the pool for one last swim before going inside to write her letter.

While the two women talked about the upcoming graduation party and Micki played in the water, Jer came home from ball practice and dived into the pool. He tormented his little sister with splashes until she cannon-balled her body at him. Tildie watched her son pull his long frame from the pool with ease and dive in again.

"I don't want to lose him," she said to Sally. She'd lived through his every phase from infant to young man. "Is it selfish of me? Would he be better off with a man around?"

Sally shrugged. "I'm glad Robbie had his dad, but who says it can't be a man other than Jer's father?"

"Mom, I need new spikes," Jer called.

"Baseball players are lovable, but expensive," Tildie said with a laugh. But she really didn't mind his requests. It wasn't as though Jer didn't pull his own weight. He watched after Micki, tended the grounds and pool at home and at neighbors' houses, and lately, did his own laundry. But with her student loans to pay off on a junior associate's salary, money was tight. She had everything for the kids outlined in her budget, every cent of the child-support money accounted for and allocated according to court orders. Next on the budget was a new suit, not baseball spikes.

"We'll meet after school at Kryder's and get you fitted for a new suit for the dance."

"I don't want to go to the dance."

"Sure, Jeremy!" Micki taunted with a toothy grin. "He wants to ask Cynthia Edgars!" Micki pursed her lips, aping her version of a primping beauty. "She's a girl at school that Jer follows aroun—" Jer doused Micki's words with a handful of water, and a splashing battle commenced. It was all Micki could do to hold her own against her big brother. Tildie watched her son dive and surface again, and she marveled at his developing muscles, undeniable evidence of maturation.

"What if Paul is right? What if Jer does need a man's guidance? I can do a lot of things for him, but I can't know what it feels like to be a teenage boy." Tildie shook her head. "I barely remember my own teen years because I was so engrossed in preparing to be a wife and mother. We were both groomed to be the consummate businessman's wife, you know that?" She looked from Micki to her sister. "But you were more successful at it than I was."

"I was lucky," Sally said simply. "Bill's essentially a family man. Paul isn't." Sally studied her sister's expression. "You have enough to worry about right now. You have this case and you have a reluctant hero to convince to work with you on it." She smiled.

"The astronaut?" Tildie rubbed her chin, contemplating what it would be like if the two of them were to work together. Somehow, only the vision of his arm around her came to her mind. "I can't figure him at all," she said with a sigh. But she hadn't waited tables, sweated over a short-order grill and studied until her eyes had turned bloodshot for nothing. She had a backbone of steel. Resolutely she announced, "Tomorrow I'll present Arthur Hillenbrand with complete, concise notes on the SynTech case and I'll knock Dane Scott's socks off—if he wears any." She grinned, thinking of the prospect, and realized she wanted tomorrow to come quickly.

CHAPTER THREE

Dear Captain Starblazer,

Mom met the spokesman of *Star Power*, who turns her cheeks red every time she talks about him. My Aunt Sally says mom's frustrated. I think that's something sexual, don't you? I think she should talk to you, because you are the Defender of the Planet. I know you could help her.

I know you'd like mom cause she's smart, pretty and she doesn't get flustered when things go wrong. So you wouldn't need to worry about her screaming if the retro-rockets didn't fire or if the lasers jammed or the milk spilled.

Maybe you'd like her so much that you'd marry her. Then you'd be my dad. Would you like a daughter? I don't eat much and I pick up my room sometimes. Maybe if you weren't too busy you could come to my birthday party to meet mom. My birthday is June 8. I would not object to presents. Say Hi to Spinner. He could live with us, too.

Love always,
Micki Moore

Dane systematically tapped the letter from the match-making kid with his pen and watched Charlie Patrick slowly circle the ultramodern circular office as he read aloud the evidence stacked against Matilda Moore. She had appeared just before the bugs were found; she'd been discovered in a hallway that provided access to every office in the place, including the design room, where the devices had been found; and she had recently moved to a wealthy Columbus suburb. The fact that she was living in a house that didn't belong to her didn't look good, either. But the really damaging news was that Nigel and Associates was retained by Fun Design's very aggressive competitor, SynTech Incorporated. Matilda Moore had visited their head office just the day before she had gotten the grand tour at Fun Design.

Every time Dane attempted to picture her as an industrial spy, he remembered the feisty, righteous attorney trying to needle him into joining her cause. He had promised himself that he wouldn't care about anything again. But Matilda Moore had the irritating quality of reminding him that he'd done too little, too late. Moreover, whenever he managed to convince himself that his preoccupation with the lawyer was only leftover disillusionment, his brain would flash back to Matilda Moore wrestling to free her stuck shoe. Her sophisticated mask had slipped a bit to reveal a down-to-earth beauty, as she sat on her heels, her thighs seductively and naturally apart.

Dane considered the letters from Micki. They were written by an intelligent, honest, lonely kid, who reminded him of his younger sister. He could not deny that the marriage proposal had triggered several sexy fantasies, all involving the cool, collected attorney melting in his arms. He'd never been overly impressed or taken in by beauty. But there was something about Matilda Moore that set her apart. Maybe it was that self-made-woman tilt of her chin. Perhaps she *was* moonlighting as a spy, he thought. She certainly looked the part. But no, she was too uptight and straitlaced. Maybe that was why his blood surged at the unlikely thought of her letting loose in mindless passion.

The closer Charlie got to the conclusion of his report the faster he walked. Dane considered himself lucky to be seated in his swivel chair. He turned as the chief rounded each bend. Bert, in the chair across from Dane's desk, did the same thing and nearly screwed himself into the floor.

"So you're saying Matilda Moore is an industrial spy." Dane had hoped that in the clear light of a new business day the facts would favor the attorney. He wanted her to be who and what she'd said she was.

"I think I make a case. She shows up just when a new line is comin' out," Charlie pressed. "She wanders into restricted areas. She would've had time to plant bugs. And how is it she lives in a neighborhood well above her visible means?"

"That question applies to half of suburbia, Charlie. Would you mind walking the other way around the room, so I can unwind?" he joked, but the chief wasn't laughing. Dane wanted Matilda to be real. She was a pain, granted, but she wasn't in it for the bucks—he felt it. "I personally think it would be great if she were here for the reason she says—"

"For the reason she pretends," Charlie said flatly.

"To protect children as consumers and to—"

"There's a snowball's chance. What major law firm like Nigel and Associates, which only caters to the wealthiest clients, is going to fiddle with Mickey Mouse stuff like the Television for Squirts group? She's being paid by Tech Toys."

"Maybe Ms Moore is a different breed. Your report said she took extra jobs as a waitress and a cook to work her way through law school at night. It's a heartwarming tale, nearly enough to restore one's faith in the legal system. Why would she jeopardize the career that she worked so hard—?"

"Money. For a smart guy, Scottie, you're acting pretty dumb. I think the chick has you snowed," Charlie said, putting a thick finger to his temple. "Money is a great motivator."

Money. Yes, it had made a good man like Marty Bauer, a friend and NASA director, accept military payloads, while a lack of funds forced whole projects to shut down. During the last couple of years Dane had been at NASA, it hadn't been the same. There had been too much pressure to work too fast on projects he didn't believe in. The lucrative contracts for military payloads had altered the thrust of the agency. The design requests had started out simple at first—just odds and ends of retrorockets and external robotics for orbiting spy labs. But eventually the requests had become more suspect. When they had asked Dane to design a manned orbiter that would be nearly impossible to detect, he began to question the real purpose of the probe. The picture became deadly serious. He promised himself he wouldn't design another spacecraft because there were people hell-bent on cluttering the galaxies with destruction.

While working at Fun Design, he had relaxed his guard, not worrying about budget overruns (toys were made of relatively cheap molded plastic), and never giving a thought to the balance of power in the world (on *Star Power* good won over evil every day). Instead, he simply tried to bring the wonder of the "great frontier" to curious children, kids like Micki.

Charlie's accusing voice interrupted Dane's reverie. "And how do you explain that she was at the corporate offices of SynTech just two days ago? They know her up there in Cleveland. She's expected to return this afternoon."

"Maybe she's working on another case."

"Sure, they can say that, but how do you explain the bugs and the suspect showing up on the same day?"

"Coincidence?" Dane thought Matilda Moore radiated pure innocence, with her solemn angel's face and her creamy skin.

"If you wanted to hire a spy, wouldn't you choose one who didn't look like a spy?" Charlie asked with a sigh, as though he were explaining the simplest of procedures to a rookie. "It's my job to protect your work. So let me do my job, okay?"

"We really don't have anything to take to the police," Bert stated and added before Dane could interrupt, "There's been no real harm, and what if she really does make a report to the FCC? We can't afford to be in hot water with them. Why don't we let her into the plant and keep an eye on her?" Bert was trying to appeal to both sides, and he looked questioningly at Dane, then Charlie.

"Let the fox in the hen house? When the lights go out don't be surprised if your toy and the woman are gone," Charlie argued.

Dane tipped back in his chair and tried to analyze the electric surge he felt when he considered seeing Matilda Moore again. He didn't trust or understand the feeling, and he promised himself he wouldn't let it overtake him again. Suddenly he sensed that both Charlie and Bert were looking at him. And indeed they were—as though they expected an answer to a question—what, Dane wasn't sure.

"If we're going to make the Christmas deadline, spies or not, we have to get the models to Roy," he ad-libbed as he crowded Matilda Moore out of his mind.

"Dane's right, Charlie. We are trying to do business here. These security glitches cost us. Production wants 250,000 units by September first." He turned to Dane. "Do you have the mock-ups?" Bert asked eagerly. "Are they in the safe?"

"Don't worry." Dane opened a desk drawer, flipped the switch to deactivate the alarm and walked over to the liquor cabinet and slid back a secret panel to reveal a wall safe.

"Don't forget the auxiliary alarm," Charlie reminded him. Dane flipped another switch before he ran the numbered combination smoothly. Then he pulled the shiny painted models out, one at a time. First came the new Evil Fortress, from where Cyclon aimed to destroy the Star Power Alliance along with its superhero, Captain Starblazer.

"Where's the other one?"

Surprised by Bert's enthusiasm, Dane pulled the next model from the safe with a proud introduction.

"Gentlemen, the Star Command Station." Until now, Dane had been the only person to see his favorite model or any of its sketches.

"What is this?" Bert asked. His dark eyes scanned the octagonal space station. Bert didn't seem to trust the faceted podlike shape, and he said, "This isn't like anything I've ever seen."

"That's the idea, isn't it? Something new? Something different?" Dane turned the piece with its glossy blue angles over in his hands. "I let my imagination fly on this one."

Despite its apparent simplicity, painstakingly detailed extras covered the external surface of the three jointed pods: communication disks, defense lasers and docking platforms that accepted the already popular Star Cruiser ships. Each element was to be sold separately. Bert stared at the intricate details on the sprawling craft.

"See these?" Dane pointed to an ingenious adaptation of a joint at the end of each arm holding the pods together. "I designed these so that the kids can interchange the pods and features." Dane demonstrated by unsnapping a landing platform and a communications disk and clicking them into compatible joints on different sides of the pods. "She's as adaptable as a real space station should be, only the kids won't have to use mechanical arms or a two-man EVT crew to move parts around."

"So more toys can be made to attach to this one." Bert narrowed his eyes, computing new sale possibilities. "Eat your heart out, Tech Toys!"

"It could be fun." That's what Dane Scott enjoyed about his work these days—fun. His last few years at NASA had been filled with disillusionment and changing priorities. "On Christmas morning thousands of kids will play with these." Dane wondered how many future scientists the Star Command Station might foster. He liked the idea of enticing young minds to the new frontier. "That's why they'll be well designed and balanced, so a kid will be able to hang her up with one fishing line and she'll fly right." That didn't sound like the skeptic he wanted to be. Someone had needled him out of his comfortable numbness. "It's imaginative, flexible...." Dane analyzed the main body of the model with discriminating eyes. Yup, designing her had been fun, he thought.

"It's worth millions." Bert flicked one of the joints, then gave the model back to its creator, his possessive eyes conveying that it just might be worth the hassle of being in the toy game. "Are there any drawings?"

"One set. In the safe."

"So we're the only ones who know where they are?"

"Unless someone has planted another listening device."

"I scanned the room; it's clean." Charlie had already attacked with the machine that looked like a glorified vacuum sweeper. "You'll use this," he said as he hoisted a leather briefcase onto the desk, "to transport the models down to production. It's fire and bullet proof." He popped the latches open and pulled out a sturdy chain and handcuff. "You attach the case to your wrist," he said above Dane's objections, pulling what appeared to be a ballpoint pen from inside. "This pen scans for bugs; it flashes when it finds one. This cigarette lighter—"

"Sorry. I don't smoke."

"This is serious, Scottie. I'm talkin' white-collar crime here. Just because it's neat and clean doesn't make it legal. There are some real bad guys getting into it 'cause there's a lotta money in it. Right, Bert?"

"Right." Bert seemed unconvinced. "Right!" he said with more conviction. "A lot of fingers point to Ms Moore. Maybe all her complaints about our advertising is just a smokescreen."

"You know people at Larensen Toys. Why don't you call there and see what they know about the FCC hearing?" Dane said to Bert, who shrugged noncommittally.

"There's nothing says she can't be doing both. Use the case when you move the models," Charlie said flatly.

"She's a mother with a little eight-year-old girl, not a spy," Dane defended. Why did having children to care for give a woman more...integrity? Because, he thought, mothers were so...real, so honest. "Her daughter, Michelle Moore, has sent Captain Starblazer a couple of letters." Seeing Charlie's facial expression at that statement, Dane knew it had been a mistake to mention the notes.

"Letters? It could be a setup. She could have sent them to throw you off the trail. And it worked, didn't it?"

"The letters are real. One warned the Captain that her mother was coming to investigate the company and another invited him to a birthday party." Dane shrugged.

"Perhaps you should cultivate that friendship," Bert suggested thoughtfully. "If, like you say, Matilda Moore's purpose is legitimate, it may help to have her kid on our side going into the hearings. And if the lady's a thief, we can keep a close eye on her. We'll have all the bases covered."

"That's not how I'd play it," Charlie said. "Still, I'll keep an eye on her while she's in the plant. What you do on your own time is up to you, Scottie, but I'd advise you not to get involved." And with that, Charlie walked to the back door of the office that led into the hallway.

Of course he wouldn't get involved, Dane thought. What intelligent man would get entangled with a suspicious woman and her ready-made family?

"When we get this cleared up," the departing security chief added, "we'll move on to production, not before. Make sure you get the model back in the safe. We don't want our 'baby' to fall into the wrong hands, right, Tundry?"

"Of course not." When Charlie had left the room, Bert asked Dane, "What could it hurt to meet the kid?"

"What's the matter with you, Bert? I'm not going to use a kid to help the company."

"I didn't say use, I said, be friendly."

Dane looked up to check his sincerity, but the harried advertising executive had already slipped out the door. Dane leaned back in his comfortable chair and hiked his fuel-splattered Nikes up onto the curved desk, one that blended beautifully with the rounded walls and the large aerial photograph of the Earth's surface on the wall. The futuristic decor had been intended to make Dane feel more at home in the world of business, but the experiment had failed. He did most of his doodling at his apartment, at an ancient rolltop desk that had belonged to his father and had been in his own office at the Space Center. The Fun Design office remained foreign territory, especially now that things suddenly turned very serious at the "fun capital." Industrial spies stealing secrets, getting "friendly" with a kid to help roust the spies...? He reread the words that had been pressed onto the grade-school type yellow paper by a dull lead pencil and smiled. He had to admit he wanted to meet Micki Moore, and he knew that desire might make him act beyond his better judgment.

He always answered the Captain's mail personally. That was the task he enjoyed most about his job as company spokesman. Maybe he *could* add a personal appearance at a birthday party. Involuntarily he pictured Micki as looking like his sister, Annie, when she had been nine. What poor, love-starved kid ordered a father from a toy company? The words echoed through his head: love, kid, father. He remembered his own father and how his arms had closed so naturally around him, his little sister and his mother. He remembered how lonely Annie had felt after her father had died. The two had had a relationship that an older brother couldn't hope to replace, Dane had discovered after the funeral.

His father had been a brilliant geologist who could have written his own ticket at Exxon or Marathon, but he had seemed content to come home from his high-school science classes to have Annie run into his arms. Dane squashed an image of himself coming home to a little girl who ran into his arms and hugged him as though he were the most loved person in the universe. A larger version of Micki—her gorgeous mom—followed on the little girl's heels, her soft, warm body flowing into his arms, her full lips curved into a homespun smile. Somehow the image didn't fit the sophisticated attorney. He grinned, recalling her uninhibited moxie when she had gotten down on her knees to retrieve her shoe from the grate. He couldn't forget her momentary lapse of self-possession, or her creamy, inviting breasts beneath her pale blouse.

He folded the letter and stuck it in his notebook, deliberately putting it out of sight and, he hoped, out of mind. Was the woman an industrial spy? Or was she a crusading attorney so busy saving the world from the *Star Power* cartoon show that she didn't have time to spend with her own daughter? And what about the kid's father? Where was he? More importantly, Dane asked himself, why was a busy toy executive and a sworn cynic worrying about an eight-year-old girl he hadn't even met? He picked up the models and put them back into the safe, remembering to punch in the digital combination to reset the alarm. *What would it hurt to meet her?* a niggling voice questioned.

The latch on his office door rattled, alerting him of an intrusion. "I know your conference is over and I'd like to speak with you, Mr. Scott." The voice that burst through the door was unexpectedly sexy. "Mr. Scott?"

Did he hear disappointment in her voice? He resolved to remember that she was an espionage suspect. He closed the panel to hide the safe, and turned around, determined not to let her fill his mind, but the in-the-flesh presence of the lawyer took his breath away. His eyes scanned her precisely painted lips, her carefully darkened lashes, her cornsilk hair, and her gracefully draped blouse beneath a tailored jacket. A matching mauve skirt, stockings and shoes completed the gorgeous picture.

"Ms Moore. Good morning." What a pleasant tradition could be starting. He would say good morning to her, she would smile and say good morning to him . . . a little give, a little take.

It took a marvelous moment for her welcoming eyes to cool as she glanced at the liquor cabinet, then to the bottle at his feet.

He gestured toward it. "Would you care for a drink?"

"It's nine-thirty in the morning!"

"Irish coffee then?" He loved the way her pink lips parted when he said something to get her dander up. Those magnificent eyes almost made him forget that he was angry with her for neglecting her kid. "I think I'll have one." He picked up the bottle, turned and gathered the tools for mixing the drink—to cover why he was really at the bar. Discreetly, he slid the panel over the safe and closed the cabinet doors.

Just then Maggie ran into the room, puffing. "I'm sorry boss. She did an end run around me."

"That's all right, Maggie. I can see she's very athletic; it's all in the legs." When he looked up again he saw Matilda's nostrils flare.

"I'm going to talk to you like an adult, Mr. Scott, if you think you can handle that?" Her voice held all the charm of a Doberman's growl, but her clear, honest eyes and the tint on her cheeks entreated him. "I'd like the same courtesy, if you don't mind?"

"Should I ring for Mr. Patrick?" Dane's secretary asked immediately.

"No, Maggie. No harm done. I'll take the responsibility." He stole glances at his visitor while he mixed a concoction of club soda and—tequila? He gritted his teeth and smiled. "We'll talk." He gestured for Matilda to take a seat on the free-form divan that was large enough for two, but she settled into the chair in front of his desk, instead.

Dane walked toward his desk, slowly, circling close behind her on the way. His gaze on her back sent a thrill down Tildie's spine. She closed her mauve skirt where a smidgeon of lace was showing through the discreet slit. "Nigel and Associates must have more pressing cases to cover, Ms Moore, yet you spend so much of your time with us." He stopped beside her and stirred his drink. "Certainly Better Television for Children is not one of your wealthier clients.

I heard your firm has an important interest in Cleveland. Is that true?"

"We have clients from all over the state," she answered pointedly, letting him know that their client in Cleveland— SynTech—was not open for discussion. "Better Television for Children is a national grass roots organization with a good idea. They want me to share it with you since you are the creator of *Star Power*."

He moved around his gray chair, sank into it and tipped back. His steady gaze gave Tildie the impression that he enjoyed studying her form almost as much as the forms he incorporated into his designs. He scanned a line here and a curve there, which gave her a curiously pleased sensation and made her angry with herself at the same time. Meanwhile, she studied him. Wearing a light gray polo shirt, which emphasized the energetic lines of his torso, and neat casual slacks, which hugged his narrow hips and suited his boy-wonder style, he looked more like a relaxed golfer than a busy executive. He sipped his drink, shuddered with a grimace and set the glass on his desk.

"Drinking this early in the morning doesn't set a good example for children," she said.

"You're right. I'll save this for lunch," he returned, quickly opening a drawer in his desk, sticking the glass in and closing the drawer again.

She exhaled slowly in an effort to ignore his contrite, innocent expression.

"I'd like to talk about the content of *Star Power* and its effects on children."

"Kids love it. I know, because I read the letters they send to the Captain. I answer them too." He tapped his notebook. "One little girl likes the show so much she wants the Captain to marry her mom."

Tildie rolled her eyes at his conceit. He made it sound as if the juvenile proposal had been meant specifically for him.

"Some children are very imaginative. They think it would be romantic to have a famous father."

"Romantic?" He lifted a brow. "Interesting." His slow smile grew more personal.

"Hero worship," she clarified. "It's not uncommon."

"How should the Captain handle this situation?" His sincere-sounding voice gave her an uncertain feeling.

"Gently, of course."

"That goes without saying." He waited for further words of guidance, and she wondered why he was acting as though she would play an important part in the outcome.

"The girl obviously loves the Captain, so..." His clear, curious eyes grew more personal, and she knew it was time to swing the conversation to her concerns. "It's my turn to ask a question now. Do you realize that Captain Starblazer is with *Star Power* fans five solid hours a week?" She spoke in a rush. "Nearly one hour a day. That's more time than most fathers spend with their children."

"Pretty sad commentary on family life, wouldn't you say?"

"Sad but true." For a moment she lost her train of thought in his gray gaze. "Captain Starblazer spends about 250 hours a year, with the children in his viewing audience." He watched her lips as she formed each word, and she tried to quell her sudden nervousness. "The Better Television for Children protection group would like those hours to be quality time."

He crossed his arms over his chest. "They see Captain Starblazer as a father figure?"

"Yes. Someone wise and dependable."

His sudden quicksilver smile warmed his clear, cool eyes.

"Children like to think of their fathers as heroes," she said, her eyes judiciously avoiding his biceps, which were cleverly revealed by his snug shirt sleeves. "It's not that unusual," she said, wishing once again that he dressed more conventionally.

"If dads are too busy and moms are doctors or lawyers, who is taking care of the kids? Is that why little kids are writing to an imaginary superhero asking him to be their dad?" He paused. "Shouldn't the parents share the job of child rearing?"

"Ideally. Especially since the days of the single-income family are nearly extinct." She felt inadequate and proud at the same time. She and her kids had survived on a single income and minimal child support for years. Not always well, but they had hung in through thin and thinner. "However, we're discussing *Star Power*, not the economy."

"I thought we were discussing a little girl who needs a father?"

She coughed, slightly unnerved by his careful study of her. "There are points that BTC would like to—"

"Advertising practices you'll have to discuss with Bert Tundry. He's the marketing strategist."

Apparently he was suddenly anxious to be rid of her. "I will, but—"

"I'll get him for you." He pressed a button on his desk console. "Maggie, would you see if Bert Tundry is free?" He informed Tildie, "You should be able to see him soon."

"You're a very important man in the company, a national hero. . ." She sensed that his eyes were striving to snag her roving gaze. "Better Television for Children feels that you could be a valuable ally in the effort to make the cartoons children watch healthier for them."

"And how do you feel? Would I make a good ally?" He leaned back in his chair and put his hands behind his head.

He did not lack confidence, she decided. "The group hopes that after hearing their points, you'll help modify *Star Power* so it's more suitable for children. That's what the hearings are all about." She blindly checked her notes. Had she let her gaze linger too long on him? Had she involuntarily returned his contagious smile? "One point that needs to be addressed concerns interpersonal relationships as portrayed on *Star Power.*"

"Sounds interesting. We could talk about it over coffee."

"No, we can't," she said coolly.

"What if I agreed to help the cause. Would I work mainly with you? I just want to know how much trouble would be in store."

"I could furnish you with a list of BTC members in the area who—"

"Suppose I said I've been against the violence in the cartoons all along and that if we worked together, we could make the difference? We could discuss the possibilities over coffee." His eyes brightened.

"No. I don't think that would be possible." Work together? Work with an irritating man with a smile that could melt the Rock of Gibraltar? Glancing up from her notes, she chanced a look at him. "No, definitely not."

"A moment ago I was a valuable ally." Searching eyes questioned her. "I'm not following this too clearly, counselor. What am I missing here? I may be offering my help, not to mention a free cup of coffee. But now you don't want my help?" His eyes narrowed and gave off a laserlike beam. "Maybe the children aren't your main concern in this project, Ms Moore? Maybe you have other reasons for being in this factory?"

"I simply feel..." Complicated emotions collided inside her, and she could hardly get the words out. "I feel that it wouldn't be wise for us to meet on a social basis before the hearing—like for coffee, for instance." Coffee could lead to lunch and to dinner and to...

"This isn't a court case. Is it?"

"No, it isn't." But her thoughts were on another case—an upcoming custody suit. "But a conflict of interest may be construed." She couldn't meet his skeptical eye, so she checked her notes again. "The BTC wants your help, but our meetings would have to be recorded, because of the...hearing." She nearly forgot why she was there. "It's nothing personal, really." She could feel the heat of the lie warm her cheeks, as she quickly launched into another point. "Now if we could continue? Usually Captain Starblazer only interacts with other human beings when he is being confrontational—with the villain, Cyclon, or his evil henchmen. This could send the subconscious message to children that people in general are bad. This is compounded by the fact that the Captain seems isolated, since his only friends seem to be machines."

"What do you mean, it's nothing personal?"

She ignored his question. "He gets detailed information and opinions from his on-board computer," she said. "He speaks of his spaceship as though it were a person, and he talks strategy with his robot sidekick, Spinner, who also acts as the main source of humor and warmth in the story—"

"Wait a minute here," Dane interjected. "I'm amazed that you can't see that Starblazer is a nice guy!"

"—and all this could dehumanize the children watching—" she went on as if he hadn't spoken.

"But of course if you're so interested in being professional that you can't drink a simple cup of coffee..."

"—and they may begin to trust machines more than people!" she finished, nearly shouting over his interruptions.

"Why not?" Dane asked, pleased at the sudden silence. "Machines don't change their minds or have ulterior motives."

"But how much companionship can they get from a machine?" she asked, searching his angry, glittering eyes. How much companionship could she get from her work? she suddenly asked herself. Did she need more? Was Sally right? Did she need to get on with her life? How threatening could one lousy too strong, too black cup of coffee be? She had no idea where the anger that had welled up inside her had come from. "I'm sorry," she said finally. "I don't think this is going to work. I mean maybe we can't work together."

"I think you're right." His eyes mellowed. "Perhaps you'd rather work with my associate." His eyes were at once daring and sincere. "And my friend."

A tiny electrical murmur came from behind the desk and soon a thigh-high robot rolled around to meet her. Despite the tension she felt, she smiled when she saw Spinner there in the flesh, so to speak, his yellow and orange lights blinking, his gleaming Plexiglas skull spinning around on tripod legs with smooth ball-bearing feet. He rolled up in front of her and stopped, turned an electric eye her way and whined a high-pitched wolf whistle.

"You'll have to forgive him. He has an eye for the ladies." Dane returned her smile with a quick, innocent grin. "Spinner, I'd like you to meet Matilda Moore. Behave yourself now, buddy. She's a crackerjack attorney who wants to write you out of the script." A robotic arm swung up in greeting. Tildie couldn't help but giggle as she shook his hand. She felt so silly. "Talk to him, it's okay. I promise I won't tell the BTC. Go on. He likes pretty ladies to whisper to him."

She bent forward to talk more personally. "Hello, Spinner."

The robot responded with a chortle of electrical sounds that ended with a croon.

Tildie laughed.

The former astronaut inclined his chin, studying her, while the robot responded to her laughter. "You should laugh more often, counselor."

She looked up and smiled at Dane Scott, then chuckled again. "Spinner is very cute."

The robot rocked a little on his rollers and rattled off another round of bleeps and clicks.

"Don't tell him that—he'll be impossible to live with."

She laughed again and shook her head, knowing that one little girl would have given anything in the world to have been here to meet Spinner, to see—she looked again at the warm expression on Dane Scott's face—the Captain and his faithful companion. She was suddenly embarrassed at his flagrant observation of her animated features.

"Friendly, isn't he?" Dane said. "I designed his body, but a friend of mine put in his brain."

"The Wizard of Oz?"

He smiled at her joke. "A computer genius with NASA."

"And he took the time to tinker with a toy?"

"Why not?" Dane's sober expression and consideration of her question surprised her.

"I would think his time and talent were too valuable and much too important to—"

"To waste on children? Hardly the right attitude for a children's advocate. Could one not say the same thing about high-priced attorneys from high-powered law firms?"

She felt foolish forgetting the main lesson of Courtroom Dynamics 101, which was: never allow a question to place you on the defensive. "Children do deserve the best talents and minds working on their behalf."

He looked pleased. "Spinner's speech is voice activated. So when you talk to him he talks back. Not much in the grand scheme of things, but fun. I believe Tech Toys has something on the drawing board along these lines. Have you heard about it?"

"No, but I like your robot very much," she said truthfully.

"That's a start. Hard to believe you can have fun with a machine, isn't it?"

She could feel his eyes on her as she played with Spinner. "He is very sweet." She felt her resistance to his creator slipping away, too, as she met his gaze across the desk. But she looked away to touch the mechanical hand again.

The robot responded with another wolf whistle.

Tildie laughed in spite of herself.

"Does that mean you'll go out to dinner with us?" The tilt of his chin and the hint of dimples in his lean cheeks were tempting.

"That wouldn't be wise." What an understatement! Already an invitation for coffee had escalated to dinner. She saw the remote control unit in the astronaut's hand and knew that he'd carefully designed this whole scene.

"You're right. Spinner's a messy eater anyway. I can dress him up, but I can't take him anywhere."

She laughed at Spinner's chattering protest, even though she realized the two clever con artists, or one, anyway, were collaborating on chipping away at her resistance.

"Maybe you and I could go out and leave him at home?" he inquired as he walked out from behind his desk to sit on the front edge, arms folded over his chest, his adorable robot at his feet—Captain Starblazer in the flesh. "His batteries need recharging anyway."

"No, dinner is out of the question." She collected her notes for a quick retreat. Why did his gold-flecked eyes dance over her? She looked away to the vivid blue shades of the photograph of the Earth on the wall as she stuffed the papers into her briefcase. "It's obvious we aren't going to be able to work together on this, Mr. Scott. You apparently aren't taking this FCC hearing very seriously."

"You could be on the threshold of enlisting me for your cause." His handsome face and his vital body were too near, so she headed for the door.

"Why this sudden willingness to cooperate?"

"You've been asking for my help for two days." He followed her step for step. "You've worn me down, counselor." She could hear the smile in his voice. "How bad could dinner be?" She feared it wouldn't be bad at all. "A little good food. I promise I use utensils." She stopped and stared at him. "Honest," he grinned. "Who knows? You may even find that it will be a very pleasant evening. Miracles have been known to happen." He reached out his hand and tilted her chin. His gaze flickered to the curve of her lips, to the wisps of hair tucked behind her ear. "Some even think I have a certain charm."

"To say nothing of a galaxy-sized ego."

"So I'll order crow. Have dinner with me tonight." He said the words with little conceit. "I like to eat; you like to eat. There's no conflict of interest there, counselor."

"Dinner is out of the question for tonight. I'm on my way to—"

"To Cleveland?"

"How did you—?"

"Is that why you're so anxious to get out of here?"

She slipped past a chair to get farther away from him. "Dinner isn't possible now or—"

"Tomorrow night then? The eighth?"

"I...I have a family barbecue. Just the three of us." She was finally at the door and she flung it open.

"I accept." A knowing smile caused the dimples to appear in his tanned cheeks, and the lines around his eyes to become more sharply defined. "Four's a better number, especially at Micki's birthday celebration."

"How did you know—"

"Well, Ms Moore!" Bert Tundry blocked her path on his way into the office. "I assume our genius impressed you?"

She glared at the confident smirk on Dane's face.

"You must know by now why we feel so lucky to have wooed our nation's top physicist and aeronautical engineer away from NASA."

Tildie did a double take. So this was the Wizard of Oz.

"What can I say?" The designer's brows furled with feigned humility under Bert's hearty praise.

"Yessiree, we stole Dane away from NASA and we're proud of it."

"And here you thought the toy business was all fun and games?" Dane smiled at Tildie's confusion. "We'll talk more over dinner tomorrow evening." He smoothly overrode her heated objections. "No need to thank me now." Dane Scott sent Matilda Moore on her way with a quick sly smile before he closed his office door.

CHAPTER FOUR

Dear Micki,

Spinner and I would like to be there for your birthday party, but we don't know whether we'll be in your galaxy by the eighth of June. I hope your ninth birthday will be the best yet.

I've been so busy defending the planet from superpowers, I never thought about being lucky enough to have a little girl of my own. If I did have a daughter I'd want a smart, sweet one like you. Happy Birthday, Micki, and many more to come.

Your Friend Always,
Captain Starblazer

Micki was standing on the sofa, bent at the waist so that her head was burrowed in a cushion and her fanny was lopped over the flowery back. She admired her letter for the hundredth time. She didn't need to read it; she knew it by heart. Every night for a week she had wished on the first star that the Captain would come for her birthday barbecue. After all, wishes came true sometimes. But not very often, she knew. Her father only needed to drive 350 miles from Chicago, but he hadn't showed up for any of her birthdays yet. *He may as well be in another galaxy,* she thought listlessly. Her dad was always too busy for her—she had figured that out when she was just a little kid.

Micki wondered what it would be like to have a father. Her friends, Cindy and Jill, played with their fathers, but not Heather, who didn't like her dad because he drank too much and made her mother cry. It was like a lottery; no one had a choice when it came to natural fathers. If she could have chosen, Micki's father would have been brave and wise—like Captain Starblazer. And, of course, he would have loved her whether she were good or bad.

Jer had told her she was too shrimpy to remember how it used to be when their father had lived with them. But she did know a few things about Paul Moore: he worked in a huge building in Chicago; he looked like A. J. Simon on TV, only older; he smelled good, but he hugged all stiff, like he was afraid a kid would bite him. There were some things she couldn't figure out about him. For instance, if he were as smart as Jer said, why had he married Lisa with the orange hair and the red lipstick, who wasn't nearly as pretty or as nice as mom?

Lisa had called Micki Sugar, as though she'd been talking to a toy poodle. Micki could have spoken about anything from the rings around Saturn to Great-Aunt Mattie's surgery, and Lisa would have treated her like a know-nothing kid. That made Micki sick, so she really hadn't minded when her father requested that only Jer come to Chicago to live with them in their apartment, which sounded like a castle. But Micki couldn't imagine living anywhere without Jer. Mom and Jer and her had always been together. They should stay together, she thought firmly.

Things were supposed to have been better when mom had gotten through school. But now her father was trying to break them up. Fathers were supposed to keep families together no matter what. She knew if Captain Starblazer were her dad he wouldn't let anyone take Jer away. He wouldn't let her down; he'd always be there. That's why she had wished on the stars. Besides, the Captain thought she was sweet.

Things were unsettled now and her birthday made it all the worse because everyone was *supposed* to be happy. But mom was nervous and Jer was grouchy. Birthdays were the pits.

Her mom whisked through the dining room on her way to the kitchen, looking funny upside-down, as though Cyclon had zapped her with an anti-gravity ray.

"Mom, do you think I'm sweet?"

"Sweet?" Mom stopped dead in her tracks, turned, and took slow, exaggerated steps toward the living room. "Who told you that?!"

Micki giggled, because she recognized the game her mother was playing as she stalked toward her. She realized it was childish, but today it felt good. "I mean, if you weren't my mom would you want me as your kid?"

"Would I want a kid with a monster face?" Soon Micki was convulsed with laughter, as her mom's fingers wriggled over her ribs with millions of tickles. "Who stands on her head?" She tickled behind Micki's knees and the bottom of her waving feet, until Micki gasped and cackled. "Who eats pizza while playing backgammon and gets the dice sticky?" Micki collapsed, crumpling her prized letter and rolling off the couch onto the floor, red-faced, happy, without a care in the world. Tildie grinned. "Yeah, I'd take ya. Why not? You're one of my two most favorite kids." She gently flicked a pigtail before she walked from the room. Micki's mom had told Micki that since she could remember and it was still true.

"Where are you goin'?"

"To start the coals for your birthday barbecue. Want to help?" she asked, hurrying on to the kitchen. Mom always walked fast—she had very long legs.

"I'll make the hamburger patties."

"Okay, in a bit."

Before Micki could retrieve her letter and sit back on the couch the doorbell rang. She went to answer it, even though she figured it was one of Jer's friends. She swung the heavy front door wide.

"Hello, Micki. I happened to be in the galaxy, so I dropped by."

She took in the golden hair, the kind eyes, the dent in the chin, the friendly dimples and the bright blue shirt that only lacked a silver star. She had wished it, and now he was standing at her door.

"Captain Starblazer..." She whispered and swallowed.

"Happy birthday, Micki. I came for your birthday party." His eyes smiled and his voice sounded much nicer than it did on television, comfortable and fuzzy like a teddy bear's. "You are having one, aren't you?"

"Yes, but I'm not supposed to let anyone in until mom comes to the door. She still thinks I'm a child." Micki rolled her eyes, embarrassed at having to admit such a thing to a superhero.

He smiled. "It's best to be safe. Why don't you go get her? I'll wait here."

In her excitement Micki slammed the door in his face and ran to the patio. "Mom! Mom! He's here! I knew he'd come! He came for my birthday! He's at the front door! Hurry!"

"Who's here?" A terrible thought struck Tildie.

"It's Captain Starblazer!" Micki squealed.

That was what Tildie had been afraid of. He had come despite her objections and despite her note and telephone message late yesterday, reiterating the possible conflict of interest. She *hadn't* told him that many of his recent comments had spooked her, confirming her belief that avoidance of him was a wise strategy. He knew where she lived and things about her family, for instance. She figured that the security chief had gathered information on her, but why was Dane so preoccupied with her trip to Cleveland? Was he trying to get something out of her? Why was he here?

"He's here for my birthday! I can't believe it! It worked!"

"What worked?"

"Come to the door, please, mom. It's not nice to keep a gentleman waiting." It was all the girl could do to contain her excitement.

"He won't be staying long, Micki," Tildie warned. "I'm sure he has a lot of missions to fly today." The nerve of the man, using company information for his personal use. She had told him that they couldn't have dinner and he'd invited himself to her home. Dane Scott—or Captain Starblazer—wasn't going to get away with this. She couldn't afford to entertain a man in her home. What if Paul's lawyer had detectives watching her? Captain Starblazer or not, she'd send the toy designer back into orbit, she decided as she marched to the foyer. She heard his familiar voice when Micki opened the door.

"Did anyone ever tell you you're a lot like your mom?" he said to her, laughing. "I hope you're not planning to slam the door again, honey. Is your mom home?"

Tildie swung the door wider and faced him.

"She certainly is." His pleased gaze wandered over her, from her tousled hair down to her smooth thighs and shapely calves. His sparkling eyes reminded her that she was only wearing a soft, pink-and-white striped boat-neck top and crisp, pink chino shorts.

"Can mommy come out to play?" His voice sounded innocent, but his clever smile warned her. "Or may I come in?"

"You can stay for the barbecue! Can't he, mom?"

The excruciatingly endearing furrows in his forehead and his furled brows echoed the questions.

"Micki, I'm sure the Captain is very busy."

"Never too busy for a friend." He smiled at Micki before he addressed Tildie again. "And for the lady of the house, I brought something special for dinner." He presented Tildie with a brown paper bag that obviously held a tall bottle. Now she knew his scheme: with a little wine, soft lighting and music after the children were in bed, her foggy brain would forget all about the case against Fun Design.

"I'm sorry to foil your wining-and-dining plans, but you can't turn my head with this, this—" She snatched the sack away.

"Chocolate syrup—for the ice cream." Dane smiled with devilment twinkling in his eyes. "I heard it was a very good year," he teased. "Micki, would you take the syrup to the kitchen for your mom, please?"

"I'm not letting you in here, Mr. Scott," she said when Micki was out of earshot. "I won't allow you to invite yourself into my home. I told you that we shouldn't see each other in social settings—"

"I imagined it would be like this." His all-encompassing gaze confirmed her sudden suspicion that her attire was overly abbreviated. He plastered a lopsided grin on his face and relaxed against the door frame. "I swear, looking at you, I hear bells."

"You're leaning against the door buzzer."

"Can't put a thing past you, can I, counselor?" Before she knew it, he had stepped into the entryway and was looking over the house. "Very nice place, Matilda. Upper

Arlington is the best place to meet the best people. Did a wealthy client arrange this humble abode for you?"

"I resent Fun Design investigating me."

"What's there to know about an upright, uptight attorney like yourself?"

She stood with her arms folded over her chest, determined not to answer him.

He didn't seem fazed. "The place may be a tad overstated for an attorney, but very nice."

"Mr. Scott, I told you—"

"Please, you don't have to be so formal. Call me Captain," he taunted confidently, then turned to welcome Micki again.

"You can call her Tildie," Micki said, proudly introducing her mom to the most perfect man in any galaxy.

"I like it." He smiled, tipping his head to the side as he considered her nickname.

"She's named after her Great-Aunt Mattie, who just had her gallbladder out. I think that's neat, don't you?"

"Very interesting."

"My name is really Michelle."

"I think that's pretty, too. But I hope you keep your gallbladder for a while longer."

Micki giggled.

"I brought something for the birthday girl." He pulled an official Captain Starblazer decoder badge and a communicator from his pocket. "These are for you, Micki."

"For keeps?" Her blue eyes glistened.

"Absolutely." A tinge of pink emerged on his cheeks under the weight of the child's unadulterated adoration.

"Pin it on me and I'll be an official Star Command cadet!" Micki surrendered the shiny, silver, star-shaped decoder eagerly.

"Maybe your mom could...?" He looked beseechingly at the crusading attorney. "The badge has a sturdy pin and clasp that meets federal safety standards for a child over five." He stalled, apparently hoping for a bailout. "Couldn't you pin this on your daughter?"

Tildie held firm and marveled at the superhero's sudden burst of human shyness.

"No, it wouldn't be the same!" Micki insisted.

Tildie shrugged gracefully as the game cadet stood at attention before Dane. His expression of acute embarrassment and vulnerability touched her, and she watched carefully as he bent over the happy child.

He stuck his finger trying to protect the little girl.

"Maybe those safety standards should be reviewed," Tildie chided softly.

He pinned on the badge with the words, "A star cadet forever."

"I promise I won't ever let you down," Micki vowed.

He smiled. "You never could, Micki." Patches of red could still be seen on his cheeks. It seemed he could handle big girls; it was little ones who threw him for a loop.

"That's very kind of you, Mr....Captain," Tildie corrected, wondering how to break the bond that had sprung up between worshipper and worshipee so she could send him on his way without a scene with Micki. "It was very nice of you to take time away from your battles to wish one of your fans a happy birthday, but—"

"Micki isn't just a fan. We're old friends. You might say we're pen pals. She's written me several letters telling me about you, asking me to come here today." Dane patted Micki's back before he looked up to take stock of her mother's shocked face.

"You were writing all those letters to—?"

"To the Captain," Micki said proudly. "And he wrote me back."

"Very gently, of course," Dane Scott said, his gaze becoming very personal.

Tildie remembered his comments about the letter from the little girl who had wanted the Captain for a father. Micki wouldn't have! Of course she would have, and she had. Tildie could see it in the Captain's teasing and playfully possessive eyes. She wanted to kick him in the shins.

"I had never received letters like Micki's before, so I wanted to meet her."

"How peculiar that you'd want to do that just before *Star Power* is to go before an FCC hearing!"

"Mom, isn't he wonderful!"

"A real hero." Tildie spoke sweetly through set teeth.

"And you're getting along so well," the little matchmaker said, beaming proudly from one adult to the other.

Tildie felt sold out by her own daughter.

"You were certainly right about your mom, Micki. She is very pretty—and smart too. Just like you."

"She didn't believe you were a real person."

"Shame on her. Maybe between the two of us we can change her mind about a few things. What do you think?"

"Yeah!" Micki grinned.

"Oh! I nearly forgot. I brought along a friend. I hope you don't mind. He doesn't eat much." He fetched the pièce de résistance from outside the door.

Spinner rolled into the oak foyer, immediately charming the little girl. He was Dane's surefire way into the house; Tildie would be the worst kind of monster if she tossed the dynamic duo out now and she knew the ex-astronaut knew it. She watched him work the remote controls behind his back, giving the robot an irresistible personality, pleasing Micki to the point of bursting. Before she knew it the door had closed and the three of them were heading for the patio with Tildie following.

Secure in his dinner plans, Dane relaxed and looked very much at home sitting in the redwood recliner near the pool with Micki orbiting around his chair or sitting at his feet. He offered his able assistance in rekindling the struggling coals while Tildie prepared food in the kitchen. She could hear his happy laughter and Micki's giggle as she put the finishing touches on the potato salad. Jer lumbered into the room and threw his dusty baseball glove onto the counter.

"Who's that?" His eyes narrowed as he studied the handsome man through the patio screen.

"He's Dane Scott."

"The astronaut?"

Jer's quick question surprised her, since he had been too young to remember much about the Sky Lab flights.

"Yes, he works for Fun Design. Micki thinks he's Captain Starblazer."

"What a spacehead." Jer snatched a bit of salad.

"There's a resemblance," Tildie replied vaguely.

Her son's eyes narrowed again. "He looks a little like dad, only younger." Jer frowned, then checked his mother for her opinion. She offered none. "I bet he can't play ball, though. What does he want?"

"Micki invited him for her birthday." She couldn't deny that it was pleasant to see Micki so happy.

"Man, he's short! I bet I'm taller than he is."

"He's small and as irritating as a splinter," Tildie said lightly. "He's the executive at Fun Design I've crossed swords with this week." Watching a totally comfortable Dane talking with her daughter, it was hard to believe that he had agitated her so much. "It seems they're pen pals. Remember how Micki insisted that the Captain was real? She had the letters to prove it." It was definitely a flesh-and-

blood man who sat on her patio; not a piece of celluloid—
a man who sent her blood pressure zooming up with jibes
about her wealthy clients and jeopardized her family unit by
his mere presence in her home. She would make the best of
it for Micki's sake and then he'd be on his way. "Would you
talk to Mr. Scott while Micki comes in and helps me with the
burgers?"

"No, ma. I don't want to. He's short, he's—"

"He's our guest," his mother insisted quietly.

"Hi, Jer," Dane called through the screen, having realized the boy was home. "How was practice? Micki tells me
you're quite the baseball player." Tildie heard Micki fuss
about having to leave the Captain to go help her mother. She
wasn't sure if Jer answered Dane or not.

Once in the kitchen, Micki continued to admire her hero
from afar through the window screen. "Isn't he wonderful!?" she sighed, sounding more like a teenager than a
nine-year-old. Tildie guided the star struck youngster to the
sink and gave her a bar of soap for her hands.

"And probably hungry. You'd better get the burgers
made."

"I think he's cute, don't you?" she asked as though she
were sizing up Tildie for a wedding dress.

How would she break the news to the incorrigible romantic? Micki had been trying to marry her mother off to
box boys or movie stars since she was four. "He's a bit short
for me, don't you think?" She kept her voice flippant.

"No." Micki shook her head solemnly. "I read in Aunt
Sally's *Better Homemaking* that short men are very compatible and *very* sexy." She wiggled her eyebrows.

"No more reading Aunt Sally's magazines. And don't
bother to even think that anything could possibly happen
between . . . the Captain and myself. Agreed?"

"I think he's cute and compatible," Micki repeated, lifting her nose into the air. "Maybe I'll marry him myself." She flattened the reddish hamburger meat between her palms.

"I'm afraid he's too old for you."

"Not for you." Micki gave her a quick grin. "You're old, too, mom. You'd be perfect together."

"Thanks." Tildie rolled her eyes. "You do know that he's not really Captain Starblazer? And that he's caused me more aggravation than you could possibly know?"

"He's Dane Scott, isn't he?" The child's intuitiveness always took Tildie by surprise. "I heard you and Aunt Sally talking. What does evicted mean?"

"You weren't supposed to hear that! You've got ears like an elephant!"

"AM I SUPPOSED to call you Captain, too?" The bored teen was standing on one leg, leaning against the wall and checking Dane out without a smile. He was glad his mother and silly little sister were in the kitchen.

Dane tried to defuse the threat. "I'm Dane Scott." He offered his hand and Jer took it reluctantly, then stuffed his hands into his pockets. Dane eased back in the redwood chaise longue, wondering whether it would be worth his while to try to beat his way through the boy's hostility. He remembered Micki's excitement at his arrival and he told himself that was enough motivation. "How was ball practice?" he asked.

"The usual." The boy's face held the sullen, stubborn expression of any thirteen-year-old who felt he or she was being challenged. Dane recognized some of the symptoms. He had been much older—nearly nineteen—and away from home, when his widowed mother had started to date other men, and Dane hadn't liked it much, either.

"Must have been pretty hot today."

"Not bad." Tiny protective lines that seemed to say, "Don't hurt me or mine" appeared at the corners of the boy's mouth.

"You remind me of your mom."

"No one ever says that," the boy said in a bored tone. "It shows how little you know about my mom or me. Everyone thinks I look like my dad."

"But you have your mother's mouth."

"People say I play baseball like my dad used to. He was nearly drafted by the Reds. He would've played with Pete Rose and Johnny Bench." Jer crossed his arms over his chest. "I bet you never played baseball."

"No, I was—"

"Too short to play first base?"

"Right." Dane nodded. He could almost picture Tildie pitching the same zinger. "But my size came in handy later. NASA couldn't afford space suits for the big guys." He smiled easily.

"My dad's big. Six feet, four inches. He's a commodities broker on the Chicago Board of Trade."

"Very competitive work. It pays to be tall in that field. Sounds like quite a guy."

"Yeah." Jer nodded. "He'll probably be here tonight." He stood like a statue, casting protective glances toward the house. "He'll probably be here any minute."

"Micki didn't think he'd come at all. That makes her feel sad," Dane said cautiously.

"She's just a kid with a big mouth," Jer said, looking away.

"Little sisters are like that sometimes, but they are also kind of—special." Dane leaned forward to confide in Jer. "I know, I've got one myself. But I don't tease her anymore because she has very powerful friends. One is a gorilla and another is an elephant called Simba."

"Does she live in the jungle with Tarzan or something?" Jer mocked.

"Close. Her husband is a linebacker for the Chargers and she's a veterinarian at the San Diego Zoo."

"That's pretty neat."

"Yeah. You should see her with that elephant." He smiled, picturing her. "Annie's a little taller than Micki, but there are many similarities between them."

The boy tried not to smile. "My mom thinks you're a pain," he said flatly.

"My feelings about your mom are similar." He rolled his eyes and laughed. "Actually, I came to see Micki today. And now that I've met her in person, she reminds me even more of my kid sister when she was her age."

The boy's eyes narrowed. "You mean you didn't come here to see my mom?"

Dane pursed his lips. He had to give Jer credit for his cards-on-the-table attitude. "I think your mother is intelligent and—"

"And you'd like to go out with her because she has a great personality?"

"No, actually."

Jer held his head at an angle, trying to decide whether Dane was sincere or just a smooth talker.

"She's much too serious for me. But against my better judgment, I'd go out with her if she'd ask me nice," Dane said, trying to censor visions of Tildie's long, smooth thighs and the pink shorts wrapped snugly around her hips. He got up to check the coals and spread them out in the barbecue pit. "Now that we have that over with, can we relax and enjoy what's left of the evening? Would you like to run the robot? He's fun to play with." Dane extended his hand with the remote control switches and Jer's eyes narrowed, then softened as he took it, accepting the fragile truce. "These coals are perfecto," Dane called happily. "Bring on the burgers!"

Almost on cue, Tildie and Micki came out to the patio, Micki with a plate of burgers, Tildie with a wary smile. Like magic, Tildie saw Dane become the head barbecue chef and chief storyteller. She watched the play of muscles in his arms and his neat compact body twist as he slipped the burgers on the sizzling grill. When he caught her watching him, she looked away at the English garden bordering the patio. The spiked delphiniums nearly matched his shirt. With tanned forearms and sturdy fingers, he handled the spatula with flair, flipping the burgers easily. For long moments she forgot her suspicions about him. Happy talk was accompanied by birdsong in the tall trees and the manicured shrubs, and Tildie sighed blissfully.

Dane had wrapped Micki around his little finger, and Jer, who had been cautious at first, forgot to lower his voice as he laughed at the visitor's anecdotes. Jer's favorite was the one about Dane's car spinning off the track during a time trial. Micki cackled at his tale about his high-school rocket club's half-time demonstration during the Westerville-Marysville football game; as a sophomore, Dane had tied the principal's large, flowered boxer shorts to his Atlas and the two objects had parachuted gently down into the capacity crowd at the Westerville stadium. All three of them silently listened to the sound of his smooth tenor voice as he described the stillness and the beauty of the blue Earth as seen from thousands of miles away. When his gaze fell upon Tildie's face, she knew he could see it in her eyes: a free-floating image of their bodies gently touching in the weightless dark. She censored her thoughts immediately and hurried inside the house for burger trimmings and drinks.

She took in gulps of dry cool air at the refrigerator door to sober her thoughts. Had she forgotten that she couldn't think of any man right now. The survival of her family depended on it. She quietly cursed the custody suit and Paul's lawyers and took another deep breath. Why couldn't she shake the image of Dane Scott whispering to her, telling her that everything would be all right while he stroked her hair, kissed her mouth and—

"May I help?"

"What?" she said as she jumped. Former astronauts walked quietly, she realized.

"May I help?" he asked again.

"No, thank you. I'm used to fending for myself." But she certainly wasn't used to being so close to a man in the kitchen. She sensed him breathing behind her.

"Are you all right?"

"Someone always takes off with the ketchup."

"It's here, in the door."

Why did he have to be so helpful and so near? She busied her hands by pulling jars from the fridge.

"I came in to get the drinks," he said in a low voice, only a tantalizing few inches away. "Everyone wants milk."

"How did you perform that miracle?"

"I told them I drink it." He feigned modesty.

"Congratulations." She grabbed a partial gallon in one hand and fumbled for a head of lettuce and some tomatoes with the other, balancing them on the jars. She turned to face him, and nearly dropped the whole armload.

"We seem to keep running into each other," he commented.

"Yes . . ." Her lips parted to say more, but nothing came to mind except his impulsive dimples and his impetuous mouth that curved so easily into a smile. She clutched her load against her chest.

"Let me help." He took the milk and a rolling tomato, and closed the refrigerator door. Without her heels she needed to tip her chin up slightly to meet his eye, and she wondered whether his kiss would be gentle or hard.

"I hope you realize that you blackmailed your way into my house with your robot," she said.

"Just another NASA success story." Why did his honest Boy Scout eyes always take her steam away? She stepped aside, but he blocked her again with his compatible body.

"Your presence here compromises my integrity on this case," she muttered.

"I would like nothing better than for your integrity to stay intact, lady lawyer, for your kids' sake," he said cryptically.

"You're putting me in a very bad position."

"Actually I think just the opposite is true." His intent gaze brought heat to her cheeks. "Contrary to what you think, I am a good influence on your children. And that, counselor, makes me good for you." His dimples appeared.

"Does all this come naturally to you or do you practice in front of a mirror?"

His eyes narrowed as he studied her. "That's what really needles you, isn't it?"

"You don't bother me at all, at least not the way you think."

"It's understandable. You see me having a good time with your kids, so you find yourself attracted to me, and you're mad at yourself for that."

"I think your brain was permanently damaged in the high altitude, astronaut Scott."

Stepping around him, she unloaded her armful of jars on the counter. He propped himself up against the counter and looked totally bewildered as she blazed into her short-order cook speed. She bustled around the kitchen, grabbing small bowls for the condiments, slicing and dicing onions and tomatoes, and magically producing trays on which to transport them.

"Actually the consensus seems to be that I'm a very compatible and sexy fellow," his low voice teased as he leaned toward her. "At least according to your nine-year-old daughter and *Better Homemaking* magazine." He pursed his lips to keep from laughing aloud at Tildie's mortified look. "Between my diminutive body and your long gorgeous legs we're meant for each other. Why fight it?"

He took a ready-to-go tray from her and slipped out the patio door before she could regain her breath and say another word.

Tildie ignored Dane's curious gaze as she stepped out onto the patio, a few minutes later, carrying four glasses of milk.

"Maybe you should ask your mother," Dane was saying to Micki.

"No, you tell us. How did you meet? Did you think mom was pretty? Was it so very ro*man*tic?"

"Knock off that mushy stuff," Jer warned his sister.

Micki ignored Jer's threat and looked from her mother to Dane with an expectant grin.

"I guess you might say we met by accident," Dane said. "Your mother still hasn't explained what she was doing in that hallway, which was off limits to unauthorized—"

"We ran into each other outside his office door," Tildie clarified while she organized the patio table for dinner. "He was sneaking out of his meeting with me." The girl's happy face indicated that the story could well become one of her all-time favorites.

"Really, your mom bumped into me." Dane waited for Micki's giggle.

"I object," Tildie said.

"Did she fall into your arms?"

"Micki!"

"Not until the second time we met," Dane laughed.

"I knew it! She's watched all your cartoons a hundred times. She even sings the *Star Power* song sometimes, don't you mom? You're her first real case," Micki announced.

"Well, I'm flattered." His knowing eyes glowed.

"We're going to be rich someday."

"Oh?" Dane swung his head toward Tildie.

"It may take a few days to get my career established," she quipped, trying to hide her embarrassment. Changing the subject, she said brightly, "Dinnertime, everyone."

The meal was simple and colorful, with cubes of orange cantaloupe and pale melon in a fruit bowl, and cool green lettuce and tomato wedges in a festive salad. Tildie was glad she had exceeded her grocery budget on this week's bill. And there weren't even any catastrophes during the meal, except for Micki's loose tongue.

"Your mom has spent a lot of time at Fun Design," Dane told Micki between hamburgers. "That surprises me, because I know that she must have a lot of other clients, smart as she is. How many does she—"

Tildie cut the question short. "Micki, would you pass the salad, please?"

"She has one in Cleveland, right, mom?"

"Micki, that's not for you to say."

"It's with SynTech—"

"Micki, my clients are confidential." From the corner of her eye, she glimpsed the astronaut's raised brow.

"SynTech Incorporated, I presume?"

"Uh-oh. I wasn't supposed to say confidential stuff, but you're a friend." Micki glanced away from her mother's reproving look.

"Maybe we should talk about something else," Dane suggested with a smile.

"Right. Did mom tell you that she doesn't think you have enough women in your life?"

"No, she didn't."

"More feminine role models in the cartoon was what I meant," Tildie explained with a hint of color on her cheeks.

"You didn't mention that yesterday."

"It didn't reflect the opinions of my clients." She decided to explain her view. "I just think since so many young girls watch *Star Power* it would be good to show that women can help in the struggle against evil, not just be pretty ornaments."

"And the Captain could have a girlfriend and get married and live happily ever after," Micki sighed.

Tildie look pointedly at Dane. "See what I mean?"

"Couldn't we ship the little tweety bird off someplace?" Jer complained.

"You wouldn't say that if Cynthia Edgars were here," Micki said accusingly.

"A girl, huh?" Dane stifled a grin after noting Jer's threatening face. He managed to smooth over the children's argument by guiding the conversation to safer topics like race cars, robots, baseball games and summer vacation. Micki blew out all ten candles on her cake, including one for good luck, and informed everyone that she'd made the same wish on the first star that had glimmered in the evening sky, but she refused to tell anyone what her wish was. After they all cleared the table, Dane and Jer played catch while Micki played with Spinner and toasted marshmallows. Tildie found herself regretting that the day was winding down to a neon pink finish. The tall delphiniums turned a purplish shade as the sunlight eased into twilight, as gently as the light rock playing on Jer's radio.

Tildie hated to say, "Micki, it's time for bed. There's school tomorrow."

"It's not dark yet," she complained. Receiving no response from her mother, she turned to Dane. "I don't want you to leave," she begged as she watched him pack up Spinner.

"You be a good girl and go on to bed now. There will be more time during summer vacation to do things. I can't take you in a Star cruiser, but we could go for a ride in my plane. Would you like that?"

"Honest? Mom, did you hear that?"

"Honey, we can't expect Mr. Scott to spend more time with us." She vowed never to allow him in the house again. He'd been right: seeing the way Micki had taken to him like jam to bread had made him even more attractive to her. "Go on now. I'll be up in a minute to say good-night, honey."

"I'm going up now, too," Jer said, as though he'd made a very important decision. "I have homework."

"It was nice meeting you, Jer. I'd like to see you play ball...."

"Yeah, maybe."

"Would you like to ride in my car sometime?"

"Who wouldn't? You actually designed a car for Corwin Racing?"

"Just in my spare time."

"I bet she's built to fly." Guarded emotion, but unqualified respect shone in the teenager's eyes. "I wouldn't turn down a ride," Jer said, remembering his mother's warning to Micki about taking up too much of Dane's time. "Good night."

Micki tugged on Dane's hand.

"I think someone wants to kiss you good-night, Captain." Tildie explained her urgency.

"Oh? You must mean Princess Michelle from the Sercerian moon." He bent down to meet the giggling Micki's eyes.

"Mom is really the princess," she said, then whispered, "Do you like her?"

"Yeah," he whispered back.

"You made this my best birthday ever." She plastered his rough cheek with a juicy smacker and hugged his neck. At first his arms hung at his sides awkwardly, but then he wrapped them around the lovable little girl and he nuzzled her cheek.

"You're welcome." He set her down and tried to regain his composure.

"Good night!" Within seconds Micki scampered up the stairs.

"Good night, honey." He swallowed hard. Why had he been shaken by a child's good-night kiss, she wondered.

The mystery of his response fascinated Tildie so much that it took a moment for her to realize she was standing face to face with the toy designer in the quiet house. The soft gold moonlight filtering through the leaded glass of the front door emphasized the lines near his eyes and made him look wise.

"She's a good kid."

"Yes. And impressionable. She probably won't wash her face again." At Dane's puzzled expression, she added, "You kissed her cheek."

"Oh." A tiny surprised laugh came out as though to indicate he hadn't realized the response such a simple, natural gesture could evoke. "Kids." He shrugged casually, but he swallowed hard. "Well." His gaze flickered to her eyes and mouth. "I'd better say good-night."

"Yes." She couldn't speak with the conviction that she had maintained earlier. Maybe she didn't really want him to go; she wasn't sure anymore. "Thank you for helping get the children off to bed so quickly. Usually it's a battle.'' His smile told her it hadn't been a problem, and she admitted to herself that he *was* good with the kids. She realized the prudent thing would be for him to leave, but before she knew it, she was saying, "Would you like to stay for a cup of coffee?'' His smile told her his answer was yes.

CHAPTER FIVE

"I'LL PUT ON SOME COFFEE before I say good-night to Micki and Jer," Tildie said as she guided him into the formal library. She had no idea what had possessed her to ask him to stay. Maybe his vulnerability with Micki had won her over—or the color of his eyes in the gold light of the foyer. Regardless, the damage had been done. Anyway, she thought on the way to the kitchen, if Paul had detectives watching her, what did it matter if he stayed another fifteen minutes?

Despite Micki's romantic hints, Tildie planned to breeze back into the library, thank him for coming to the birthday party, chat for a minute and send him on his way. And that was what she told Micki would happen when she said good-night to her. But when she returned to the library she made her second mistake: she hesitated in the doorway to study the man who was apparently engrossed in a book he was holding rather far from his face as he read. She guessed his only surrender to vanity was a refusal to wear reading glasses. It was odd that the incredulously flippant Dane Scott seemed to suit the rarified atmosphere of the wood-paneled room. For the first time she could imagine him as a scientific wizard.

Yet he had played with a child—her child—all evening and had looked so at home, relaxed—compatible. The fact that he got along with her children *did* make him very attractive, not to mention what his own collection of physical attributes did for her, particularly the flirtatious dimples, the mysterious cleft in his chin and the impish nose that turned up. Not to mention the compact, sturdy body that wasn't overpowering, yet showed tone and biceps at surprising moments, and the character-enhancing crow's feet that fanned out from his eyes, saving him from looking too boyish. His features weren't devastating in themselves, but together they made a very pleasant combination. As well, being able to look him directly in the eye held a sweet fascination.

He sat in the leather wing chair, one ankle crossed over his knee. Her gaze was drawn to where his slacks drew interestingly snug at the vee between his legs, and she managed to embarrass herself just as he lowered the book he was reading. When his lively, intelligent eyes met hers, she couldn't deny that new frontiers had indeed become available to her....

"Counselor?" His expression as much as asked, "Can I do something wonderfully sexy for you?" She hovered in the doorway, unwilling to leave the security of the solid wood.

"Micki wanted me to tell you again that she is very, very glad that you came for her birthday." Tildie smiled nervously.

"I had gathered that somehow—between the giggles." Dane noted that Tildie's arms were wrapped around her waist, her ankles were crossed and she was propped up safely against the door frame.

"I wanted to thank you for making this a very special day for her." She could feel his appraisal, and knew he was testing her eyes for signs of sincerity.

"Micki is a sweet kid. You've done a great job raising her."

"Thank you." Tildie felt self-conscious, not because of the compliment, but because of how instantly important it had become for him to have said it. "You made her very happy today."

"And to think someone didn't want me to stay," he taunted.

"Couldn't you just say a simple, 'You're welcome'?"

"What? And make it easy for you?"

His smile was inviting. The tiny flutter in her stomach warned her that sending him on his way wasn't going to be as simple as she'd thought.

She coughed discreetly. "The fact that you're here puts me in a difficult position. Yet, I wouldn't have wanted to deny Micki the evening. But then, I think you knew that when you came."

"I believe we have agreed on something at last." His voice mellowed and his dimples appeared when he spoke again. "Micki is a special kid." He secretly stole a look at her before he rose from the chair to return the book to the shelf. "This is a very interesting library."

She walked to a wall of shelves, sidestepping his half-teasing, half-devouring gaze. "There's a special collection...here they are." Her fingertips glided over fifteen leatherbound spines and by the time she got to the last in the series he was standing beside her. "It's a private collection of diaries by some of the women who first settled in Ohio." She could feel his eyes on her as she looked at the titles. Why was he scanning her from head to toe?

"Are you interested in brave new worlds? Frontiersmen?"

"Frontiers, not men," she said, momentarily meeting his clear gray gaze. Although she knew he could tell her fascinating tales about what it was like to be in a new world, she sensed that he couldn't share them without opening intimate parts of himself. "There are descriptions of wolf attacks, tales of Indians slipping in and sleeping by the fireplace at night, and explanations of nursing techniques for treating symptoms of the 'shaking ague,'" she said quickly. He had no right to make her feel like an infatuated teenager talking to the high-school hero in the stacks of the local library, she thought angrily. She was a thirty-five-year-old woman with a teenaged son; she had no business feeling giddy.

"Do these volumes belong to Eloise Caruthers?"

Is that why he had come here, after all, she wondered. Had Fun Design needed more information on her? She suddenly felt defensive. "From Charlie Patrick's research you probably know that this house belongs to Eloise Caruthers. Eloise has been a friend of mine for many years. The kids and I needed a new place to live, so Eloise asked us to sit with her house while she's in Europe." She crossed her arms again. "The arrangement had nothing to do with any client, in case you're wondering."

His cocked brow was his only concession to her speech. "I also noticed that you're at ease in a house like this—as if you were born to it."

Her only response was to elevate her chin slightly.

"I try to be observant." He shrugged.

"I spent most of my life in a house like this, first as a child and later as a bride." She turned her back to the books and leaned against the shelves. "It was a pleasant world I liked very much."

"Why did you leave it?" he asked curiously.

"That really isn't pertinent to your company's business." She walked away from him, remembering all the courage it had taken to leave her fine home and refuse help from her family or alimony from Paul. "You've pumped us for information all evening."

"Do you have anything to hide?"

"I like my privacy."

"What was Paul Moore like?"

"Paul?" The question took her by surprise. "Was that in the report, too? Your security chief left no stone unturned."

"What was Micki's father like?" For the first time that evening Dane showed agitation and something more. "You know, the wealthy commodities broker and almost professional baseball player? Micki and Jer filled in some of the blanks," he explained to her raised brow. "But what attracted you?" There was anticipation and reluctance at once in his eyes.

"He was very much like my father."

"Let me guess: a finely dressed, aggressive businessman?"

"Did the kids fill you in on Grandpa Cabe too?"

"Cabe Fitzsimmons?" His voice held moderate surprise. The report hadn't gone that far back. "Major construction, right?" When she nodded, he continued with his analysis. "And you were daddy's little girl and Paul was handpicked."

"You're partially right. Daddy had two little girls, but he didn't have much time for either of us." She avoided his eyes. "Paul preferred and belonged to a bigger world; a house like this couldn't hold him," she said simply. She had fought hard to regain order in her life, and now Paul was threatening to upset it with his custody suit. She forced the thought out of her mind and went on, "Paul was and is a very complicated and a highly competitive man. If he sees something he wants, he goes after it, both in his business and in his private life." Tildie didn't want to think about the finances and energy he would expend to win Jer back.

"And Micki misses him." Dane shut the book he had been absently leafing through and shoved it back on the shelf. "Tell me something. If Paul Moore is so competitive, and such a winner, how is it that he managed to lose the most important people in his life?''

His blunt question threw her, and a sudden thought occurred to her: Was that what the custody case was all about? Paul Moore couldn't tolerate being a loser. Did he, in fact, care about his son, or was it all ego?

"Maybe he's not the winner the kids think he is," Dane added.

"Perhaps not." She'd been in such a panic about the custody suit that she hadn't thought about it objectively. It was time to stop reacting to Paul's claims and start developing her own case, she told herself firmly. Before this moment she hadn't even taken the time to think of valid arguments against Jer's going with Paul—other than the fact that she didn't want it to happen. This was the most confident she'd felt about the custody suit since Paul had filed in April, and it was thanks to the bothersome ex-astronaut. She could have hugged him.

"What are you thinking about?" His expression was concerned.

"Micki tried so hard to feel blue today," she said, suddenly realizing that she was wearing a tiny smile on her parted lips. "I assumed it was because Paul didn't come or call." She looked away from Dane's curious regard. "But then, I also had assumed that she had sent all those letters to her father, inviting him to..." She felt herself blush at the thought that she'd been set up on a blind date by her romantic nine-year-old daughter.

"It's obvious," said Dane, "that she'd like to have a dad. One who would give her hugs, congratulate her on her schoolwork, and kiss her mom when he gets home from work." For an instant his gaze flickered over her full lower lip. "I feel it only fair to warn you that your daughter is considering me for father material, in lieu of the Captain."

"I hate to disillusion you," Tildie returned, "but you're not the first. She's also written Kenny Rogers, Prince Charles, and a box boy at the Big Bear grocery store." She glanced away from his smile, speculating about how his kiss would be when he came home from work at night, how his mouth would feel... "You just happen to be the only one who ever showed up."

"Their loss." He shrugged. "I'm into those really long shots—like to the stars." He watched her eyes until he gave himself a mental nudge. "Fathers are very important to little girls." He spoke as if from experience. "Evidently," he said kindly, "Micki misses hers very much."

Tildie had been so concerned about a father's relationship to a teenaged boy that she hadn't given a father-daughter relationship much thought—probably because she hadn't had much of a relationship with her own father. But she had made it, hadn't she? At thirty-five, with a broken marriage behind her, a career ahead of her, and two children to brighten her life, she was finally on her feet.

"Actually, Micki never really knew her father," Tildie said. "She was only two when Paul left." She didn't offer any more information and he seemed relieved. "Your visit today made her happy." Tildie was pleased that he had helped Micki, and happy that he'd made her feel more confident about the custody suit. She placed her hand on his forearm. "You were a hero today, Captain Starblazer. You saved a little girl's birthday." Warmth spread through her body as the gold flecks in his eyes shone invitingly, like fool's gold at the bottom of a clear, rushing stream. He leaned toward her as though he were being pulled by an irresistible force, and she felt herself being drowned.

"I'd better get the coffee," she said, breathing deeply, giving herself an excuse to break the trance. Yet her hand remained on his hard forearm a moment longer. "Thank you for helping Micki."

"What are superheroes for if they don't help their pen pals?" He shook off the intimate instant with an endearing shrug.

Tildie turned away and headed for the kitchen, her thoughts in a jumble.

As she set cream and sugar on a tray, she asked herself why Dane seemed to delight in keeping her off balance, making her feel so jumpy and nervous. For a moment in the library she had thought they would kiss, but she knew she should just forget the incident, get him out of her house and out of her system.

"Can I help with the coffee?" Dane had followed her into the kitchen. "Even superheroes are handy in the kitchen, or haven't you noticed?" He smiled.

"Why do you finish every sentence with a question?" She was angry at herself for feeling a tiny curl of anticipation in her stomach at the warmth of his smile.

"I have unending curiosity. I'm a scientist, remember?"

"You should be working on some space mission for NASA, and instead you're playing with toys." Tildie stood with her back to the sink as he casually walked the length of the U-shaped room.

"It's my job to put fun in your life, counselor," he teased.

"Don't you take anything seriously?" She looked up at the ceiling, as if for guidance. "I try to thank you for helping my daughter and you make a joke of it." She shook her head. "You make jokes, you ask questions. Why are you so interested in my clients? Why aren't you working for NASA anymore?" Tildie looked into his unflinching gaze.

"Now who's asking the questions? I'd like to see you in court someday. I bet you're very good." He tilted his head to the side consideringly.

"One tries," she said, but she wasn't going to let him off the hook. "If you *are* the best, why did you leave NASA?"

"One of the last NASA projects I worked on was a multi-module probe designed to observe Halley's Comet." He stopped. "Am I boring you? You're staring at me."

She busied her hands with the coffee pot. "No. Go on."

"The pod was designed to whip around Mercury, using parachutes and retro-rockets, so that eventually she'd run in a parallel orbit to the comet. She was going to be taking pictures, collecting particle and gas readings and so forth: it was a data catcher."

"You designed it?" She really did have a rocket scientist standing in her kitchen.

"We'd worked on the project for six years and were ready to put her into production, when a member of the Science and Exploration Senate Committee woke up on the wrong side of bed one morning and cast the deciding vote to cancel the funding. The whole project went down the tubes, just like that." He snapped his fingers.

She stared at his face, trying to fathom the rarified intellect behind his casual exterior.

"It was hard for us to believe," he went on. "Do you know what the U.S. had up there to study the comet? Zippitydoodah. Nothing." He gestured haphazardly to emphasize his point. "Oh, they sent the shuttle up to snap a few pictures. I mean, what the hell? It'll come again in another seventy-six years, right?" He laughed hollowly. "That's when I learned not to take myself or my work too seriously. Things just weren't the same as they used to be at NASA. Priorities were changing. There was too much juggling going on." He tried to act nonchalant, but there was tension in his shoulders. "Where are the cups?"

She pointed to the cupboard door, and as he moved toward it he asked, "And what about you? I would think it would be hard to handle all those cases at once—one here for the BTC, one in Cleveland for SynTech. Of course, I suppose everything would be easier if the cases were related to each other?" He peeked around the cupboard door to catch her reaction to the question.

She didn't know what he was after, but she stood with her arms over her chest, determined not to open her mouth. Her dealings with SynTech were none of his—or Fun Design's—business.

"And I would think it would be especially difficult to balance your family life and your career, especially being a single parent." He glanced at her from the corner of his eyes as he slowly removed two delicate cups with matching saucers from the cupboard. "Balance and coordination is the trick to any kind of juggling." He tossed a cup into the air.

Tildie gasped.

"It's all in the timing."

Before a sound could escape from her choked throat, the saucers and the second cup were flying in flashing arcs, until he was juggling all four pieces.

"What are you doing?"

"Juggling. Don't worry," he assured, his eyes darting from cup to cup, his hands deftly flicking and catching the continuous circle of china. "I learned to do this in zero gravity."

"Oh, then of course we have no problems," she breathed, amazed at his skill. The man was a constant source of bewilderment and fascination.

"Hey, would I let you down?"

"The last I heard we still had gravity on this planet."

"It's only because you insist that your feet touch the ground, counselor." His eyes flitted from dish to dish, and he shifted his balance slightly onto the balls of his feet. "I, on the other hand, have learned to float, not to take anything too seriously, because life is like these dishes: it goes in circles. One second you're in one place and a fraction later you're somewhere else.'' In an instant he altered the rhythm and flight pattern of the dishes. ''Things aren't always predictable.''

''We can't all be jugglers.''

''You are. Here's you.'' He made exaggerated, stiff movements instead of sticking to his calm, relaxed style. ''You juggle your job, the kids, your principles. Then something comes along to change the order of things...'' In an instant the dishes dived into a figure eight.

Tildie gasped again.

''Something or someone comes along...''

''Like a clown juggling dishes?''

''Why not?'' He grinned.

''You're right. I prefer to be serious. I require both feet on the ground at all times. And coffee in my cup.''

''Coming right up! Here, catch!''

''No!''

''Ready to play, Tildie?''

''No-o-o!'' She caught the first cup and then a saucer, and put them gently down onto the counter. Then she caught the second cup, followed again by a saucer. She sighed with relief and sank back against the counter, still clutching the cup and saucer.

''Nice catch, counselor! Maybe there's hope for you yet.''

''You're impossible.'' She flicked her silky hair out of her eyes with a toss of her head and allowed her smile to soften her words.

''There are reasons I wasn't serious earlier when you thanked me for helping Micki,'' he said, taking in the beauty of her shiny hair and her arched brows as he stood before her. He gently retrieved the cup and saucer she was holding to her chest, put them down and said, ''Anything I do for

Micki doesn't need thanks.'' He glanced away from her for a second, and then returned his gaze to her delicate jawline. ''And if I hadn't kept it light, I probably would have done something very foolish.''

''Like what?'' Her soft lips parted as she met his serious gaze.

He leaned slowly toward her as she braced herself against the counter. It was obvious his lips were going to contact hers, yet she didn't stop him. She wanted the inevitable to happen so she could get her feet back on the ground. She distrusted this lighter-than-air feeling that lifted her as high as a helium balloon. Their lips would simply meet and the mystery of how his kiss would feel would be cleared up, and there would be one less thing on her mind to juggle. A moment's contact and she could get the whiz kid out of her mind and out of her house.

Her skin came alive as she felt his breath on her cheek. He hesitated for a spine-tingling moment and lightly pressed his warm lips to hers. For an instant she thought he probably hadn't kissed a woman in a very long time—he was timid and cautious. But as his mouth moved over her lips with tenderness, she realized how skilled he was, and she resolved not to respond, not to feel anything. But soon she felt her anger and determination become shivery surprise and delight as his warm mouth played over hers. The gentle caresses felt so wonderful that her body celebrated in a warm rush that flooded her limbs and brain.

The gold light in his inquiring eyes and the tiny, tight curl in her middle told her she'd made her third mistake. His mouth drew close to hers again, so she moved her face away. But he turned with her, and his lips found hers and claimed them, giving her a warm, sparkling burst of pleasure. He tasted, tested, slanting his mouth this way and that over her pliant lips. She felt gloriously alive and lighter than air.

Her hips arched toward him, succumbing to the magnetic pull of his warm body, until her smooth, bare thighs met the fabric of his slacks and her fingertips ruffled the soft curled hair at his nape. His quicker breathing kindled her own desire to return his kiss; the reasons for not doing so seemed far away. As he drew his mouth away she nipped at his full lower lip, quickly and privately, as though she had a wonderful, whispered secret to share. He kissed her again, a torturously intimate kiss this time, the tip of his tongue flicking over her sensitive lips until for an instant she knew the feeling of weightlessness, the irresistible freedom of... No, she thought. No freedom for her, no walking on air. She mustn't allow... She pulled away from his kiss, but his arm still held her.

"If you think I like this..." she murmured as his lips played over the corner of her mouth.

"Yes, I think you do," he breathed.

"No. I don't want to feel lighter than air. I need to have both my feet on the ground." She pushed her way out of the arms that were enveloping her. "That wasn't at all wise. We, we shouldn't have...done what we just did."

His disbelieving expression made it all too clear that he'd felt her very real, very powerful response. "It's called a kiss."

"No, it's called a mistake, a conflict of interest and unethical conduct and—"

"Somehow, wonderful and sexy were the words that came to my mind." He collected himself, embarrassed that his feelings weren't shared.

"I think you'd better leave."

"Without my coffee?" He smiled without warmth. "Ease up, counselor. It was a very nice moment, but chances are very good that it'll never happen again." A more genuine smile grazed his mouth when he noted her lips parting, as though she were going to object.

"I'm afraid I can't afford to be as flippant as you are," she said. "I have responsibilities. I can't live for the moment." She hurried to the other side of the room to fetch the coffee pot and came back to the counter. "I don't understand you. Here you are a scientist, one of NASA's best—"

"Hard to believe, isn't it?" He touched her arm gently to stop her from spilling the coffee. "Let me pour. You're shaking like a leaf."

"Because I'm angry."

"I don't think so, counselor." He gave her a sidelong look. "You know, I think this episode has shed new light on the possibility of the two of us working together."

"Working together?"

"I may decide to cooperate with you and the BTC." He smiled.

"No. That's impossible. We can't work together." She turned her back on him.

"For days you've been trying to convince me to become a champion of non-violence in children's programing. And when I actually offer my services, you fall to pieces on me." He grabbed a delicate cup and filled it with coffee. "This won't look good for you at the hearing, counselor. Shall we say it shows a considerable lack of concern and cooperation?"

"I'll have members of the BTC call you—"

"What if I choose only to work with their legal representative?"

"You don't even belong at a toy company. Why are you wasting your time at Fun Design?"

"Wasting my time? What happened to molding young minds and being a national hero? How soon they forget!" he said, feigning a bruised ego. "Maybe helping children isn't *your* primary goal. Maybe it's not your real reason for coming to Fun Design."

"I don't understand. What do you mean?"

"Each time I suggest we work together..." His expression signified that he was suddenly seeing things clearly. "Your mission at my company isn't about the hearing or about helping children. Either you're up to something, or it's about you and me."

"There is no you and me, Mr. Scott. And there won't be."

"Then why did you kiss me back?"

"I don't have the time or the energy to discuss this," she said decisively. "I think you'd better leave now."

"What are you afraid I'll discover if I get too close?"

"You aren't going to find anything. If you'd like to help, I'll connect you with—"

"I haven't decided yet. I'm more than a little cautious about jumping onto a bandwagon. Especially when I don't know where it's going."

He stared at her a moment in speculation, turned suddenly and marched from the kitchen. In the hallway he picked up Spinner and muttered about an uptight attorney and thieves. By the time Tildie reached the front step, his sleek scarlet car had reversed down the long paved driveway and was on the street. Her feelings churned with confusion as she hugged her body to bring back some warmth. She had wanted him to go, hadn't she? It had been a mistake to ask him to stay for coffee, a mistake to allow him to kiss her. Then why did she feel so miserable because she had asked him to leave? She had only the twinkling stars in the navy-blue sky to ask.

The rays from the old-fashioned street lamps along the quiet street shone into the huge leaded bay windows at the front of the stone Tudor home. Tildie scanned the street for a strange car that might be sheltering a detective. That was her reality. She should have asked Dane Scott to leave earlier, much earlier.

"HE'S ANGRY and he'll never come back," Micki whimpered, leaning out of an open window one floor above, out of Tildie's earshot. "Just like my dad never came back."

"Shh. She'll hear you."

"But I blew out all my birthday candles. I even wished on the first star. I'll wish again. 'Star light, star bright...'" She recited the wish in a murmured fervent litany.

"Don't be a dope. He's just a guy."

"He's a friend."

"So all right, he came for your birthday party. That doesn't mean mom's going to like him. So don't get your hopes all up and make a big deal about this, promise?" Jer demanded in a harsh whisper. The practical teen exhaled hard, as though he were carrying the weight of his sister's crumbling romantic world on his shoulders. "Get back to bed."

AS SHE REENTERED the house, Tildie remembered the sound of Micki's voice telling everyone she'd made the same wish over her birthday candles that she'd made on the first star. No doubt she had wished for a hero to call dad. How could she explain to the nine-year-old girl that she had chosen the wrong time and the wrong hero? Dane Scott and Matilda Moore were, for all practical purposes, polar opposites. Anyone could see that. He was never serious—by his own admission—and wouldn't commit to anything, while she was constantly tiptoeing a tightrope of responsibility. Yet, recalling the fascinating clown juggling the china in the kitchen brought a warm smile to her lips. He had seemed relaxed and carefree as his quick, sure hands, darting eyes and agile body had responded to his mental commands. He had controlled every piece with the lightest touch. For an instant she wondered how her body would respond to his sure hands. Would he be quick and careless, she mused, or breathlessly thorough? She chastised herself for the fantasy.

There was only one thing to do. She would arrange for expensive telephone interviews with the *Star Power* writers and animators in Chicago. They would cost the novice attorney dearly, but being seen with Dane Scott might cost her more. She'd use her notes from those interviews to finish her preparations for the FCC presentation. She wouldn't see or think about the ex-astronaut-turned-toy-designer-and-juggler again.

CHAPTER SIX

TILDIE WAS PERCHED on a faded bleacher bench at the baseball field at Hilliard Junior High, surrounded by a small group of cheering parents. Hiding behind her Foster Grants, she absently watched puffs of dust blow up from pounding baseball spikes, her mind wandering away from the game.

She asked herself for what seemed the thousandth time if Jer needed a man to guide him through his teen years. She wanted to make the best choice for her son, no matter how painful it might be for herself. She knew the main argument Paul's attorneys would use: a growing young man needed a male role model, someone who could guide from experience. No matter how hard she tried, Tildie would never know what it was like to be a teenage boy or a man. His father could identify with him, relate. But as Dane had suggested the other night, did Paul only want him back because he couldn't tolerate losing? Paul didn't deserve to have Jer—and wouldn't be much help to him—if he only wanted the boy to soothe his ego. Jer deserved better. Maybe a loving mother *was* better, no matter if she didn't pretend to know everything about men. Dane Scott certainly had her confused. Yes, she sensed he had set her on the right track about Paul. She should stop feeling guilty about depriving Jer of his father, she told herself, and fight to maintain custody.

But what about her daughter? Did she need a father, too? She certainly wanted one badly. Tildie brushed the thought away. It had been three days since Dane Scott had marched out of her house. She would finish this case with Fun Design and that would be the end of it. So why couldn't she erase the man from her mind, she wondered, exasperated. He had waltzed into her home and her life and had threatened her family unit, for heaven's sake.

Drawing her eyes back to the game, she thought again how her attention had been focused on Jer's need for a father more than Micki's. *Little girls need fathers.* Wasn't that what the toy designer had said? She remembered the clear sincerity in his eyes. She wondered what experience he'd based his heartfelt statement on. Did he have a daughter of his own? The sudden vision of him returning to a house, with a little girl running into his arms and a loyal wife greeting him with a warm peck on the cheek and a playful hug, stunned her. Maybe he got along with her children so well because he was lonely for the ones he'd return to soon. But she quickly dismissed the scenario. She'd come across a few disloyal married men in her time, and Dane hadn't revealed any of the usual signs—secretiveness, jumpiness, or just plain sensitivity.

Tildie had always craved a marriage, home and family of her own. She had married a man much like her father, too busy to spend time with her or the kids. She had thought if she kept a perfect house, all would be happy and loving—as though stitching a perfect "home sweet home" would make it so. After a divorce and a struggle for a career, she knew better. How dare Dane Scott rekindle that impossible dream, she thought angrily, on top of jeopardizing her custody of Jer. Damn the man for being so lively, vital and honest . . . and for kissing her and sending goose bumps up her spine. It was best to stick with her plan never to see him again.

As she came to that conclusion, the Hilliard outfield got the third out. During the inning change Tildie stretched and looked up to see a straight white jet stream split the sky. She knew that Dane Scott had gone higher, faster and farther than the silvery jet streaking across the vast cloudless sky. She had felt goose bumps on her spine when he'd talked about seeing the planets from outer space; yet he had walked away from NASA. Why did she let his inconsistencies needle her? she wondered. But she couldn't help it. Bragging that he didn't care about anything didn't jibe with his apparent weak spot for Micki. What was the matter with her, anyway? Other men paid attention to her—reliable, traditional men, more her type—and she had no problem resisting them. So why had fate placed this brilliant scientist in her path? It was a puzzle.

Micki was right; he really was a hero. A lazy smile curved her lips as she imagined him juggling in zero gravity. She visualized his compact body in the Sky Lab capsule, a confident smile plastered on his boyish face roughened with a four-day growth of beard. Without warning a powerful desire to have his beard brush her bare breasts suddenly possessed her. Her eyelids closed behind her glasses, she could almost smell his honest scent of soap and maleness. For an instant it felt as though the sun was being blocked, and when she opened her eyes she saw that Dane Scott was sitting, in the flesh, beside her on the wooden bench. Her sensual fantasy vanished instantly, replaced by hundreds of real sensations. She didn't speak and tried not to look at him.

"Did I miss much?" His voice and attitude dripped nonchalance, as though this was the most natural place on earth for him to be—by her side.

"It's the bottom of the final inning. Hilliard's behind 4-3. Jer is the cleanup batter." Her mouth managed to form the words, even when all she wanted to know was what he was doing there. Meanwhile, he was filling her senses.

"Sounds like I got here just in time." His smooth voice was enthusiastic and his eyes twinkled with pleasure.

"You shouldn't be here at all," she said quietly. There was no way that a judge would consider this meeting business-related and a jury would certainly hang her for her erotic thoughts of a moment ago. She hated herself for allowing her eyes to soak in his muscular form, shown off to good advantage by a well-fitting shirt.

"What, and miss the best game in town? I'm surprised at you, counselor."

She made the mistake of meeting his eyes and glanced down at his mouth, which was turned incorrigibly upward at the corners. He seemed to be trying to memorize her cheeks and her cornsilk hair fluttering in the breeze as he gazed at her steadily.

"Jason is up first, and my boy Billy bats next," a proud dad informed them as he leaned down between them from the bench above.

"Billy's been hitting very well," Tildie complimented him, grateful for the interruption.

"He takes after his old man." Billy Walters's father shook the bleacher seat when he laughed. "Say," he turned to Dane. "I've seen your wife at the games—" he cocked his head toward Tildie "—but this is the first time I've caught you."

"It's hard to get away from work. I'm just glad I got here today. Right, honey?" With that comment, the first batter struck out on an inside curve. One down and two to go.

"Ah, there he is." Dane gently nudged Tildie's arm and pointed to Jer, who was clambering out of the dugout to take the on-deck position. He went about the process of painstakingly picking out a bat, measuring each one for weight and comfort with a warm-up swing. "Is he good when the pressure's on, like his mom?" Dane said to Tildie through the side of his mouth. He almost smiled as she folded her arms over her chest, avoiding his testing, confident eyes.

"That's two down for you, Mr. Scott, one to—"

Mr. Walters behind them shouted words of encouragement to his son, drowning out Tildie's retort. Then he tapped Dane's shoulder and filled him in on Billy's batting average and fielding abilities. Dane clapped his hands to encourage the young batter, his golden forearms glistening in the sunshine. His knees were spread apart and he was leaning forward in anticipation. To Tildie he looked totally open, completely confident. It was as though he didn't even care about the competition—all he wanted was for the boys to enjoy themselves. She heard a thwack against the bat, and spotted a grounder scooting up the middle, past the second baseman for a single.

"Keep it alive, Jer!" Dane's enthusiasm for the youngster proved contagious. The other parents cheered, too.

Jer was swinging the heavy bat near the team bench, and looked up at his mom in the bleachers, as he'd done since his Little League days. But he stopped his warm-up completely when he recognized the man beside her. Dane gave the boy a quick thumbs-up signal. Jer's mouth dropped open, then curved into a grin as he tapped the dirt off of his spikes.

Dane stood up, clapping his hands and shouting.

"Come on Jer, bring Billy home. You can do it!"

Was Jer's stride more confident, his back straighter when he walked to the plate? Did he sit deeper in his stance? Was his grip on the bat more sure? *Did he need a man for encouragement and guidance?*

They watched a ball and a strike cross the plate. Then the bat swirled around Jer's shoulders and smacked the hard leather. Tildie and Dane rose to their feet as the ball climbed higher. Billy Walters tagged up at first and Tildie reached for the strong arm beside her. The hit was a beauty, a gorgeous high fly to center field. It sailed over the head of the center fielder, who chased it, and bounced onto the turf. It was a natural, exhilarating high. She found herself smiling into Dane's eyes and leaning against him as his arm drew her close in shared celebration. It felt wonderful, like...a home run.

She moved away from him and collected herself as she watched Jer round third, cross home plate and jump into the waiting arms of Billy Walters and the rest of the team. The win was Hilliard's, with a score of 5-4.

"That was something!" Dane said, offering his arm to her as she climbed out of the bleachers.

"Yes, it was." She met his sparkling gaze.

Fortunately it didn't take Jer long to join them.

"That was wonderful." She gave her son a hug and ruffled his hair.

"Oh, ma," Jer complained despite his grin.

"It was a beauty—sailed right past the center fielder! I'm glad I had a chance to see it," Dane congratulated the boy.

"Yeah, me too." Jer nodded. The two of them were lost for a moment, discussing the wicked inside curveball and how well Jer had handled it.

"I drove here in my Corwin Special, Jer," said Dane. "Are you ready for that ride now?"

"Yeah, sure!"

"Tonight's a school night," said Tildie. "There's homework and—"

"But there's also a home run that needs celebrating." Dane's gaze cruised over her mauve cotton blouse down to her rose slacks, a hint that he remembered an earlier celebration.

"Yeah, mom. Can I go with Mr. Scott?"

Dane's eyes were hidden behind dark aviator sunglasses, which seemed to make his skin look even darker and his thick hair more golden. He had her over a barrel again. She'd consent to the ride, only because he'd drop Jer off and that would be the last they'd see of him—or so she told herself.

"Be home for dinner," she insisted.

"We should be able to make that." Dane had easily and naturally included himself, and grinned at the pretty pink lips that opened in surprise. "I insist," he said, then added before she could object, "Have Micki ready and we'll pick you both up for dinner." He shrugged. "It's the least I can do to repay you for your gracious hospitality the other night. Besides, I promised Micki a pizza." She knew he already had Jer's vote and Micki wouldn't forgive her for passing up pizza with Captain Starblazer.

She finally murmured a grudging acceptance.

"All right, mom!" Jer cheered and tossed his glove in the air.

"How does a milk shake sound?" she heard Dane ask Jer happily. "Do you think that will tide you over until the pizza?"

Tildie began to walk away, with a backward glance over her shoulder at the jolly duo. The ex-astronaut was watching her hips sway as she walked away, and Tildie blushed at his pleased expression, despite the fact that her teenaged son was looking on.

On the way home her thoughts teetered between wanting to go out for dinner and fearing that their evening might turn up as evidence against her in the custody suit. On the other hand, she couldn't possibly see how a night out in the company of two children could be construed as a romantic evening. Soon she found herself thinking of wearing an outfit that was guaranteed to knock Dane out.

Of course Micki soon weaseled the information out of her that Mr. Scott had asked them all out for pizza. The nine-year-old was so ecstatic, Tildie was almost glad she'd agreed. Besides, she rationalized, her business with the toy designer and his company would be finished shortly. What could possibly happen in one night?

She took a leisurely shower, carefully darkened her lashes, whisked a brush through her hair and slipped into a sleeve-less sweater and full skirt. She completed the outfit with a delicate necklace and sandals. These items, too, had been borrowed from her sister, but were too summery and ca-sual for the office. Now she understood what her brother-in-law meant about Sally having enough clothes in her closet for two women. Actually, Tildie suspected that Sally had purchased some outfits with the thought of bringing her conservative little sister out of her shell. When Micki whis-tled at her, Tildie had the feeling that she should go back up and change into something more proper.

But before she could, Dane delivered Jer to her and Micki ran out to greet her hero with a hug, a squeal at the sight of the car and a complaint about Jer getting to ride in it first. To keep everything proper, Tildie walked out the front door and down the curved walk as though she were catching a carpool ride to work. But when she saw Dane's warm smile and Micki's worshiping grin her very heartstrings were tugged. The doors of the Corwin Special were raised above the body like expectant wings, and Dane let Micki sit in the driver's seat while he and Jer pointed out the car's interior features to her. Dane seemed both charged and bewildered by the nine-year-old's enthusiasm.

"Are you sure you know what you're getting yourself into?" Tildie asked over his shoulder while he explained the tachometer to Micki. He lifted up his head and looked pointedly at the scooped neckline of her raspberry-colored sweater and then down her flowered skirt to her shapely calves.

Micki grinned as she looked from one adult to the other.

"Pizza with the Moore tribe can be a . . . a harrowing experience," Tildie said, stammering under the weight of his momentarily undivided attention.

"I'll take my chances," Dane said, trying to hide a smile.

"Come on, mom. Captain Starblazer is used to fighting alien invaders and Cyclon. He can handle anything—even us!" Micki scrambled into the hatch at the back of the car, singing the *Star Power* theme song. "This'll be like riding in a spaceship! Fire the retrorockets, man the on-board computer for the trajectory mode!"

"Hey, maybe we could quick-freeze the squirt and wake her up when we get to Mars," Jer said. "How many light years would that take?"

"I'm going to go there someday, just wait and see," Micki said confidently.

When she became too excited to say more, Tildie suspected it was going to be an extraordinary evening. Dane followed her around the car and watched her fingertips gently graze the low hood.

"This car is very, uh, short," Tildie commented as Dane held the door open for her. She didn't know what else to say; she'd never seen another vehicle quite like it.

"And very much fun," Dane said, watching her flowered skirt sweep over her thighs as she reached with a leggy stride to sink into the low leather seat. Tildie and Jer had to share the passenger seat in the front, and Jer insisted that his mom sit nearest to the gear shift. With the flick of a switch and the turn of a key the motorized doors swung down to latch and the engine rumbled.

"It's not exactly a family car," Tildie commented as she wedged her knees away from the air-conditioning vent, the only concession to conventionality in the vehicle.

"Oh, I don't know. It might be just the thing for a tightly knit family," Dane teased. In response to her arched brow he added, "How could we be any closer?" Indeed, his hands grazed her thigh as he shifted gears, reminding her of when her whole body had leaned against his.... His questioning glance at her warm cheeks told her she wasn't doing well at acting detached and aloof.

"I still can't believe you left NASA," she said in an attempt to change the subject. She knew her constant harping about his having left NASA for a toy company was beginning to bother him, but she couldn't think of anything else to say. And, she thought, maybe subconsciously she wanted him to take offense, so he'd get out of her life— and her mind—once and for all. She checked the cars parked along the quiet residential street for possible detectives. But it didn't seem as though they were being watched.

"What's so magical to you about NASA?" He glanced at her a moment as they traveled in and out of the shadows of the maple trees that canopied the street. "Designing space vehicles like Apollo and Sky Lab isn't very different from designing great toys."

"You helped design Apollo and Sky Lab?"

"Why else would they give a fun guy like me a ride?" He laughed.

"You must be brilliant..."

"I would be more pleased at the compliment if there wasn't quite so much surprise in your voice, counselor." He smiled at her blush. "Hey, don't worry." He grinned widely as the car veered around a corner, forcing her to lean closer to him. "I work very hard at not letting people see I'm really an egghead."

"Your head looks okay to me," Micki said, resting her chin on the back of his seat.

"Thank you." Dane bit the inside of his cheek. He turned the car sharply again and Tildie's shoulder touched his.

"Where are we going, and do we have to get there so fast?" Tildie asked, watching the trees of the country club golf course fly by.

"Isn't this a great car?" Jer was all but drooling.

"I think we should go back home," Tildie said firmly.

"Lighten up, Matilda. Relax," Dane encouraged with a smile that put a tiny flutter in her stomach.

"Relax? Going ninety miles an hour?"

"Forty." Micki monitored the speedometer. "It's all right, mom. Dane's a race driver."

"Only on weekends." Dane laughed at his pint-sized fan in the back. To Tildie, he said, "You're outvoted, counselor. Face it."

"Why would a smart man like you risk your life racing cars?" Tildie's voice was disapproving.

"It's cool, mom," Jer defended.

"Daring death isn't cool. It's irresponsible, it's—"

"Maybe it's just another way of acknowledging that the inevitable is on its way."

"So you want to speed it along?"

"I'd like to stop it, but no one wants to listen to me."

"I'll listen," Micki said. "Besides, you're too good a driver to have an accident, aren't you?"

"Absolutely," Dane guaranteed. "So let's all relax."

"It's very obvious I shouldn't have come along," Tildie said.

"Why not? We welcome wet blankets, don't we?" He glanced at Micki, then Jer.

"It's obvious that we are two very different people, Mr. Scott."

"Haven't you heard that opposites attract?" Micki said, old lady of the world that she was. "You could be like many other famous couples: Beauty and the Beast; the Captain and the Princess of the Sercerian moon." Micki waggled her blond brows.

"You've been working hard, mom. You deserve a night out," Jer reasoned.

"You have homework, I have notes to go through, we've already celebrated once this week and—"

"Can we have a pizza with four or five toppings?" Jer interrupted.

"Yeah," Micki breathed.

"We can't afford that, and besides, it's wasteful."

Jer groaned; Micki rolled her big blue eyes.

Dane's brows furled, but a smile played at his lips. "Am I wrong—" Dane checked Jer's expression "—or is your mother going to mention the starving children of China?"

"Ethiopia," Micki corrected flatly as she plunked her chin in her hands on the back of the headrest.

"There are droughts and wars in just about every country in the third world, you know," said her mother.

Jer shrugged. "I keep telling her they wouldn't like pizza anyway."

Dane stifled a grin. "But your mother's right, you know," he said, giving Tildie a sidelong glance before pulling the racy red car onto a main street.

"You don't have to patronize me, thank you. Some day people are going to wake up and realize the depth of the tragedies in our developing countries. I just hope it won't be too late." She felt too strongly about people—particularly about the man who sat beside her. "It's very plain to see that we're nothing alike, Captain. We have nothing in common." Tildie pursed her lips and swallowed. "We probably never should have crossed paths in the first place." Under her breath so that the kids wouldn't hear her, she added, "And with any luck we never will again." She looked out the window at the parked cars they were passing in a blur.

"Don't get me wrong, Matilda. Personally, I think it's great that you try so hard to save the world. In fact you've singlehandedly restored my sagging faith in humanity." His voice teased, but there was something very deep and sincere there, and she did a double take. Yet, she still couldn't tell whether he was being completely serious. "But even Superman hangs up his cape and takes a night off now and then," he said gently.

"Captain Starblazer jokes with Spinner after a long day of battling Cyclon," Micki piped up.

"I'm very serious about my work, about my responsibilities," Tildie insisted.

"We admire you for that, don't we kids?" Dane received two affirmative votes from the peanut gallery. "But you should have a chance to relax, too," Dane insisted.

But she couldn't let down her guard around him; each time she did, his smile wore down her resistance.

"I propose that for tonight and tonight only we give your mother a night off from saving all the children of the world from starvation and violent cartoons." He continued before she could protest: "For the next two hours she is pardoned from all her obligations."

If I were totally responsible I wouldn't be here right now, she thought sourly. If she could have forgotten how it had felt to celebrate Jer's home run with him or how alive her body had felt in his arms, she wouldn't have come.

"So Matilda Moore can celebrate—tonight—without a care in the world."

"But I—"

"Not a care. Just for tonight, counselor," he said firmly, their gazes fusing for an instant. "All those in favor?" She was outvoted instantly. "What do you say?"

She couldn't look him in the eye or he would know why she was really here. Staring straight ahead, she said, "I care about what goes on in the world, but you...you don't seem to care about anything serious. You don't even have serious clothes—like a suit."

"Maybe he would rather have baseball spikes," Jer mumbled.

"I may not dress like the other executives at Fun Design—"

"That's an understatement coming from a man who doesn't seem to own a pair of socks."

"But it saves on laundry detergent, and the washing machine just eats socks, anyway," Micki said in praise of his efficiency.

Dane laughed. "And you have to admit I'm very good at my work." He angled his head back slightly, toward Micki. "Do you know that your mother told me I've helped make Fun Design a multimillion-dollar company?" The car rolled to an idle at a traffic light.

"Wow!"

"A man with your talent—"

"You're being serious again." He used one hand to turn Tildie's stubborn chin toward him. "Do you promise that for the next two hours—from this moment on—you'll act as though you don't have a care in the world?" Dane's honest gaze probed her face. "Promise?"

"Cross your heart?" Micki added sternly.

"Yes. I promise," she heard herself saying, almost laughing with relief. Did she actually feel that part of her burden was being lifted from her shoulders? "But I still

maintain that a man with your brains shouldn't be designing toys and risking his life in race cars."

"You heard her—she promised." Micki giggled. "And it
sounds like she cares about you."

"See what you've gotten me into with your letters," he
complained playfully to Micki as he drove off again. His
expression was so receptive to Micki's smile that Tildie
couldn't help but ease back in her seat and enjoy the moment. "I forgot to tell you not to laugh at my jokes too
much, counselor," Dane said teasingly. "Someone may
think you're beginning to relax."

"I can't afford to have that happen," she said, smiling,
realizing that her guard was down. She would have liked to
forget the constraints of the time and place, and give him an
enormous hug.

"You gave your word, not only to me, but to your children," he intoned seriously. "Mothers can't break their
promises."

"There's still a hearing coming up—"

"Not tonight there isn't. Agreed?"

"Agreed."

"Just in time," the jolly ex-astronaut said as he pulled the
car into the passing lane. "We're almost there. I promised
this young lady the best pizza in town." He reached behind
him and tweaked Micki's nose, waiting for her musical giggle.

CHAPTER SEVEN

BIG TOP PIZZA lived up to its name, with piped-in calliope music lending a circus atmosphere, and vintage Barnum and Bailey posters plastered on the walls. They reminded Tildie that a sucker was born every minute, as Barnum—or was it Bailey?—had said, and she realized that she had been misled into yet another mistake. She shouldn't have come at all, she scolded herself. She shouldn't be enjoying the warmth of Dane's sure hand on her back as he guided her to a table, and she shouldn't want to pause long enough to feel the assurance of his toned body at her side. Without hesitation she purposefully marched down the aisles, surrounded by happy families served by waitresses wearing clown or animal costumes. After they were seated it didn't take long for Jer to spot the room full of video games and eye it longingly, and for Micki to list the toppings she wanted on the pizza.

"Please tell Mr. Scott what you'd like—within reason," Tildie told the kids.

"Would you remind your mother that this isn't a formal occasion, so she doesn't have to call me Mr. Scott?" Dane asked Micki in a mock-serious tone.

"I think she should call you Dane darling," Micki said decisively, as though she'd given the matter previous thought. "Don't you?"

A low chuckle came from deep in his throat. "That's what I'd call less formal!" he said, grinning hugely.

"Choose your toppings, Micki," Tildie insisted, avoiding the devilment sparkling in Dane's eyes.

"You promised to relax, Tildie. You're juggling too many things again." He shrugged casually. "I'll just have to demonstrate one more time." He reached for the salt and pepper shakers on the table.

"No. That won't be necessary." She stopped his hands before he sent the shakers flying. "I'll take your word for it." Laughing, she vowed again, "I'll relax, as long as everyone else promises to get their homework done and get into bed as soon as we get home." The three of them nodded solemnly.

A smile played at the corner of his mouth and his dimples deepened. She pulled her hand away from his and looked away when she realized why he was grinning so mischievously.

Finally they ordered the Three Ring Circus with the works. While they waited for it, they talked about Jer's home run at the ball game and about the field day coming up at school. Tildie loved the way the four of them were talking about ordinary things. Somehow it gave her a contented feeling. By the time the big, round pizza arrived at their table, she'd forgotten all her warnings to herself. He fascinated her: how could he field Micki's questions without losing pace, she wondered, and eat with such carefree gusto at the same time? The children chattered and laughed when Dane related a funny incident that occurred when he'd shot a round of golf with the then President, Gerald Ford, and despite herself, Tildie laughed, too.

They were nearly finished eating when Tildie did a double take at seeing her son suddenly sit transfixed.

"Jeremy? Are you with us?" Dane asked, following Jer's line of vision to a table where a couple and a teenaged girl were being seated. "I believe someone has snagged his attention."

Micki nearly turned around in her chair. "It's Cynthia Edgars," she confided to Dane, pointing to the fresh-looking teenager with distinctive dark eyes and brows, a pale complexion and light brown curls that tumbled to the middle of her back. "I think she's pretty," Micki added.

"Evidently Jer does, too." Dane smiled.

"I'd say the admiration is mutual, judging by the color on her cheeks." Tildie took note of the girl's coy sidelong glances in her son's direction and her pretty blush. Infatuation could be so awkward sometimes, she mused. And then it hit her: she was as infatuated with Dane as these two teenagers were with each other! She realized that she had blushed more in the past few days than she had in her entire life! She'd skipped that stage in her own growing process; was it catching up with her now, she asked herself. She had lived with her family until she had married Paul, an older man much like her father. There had been no blushes and no rushes.

"Jer's in love and all that mushy stuff," Micki whispered.

"What?" Jer asked, temporarily returning from Cloud Nine.

It was the first time Tildie had ever seen her son so preoccupied with a girl, and she couldn't help but share a knowing smile with the man across the table. It felt very nice to have someone to share special moments with.

"Jer, if you're done eating, you and Micki can hit the video games. That seems to be what's captured your attention."

"Ah, yeah." Jer blushed.

"Oh, sure," Micki said, rolling her eyes.

As they started toward the game room, Dane caught Micki's shirttail. "Look after your big brother, okay? I don't want him to run into any closed doors," he teased, pressing some quarters into her hand.

Micki giggled. The radical idea of her taking care of Jer appealed to her.

"This is a new phase," Tildie said after the kids were out of earshot. "It seems he's got it pretty bad." She smiled, but couldn't meet Dane's eye. *Dane darling.* Micki's less-than-subtle hint embarrassed her all over again. "This romance business is a whole new experience for us."

"He's a good kid. You'll do fine, mom." Dane glanced away.

"It sounds like you're speaking from experience."

Was it obvious to Tildie, Dane wondered, that he couldn't keep his eyes from her alabaster skin, her pouty pink lips, and the twinkling stars in the blackest centers of her eyes? A teenager's infatuation had to be a world less awkward than that of a lovesick forty-three-year-old man. He had always been so busy with work he'd never known the crush of a romance before.

"You seem to know a lot about teenaged boys," she pressed him, having met with no response.

"I can empathize with Jer," he said at last, trying to hide the fact that she took his breath away. "I was a boy once." Lord, he thought, he'd never felt this way in his life. His relations with women had always been so passionless; the few women he'd known had been colleagues at the Space Centers, so they'd talked shop mostly. But this woman had come from out of the blue, and he wanted to feel the passion that he knew was hiding behind her deep blue gaze. He managed a smile.

"I only heard about Cynthia a few days ago." Tildie was a little lost without the children. The truth was she was afraid to be alone with Dane. Every time the conversation became light and easy, she'd catch herself having too good a time.

"It doesn't take long to lose your heart sometimes." He realized now that he must have lost his the first moment he saw her. "I lost mine a couple days ago," he said now. "Your daughter, she's the cutest thief I've ever seen."

"You're so comfortable with her."

"She reminds me of someone." He looked away.

"Do you have a daughter of your own? Who misses her daddy?" Tildie was almost afraid to hear his answer.

"No." He turned back to her and frowned at the turmoil in her eyes. "I've never been married; no children, no wife."

"No ties?"

"Only to my work. Lately that hasn't been enough."

"Not challenging enough?"

He nodded. "Right, I always enjoy a challenge, and now it's not quite the same as it was...." Watching her brush a silky lock of hair from her cheek, he asked, "Why did you think I was married?"

"I thought you may have been married and divorced," she said quickly, hoping he didn't think badly of her for having thought—even momentarily—that he was an unfaithful husband. "You're so good with Micki, and she reminded you of someone...."

"Actually, she reminds me of my kid sister, Annette."

"Are you and your sister close?"

"We see each other as much as we can, but that's not often. Annie lives on the west coast."

"I bet she misses her brother, too."

"We're the only family we've got left." Matilda Moore cared about people, Dane realized all over again as he saw the real sympathy in her features. Family was the most important ingredient in her life, he guessed. She was good and beautiful, and her lips were the softest and the most welcome he'd ever kissed.

"My sister was a brainy kid and very loving, like Micki."

Tildie accepted the compliment graciously for her daughter and relaxed more as their clown waitress refilled the four soda glasses on their table.

Four was a magical number, Tildie decided: a family of four, a four-door, a foursome... She cut her reverie short. "I want to thank you for this special celebration for Jer."

"Anytime," he said, remembering how naturally his arm had slipped around Tildie's waist as they'd shared Jer's victory home run.

Birthdays, home runs and pizzas could be shared by four, or by two, she thought. She suddenly felt warm, realizing that she longed to steal more moments alone with this complex man.

"I'm glad you came tonight," he said to her in a low tone. He also wanted to tell her that she should smile more often, because her smile lit up her face and brightened the blue of her eyes. "I missed your interruptions at work the past couple of days, counselor." He looked away from her for an instant, so that she wouldn't see that he also lusted after her smile, her laugh, her voice.

"I have almost all the information I need."

He tipped his head to the side as though he were puzzled. "Do you have someone in the field advising you?"

"That may not be necessary." She didn't meet his eye.

"I could—"

"It wouldn't be right for us, for you and I.... We shouldn't even be here together now...." She had no logical explanation for why she had agreed to come tonight. He studied her and was about to speak when she said, "We really can't work together."

"If you think it's because we aren't alike or we don't have anything in common, I wasn't kidding when I told you that I admired you for caring what happens to the world."

"It's . . . I think I'd better find the kids."

"Cynthia is at the video game next to Jer's. You can't interrupt now," he said lightly, covering her hand with his. "Besides, I'm trying to tell you that we're on the same side, Tildie. We can work on the presentation together." Did she think he'd let her walk out of his life? From the moment she'd bumped into him in that hallway, she'd been on his mind. Her hair smelled like sunshine, her skin like lilacs, and her lips were softer than flower petals. Her hand fit into his perfectly, and her body had felt like heaven when they'd embraced.

"No. I'll finish my business at Fun Design tomorrow." She purposefully didn't say more.

"What's the hurry?" It was as though she wanted to get away from him. Did she think he'd let her go without a fight? It was she who had stepped into his life unexpectedly, not the other way around. Tildie and her lively kids had given him a glimpse of family life that he hadn't seen since he'd left home at seventeen. He wouldn't let that slip away any more than he'd allow her to give up on the presentation for the FCC. She couldn't pull the rug out from under him, not after she'd given him faith in people again.

She removed her hand from under his self-consciously. "I've already set up an appointment at the Federal Building to go over the presentation." If she had to answer one more of his questions or withstand another probing gaze, she thought she'd start to cry. Had she actually met someone who could complete her perfect family? Ironically, having him near could break up the family she had now. She couldn't afford to feel giddy in his arms, or want to hold the wide hand that had covered hers moments before, brush a lock of golden hair from his forehead. She remembered what was at stake and said, "I'll go get the children. We really should be going." She slipped out of her chair before he could object.

Dane entertained Micki and talked with Jer on the ride home. Unlike Tildie, they didn't know that this would be their last night together. Tildie stole glances at Dane as he told Micki a funny story; this would be the last few minutes she would see him before she jumped out of the car with the children and retreated into the house. As the car turned onto their street Dane mentioned that he did some juggling, but Jer was skeptical.

"Can you juggle baseballs?" Jer asked.

"Of course he can," Micki defended. "He said so, didn't he?"

"Baseballs, books, bats or china cups. I'm flexible," Dane said. "Some people play golf to relax. I juggle. If I have something that I can't quite figure out, I juggle until a possible solution comes to mind...." His sidelong glance took in Tildie's sweater—the color of raspberry sherbet— and the full skirt that was pulled chastely over her knees. "I think I'd like to juggle now."

"Do you have a problem?" Micki asked.

"Certainly not you." He reached back and playfully tweaked her nose.

"Could you teach me how to juggle?" Jer asked.

"You wouldn't happen to have a problem with something—or someone—would you?" Dane probed, and met Tildie's gaze.

"Could you teach me tonight?" Jer asked seriously.

"Jer," admonished his mother, "I'm sure that's not something you can learn in one night, especially without zero gravity."

"They only have five percent gravity on the Sercerian moon," Micki informed them.

"Yeah, you'd be floating if you were there, mom," added Jer.

As Dane pulled the car into the driveway, he wondered if Tildie would float into his arms later in the evening. . . .

"I prefer to keep both feet on the ground," Tildie said, trying to ignore Dane's curious smile. No doubt he was remembering how she had responded to his kisses.

Tildie played the heavy, reminding everyone it was a school night as they scrambled up the walk. "Homework and to bed. You promised." Dane began to follow them in, but Tildie cut him short at the bottom of the front steps.

"The children really do need to call it a night."

"We'll be far, far away, up in our rooms doing yucky homework, so we won't be able to hear you talking downstairs," Micki hinted with a wink and skipped happily up the front steps.

"Thank you, we'll keep that in mind," Dane laughed.

"Look out, squirt," Jer said, stepping around his sister. To Dane he said, "Thanks for the pizza and for coming to my ball game."

"Sure. We'll work on the juggling another time."

"Will you walk me in, Dane darling?" Micki said melodramatically as she waited for the adults to catch up with her. Sighing, Tildie wondered why her own kids always seemed to be conspiring against her. Micki took Dane's arm when he met her, and he happily escorted her into the house.

At the bottom of the stairway he said, "Good night, my dear," playing it out.

"Parting is such sweet sorrow!" Micki hammed, batting her long lashes.

"Micki," Tildie warned. "Homework."

Dane laughed again. "I think your daughter is a woman after my own heart," he teased.

Tildie smiled tightly, thinking her own daughter had fed her to the lion once again.

"Good night!" The little girl kissed Dane's cheek.

"Such a cute kid," he said, after Micki had scampered up the stairs and out of earshot. "You and I do have something in common. We both think those two kids are great." He gestured up the stairway while he gazed steadily at her eyes and reddening cheeks.

"Thank you. And thank you for dinner. But you really should go. We don't have anything to say." She walked to the door.

"You know we should work together."

"It's nothing personal, Mr. Scott."

"I think it's very personal."

"I told you I'll be finished with my interviews tomorrow. Then my business with Fun Design will be over."

"Would you like to know why I really walked out on NASA?" Thank goodness he could still count on her curiosity. "You don't think we're anything alike, lady crusader?" He smiled at her warm blue gaze that was lapping over him like gentle ocean waves. "I left NASA because I didn't like the change of priorities and the adoption of the bottom-line philosophy everything for a buck. I protested. Doesn't that sound like something one very beautiful attorney would do?"

"Please, I don't want to hear this. You needn't—"

"The Agency would ship any payload," Dane went on relentlessly, ignoring Tildie's efforts to make him leave, "including military ones, on any schedule if there was money in it." He leaned against the newel post and crossed his arms over his chest. "Maybe they thought that was the only way to keep the worthwhile programs going; I don't know." He shook his head. "But it wasn't right. People were working too fast and putting in too many hours on projects that could jeopardize world peace or the planet's very existence." As he spoke Tildie realized she'd known all along that there was a part of him that lay much deeper than his dazzling smile. "When I finally wised up and realized what my last project could be used for, I told the director to drop it or I'd walk out." He leveled his gaze at her. "I do care what happens to the world, counselor, especially to three very dear people in it."

His words began to sink in as he walked toward her. She *did* care. "That means the project is still going on?" she asked, barely getting the words out.

"The frustrating thing is I can't say anything about the project without being arrested for treason. Not to mention the field day the Soviets would have with a negative statement from a former top NASA scientist. I'm positive that they're working on a system similar if not more devastating; it doesn't just involve near Earth space, Tildie. It could mean military bases on the moon."

"What can we do?"

"Maybe teach little children how important space can be." He wasn't smiling. "You know, after I walked out of NASA, I tried not to care. But then this crusading dynamo bumped into me one day and disturbed my sleepwalking." His gaze roamed along her delicate jawline to the high curve of her upper lip. "You made me care and feel again, Tildie." He shook his head and smiled at her round blue eyes and her parted pink lips. "I don't know whether to thank you or blame you."

The smoky emotions churning in his eyes scared up a flutter of butterflies in her stomach. She couldn't speak.

"I only know that I'm not going to let you give up on the fight against the violence in *Star Power*."

Tildie checked the powerful sincerity in his clear gray eyes. For a wonderful moment he wasn't a threat to her security, but only a very warm caring human being and ally—someone who wanted her to win, to succeed. She wanted to throw her arms around his neck and hug him, but . . .

"Do you want to protect the children?" he asked.

"Yes." How could he doubt that?

His smile frayed the seams of her defenses.

"Me, too. When I first proposed *Star Power*, Auggie hired a group of writers that immediately wanted to turn it into a *Star Wars* clone, with battles and weapons. I protested and nearly lost my job again, because I was told that I didn't understand what sells. We were down to the bottom line again."

"So you suggested Captain Starblazer—to always be there to defend the planet." Her voice was sympathetic. "To save the day." She shook her head and smiled. "You are the Captain, aren't you?" As she spoke the jet-black centers of her eyes sparkled with stars, and her full lips pouted a soft invitation. As he leaned toward her, he rationalized that he'd only brush his mouth against hers for an instant. But as his lips hovered near hers and he inhaled a warm breath of summer sunshine and lilac, he knew he had to hold her.

As his mouth gently met hers his hands trailed down the gentle slope from her pale swanlike throat past the warm nubby yarn of her sweater that covered her shoulders. When they reached the small of her back, he pressed her hips to his. An incredibly powerful feeling swept through him the instant her long, luscious body relaxed naturally against his and her lips answered his kiss.

This was the first time he'd told anyone why he'd left NASA and he felt relieved, unburdened. The heart and compassion of Tildie Moore took some of the sting out of the experience he'd had there. His protest hadn't accomplished anything, yet she had appreciated that he'd tried, that he'd cared. To her he was a hero. He suddenly felt able to leap tall buildings in a single bound. Her body was nestled against his and her arms were gently wrapped around his neck like a hero's laurel, and as her fingertips toyed with the hair at the nape of his neck, months of confusion, disappointment and bottled-up fears rolled away. A new, wonderful feeling took their place.

He cares, he cares, were the words that went through Tildie's mind over and over as her lips caressed his. He had tried to change the course of the future; he had wanted to save the world. He kissed her so tenderly that she couldn't resist returning his goodness. She felt dizzy as his gentleness gave way to urgency and his kiss expanded to test the pursed corner of her mouth and to tug gently on the fullness of her lower lip. She'd felt a slight chill when Dane had told her how he'd tried to stop the destructive project at NASA, but now she was covered in goose bumps as she realized the depth of compassion and commitment his action had indicated. He was a hero; he was the Captain; he was always there.

The muscles of his back felt hard and tight under her hands. His compact energetic torso felt immovable against her breasts and his rocklike thighs made her keenly aware of his strength. He tasted her lips again and again in a series of nibbles that lightened her head until she wound her arms tighter around his neck so that she wouldn't float away.

A man could live and breathe on her sweet appreciation and her wide-eyed admiration alone, he decided, until her soft breasts flattened against his chest and he suddenly needed more. One hand slipped under her sweater to the hollow of her back and glided over her smooth bare shoulder blades. The mellow intoxication he felt at touching her velvet skin buzzed through him until every cell of his body, from the soles of his feet to the roots of his hair, craved a slow, breathless fix.

Hearing his breath become uneven, she realized that her own heart was pounding. She arched her long neck with a sigh as his flicking tongue played a happy game of thrill-and-seek between her parted lips. Both of his pleasure-giving hands stroked her back until one eased over her hip and took her breath away as it edged up her ribs. His thumb confidently tested the weight of her round breast as he caressed her mouth. His fingertip whispered along the sweetheart line of her satiny bra, teasing the upper curve of her breast with feather-light touches, drawing a choked sigh from her.

God, she was actually moaning, Tildie suddenly realized. She had two curious children just up the stairs who were no doubt trying to listen to every word, every breath, every murmur. Her body stiffened in Dane's arms as reality set in. This had gone too far. She wasn't supposed to melt in his arms. She pushed away from him, breathing hard. "I'm going to finish my business at Fun Design tomorrow. I don't want you—"

"That message doesn't compute, Tildie," he breathed. "Not after your response a moment ago."

She was still reeling from the realization that they hadn't even taken the time to move from the foyer before she had allowed him to make love to her. Dane Scott was an irresistible irritant, who had had her running in circles from the first moment they'd met. She'd been telling herself that he wasn't her type, wasn't worth the risk, that she didn't have the time or energy for a romance, yet tonight he had conveniently said things he knew would melt her resistance and she'd willingly jumped into his arms.

"I'm never going to see you again." She knew she shouldn't have seen him tonight. "I don't want to see you again."

"Would you repeat that under oath, Tildie?" His eyes held a confident glint.

"Please leave. The children are upstairs."

"This may come as a surprise to you," he said, barely containing his frustration, "but at least one of the two children upstairs is cheering us on. Micki thinks we make a charming couple." He gave her a sidelong glance. "Out of the mouths of babes..." His eyes were at once testing and teasing.

"We haven't known each other very long. We aren't going to see each other after tonight. I don't have the time or energy for a romance—"

"You're full of energy and passion—and wonder."

Tildie was struck by the urge to tell him about Paul's custody suit, but she knew that doing so would only draw them closer, and right then she wanted nothing more than to be safe and secure again.

At that instant as his gaze focused on the confusion in her eyes, he knew instinctively that he would make love to Matilda Moore one day. Despite the fact that the woman was doing her damnedest to throw him out of her house, he realized that someday he'd find a passion in her arms that was meant for him alone. He knew she could feel it too. He wanted to make love to her until all her righteous fury ignited into passion. He smiled at her because she was so beautiful. For a moment he could only hear his heartbeat, until his foggy brain registered what her lips were saying.

"Please, leave... we can't see each other..."

Her eyes didn't match what she was saying. He wanted to reprogram the information. But how? The woman was throwing him out of her house, saying a permanent good-bye.

"What's the bottom line, Tildie?" She had made him trust people again and now she was knocking the wind out of his sails.

"I have more to lose than you do," she said, lifting her chin.

He frowned. "You're the one person I'd never have guessed would turn this into an accounting game."

She swallowed. "Please leave."

He studied the eyes that were the color of a western sky just before the stars appeared. He could wish upon those stars in her eyes, he thought. He had to be crazy, he decided, as he let his gaze linger on the dazzling layers of sunshine in her shiny hair and on her luminous pale skin. He remembered the shape of her breasts.

"Sure," he breathed out, so he wouldn't pull her into his arms again. "I'm leaving."

"Fine!" She folded her arms over her waist and breathed through her flared nostrils.

"You can relax now, counselor." He teased her with a tantalizing smile of what might have been. "Oh, and about what I said earlier—about NASA—just forget it, all right? I made it up." He pursed his lips and waited for her reaction.

"Fine." She saw uncharacteristic tension in his shoulders and lines between his brows that weren't normally there. "It's forgotten." By the shift in his jaw Tildie sensed that Dane Scott had indeed been open, honest, and intimate when he'd talked about NASA earlier. It was the present attitude he was fabricating.

"Fine," he said, exhaling quietly. His eyes studied every last detail of her features until she looked away.

He was honest, good, caring....

"Do you know the best part about you, Matilda-Fitzsimmons-Moore?" he asked as he moved toward the door, opened it and stepped out.

Tears were pushing hard behind her eyes, so she only lifted her chin.

"Although you have many commendable attributes—" his eyes roamed briefly over her sweater and back to her steely eyes "—your two kids are definitely the best part of you. They're great."

"I know." She swallowed hard. "That's why I'd like to keep them."

Expressive brows furled over questioning gray eyes. "Goodbye," was all he said.

In another moment, with only the sound of the door closing, he was gone.

CHAPTER EIGHT

DANE DIDN'T WANT to remember how tender Matilda Moore's velvet skin had felt the night before. She had no right to be in his thoughts or in the silky memories of his fingertips. Yet as he talked with Roy Baker in the harsh light of the noisy Fun Design assembly room, he fantasized about touching her again.

"I'll bring the models to you this afternoon, then," he said vaguely. Matilda had said she'd be at the plant today. He'd decided late last night, when he should have been sleeping, that he would make a point of talking with her again. Maybe he had rushed her last night.

"Right," Roy agreed. "If my crew has a few hours to measure and prep them we'll be able to work on the molds over the weekend and not lose much in production time," Roy Baker explained.

Time. How could Matilda Moore have possibly finished her research on Fun Design so quickly, when she had originally spoken about needing a couple of weeks? He needed more time with her, time to make her melt in his arms as his hands moved slowly over her....

"What's the hurry? I thought nothing was to be done for a week or two yet?" Bert Tundry had joined them, and though he tried to sound casual, it seemed to Dane that Bert was reluctant to start production. But Dane had other things to think about.

"We promised Charlie we'd hold up for a few days," he replied absently. For a fleeting instant he considered that Charlie Patrick may have been right. Maybe she was an industrial spy working for SynTech Incorporated. Maybe she had all the information she needed. But he knew that wasn't true; he'd locked the models and drawings in his safe only moments before. Besides, she cared.

He had looked into her eyes last night and he had felt her heart soften. When he had told her why he had walked out of NASA, she had wound her arms around his neck and kissed him as though he were her hero, and suddenly life hadn't seemed meaningless. Maybe he *could* save the planet with her beside him. Damn, the woman had him feeling again. He cared about what happened to her daughter, to the world. She had no right to walk out after she'd made him care again.

"There haven't been any more listening devices found, and the prime suspect is leaving the plant. Matilda Moore is wrapping up her case today." Roy nudged Bert's arm. "Haven't you noticed how distracted our chief designer is this afternoon?"

"I'll bring the models over later," Dane repeated, then looked up into Roy's sympathetic face. "I liked her kids, that's all," he said with a shrug. "Did I tell you about Jer's home run yesterday?"

And then he thought, what in hell had Tildie meant when she'd said she didn't want to lose the kids? How could she lose them?

"Yes," Roy said. "About a dozen times. The little girl stole his heart, too," he informed Bert with a shake of his head.

"She's something else," Dane said. Micki had untapped an energy in him that he'd never felt before. Had his own father felt the same when his sister Annie had hugged him?

Had he wanted to protect her and wake up every morning holding her mother in his arms? He tried to push the images away. A rational, intelligent man didn't fall in love in five days and take on a ready-made family, he reasoned.

Matilda Moore had shaken him out of the comfortable niche he'd found at Fun Design. Now he felt at loose ends; that was why he was so vulnerable, he rationalized. That was what made him so susceptible to Micki with her cute giggle and to her gorgeous, irritating, uptight mom. Again he wondered what Tildie had meant when she'd said she wanted to keep the kids.

"...Scottie?" The pinched, impatient tone of Bert's voice registered more than his words. "How long will it be before you bring the models down to Roy?"

"I have a few things to clear away in my office," Dane replied. "How about an hour?"

"We'll be ready and waiting." Roy smiled, but Bert looked paler and more nervous than usual as he popped a white antacid tablet in his mouth.

It wasn't any easier for Dane to keep his mind on his work as he sat at his desk. He had instructed Maggie to signal him the second Matilda Moore finished her business with Auggie Klopperman. He'd speak with her once more before she left Fun Design. He wanted to pretend that would be enough for him, but then he'd remember Tildie's smile, her laugh that bubbled deep in her throat and how she had kissed him....

He realized, too, that he wanted all three of them: the beautiful crusader and her freckle-faced kids. Together with a defrocked NASA designer, they made an unlikely combination. Yet anyone could see that they were good for each other. He liked Tildie's kids and they liked him. So what blinded their mother? Why wouldn't she admit she was at-

tracted to him? Why was she in such a hurry to get away
from him?

He absently picked up a paperweight, his rotary file and
a Sky Lab model from his desk and began to juggle them.
But answers wouldn't fall into place. If the three of them
were so happy on their own, why did the little girl write him
letters? Why did Tildie melt in his arms so her body fit
against his in a way that drove him crazy? He tossed the rotary file and paperweight higher and grabbed a stapler to
add to the bunch. That felt more comfortable—four objects circling through the air. Four: a very stable number, a
good number for a birthday party. A husband, a wife, a
couple of kids. Four felt comfortable.

Finally Maggie buzzed to tell him that Tildie was leaving
Auggie Klopperman's office. He caught the stapler, the file,
and the paperweight, and tossed the Sky Lab model up in
the air one more time. Four. Dane hurried out of his office
and down the hall.

As she made her farewells to Auggie by the door to the old
man's office, Tildie didn't notice Dane, who saw a silky,
satiny, heavenly vision of lilac and lavender. She wore a sophisticated outfit with a shiny cardigan, which emphasized
her beautiful, proud shoulders, and softly draped dress that
attempted to disguise her curves.

He had intended to say his piece with calculated distance
so she wouldn't know how much she mattered to him, but
after one look at her he wanted to make love with her so
badly that his voice nearly disappeared. He came up on her
blind side and waited for her to finish her goodbye to Auggie Klopperman. Finally, she turned to leave.

"Oh..." She met a pair of clear gray eyes head on, and
they nearly took her breath away. His lips were pursed
slightly and dimples softened his tan cheeks. She hadn't

wanted to see him again, but now she couldn't resist feasting her eyes.

"It seems this hallway isn't big enough for the two of us." He'd meant for his words to be light, knew he hadn't succeeded. And now all he could do was study the series of emotions that flickered over her features until color brushed her cheeks.

"I suppose you've already met the man most responsible for Fun Design's success," Auggie boasted broadly, having heard Dane's voice and come back to the door. Yet neither the man nor the woman looked his way when he spoke.

Dane inhaled lilacs.

Tildie caught a reckless breath. "Yes, we've met." She hoped her gaze was unflinching and her voice carefully modulated. She was determined to hold herself in restraint today, unlike the night before.

"Ms Moore and I have had interesting encounters in hallways and foyers." He remembered how marvelous her body had felt, the tiny catches in her breath, the low "coo" deep in her throat at his touch. . . .

"But we don't have anything more to say to each other."

"I believe we do," Dane insisted. The fact that she didn't want to see him again wriggled under his skin and smarted like a sliver.

"My business is finished with Fun Design and with Mr. Scott," she explained, suddenly realizing that the company founder could act as a buffer against Dane Scott's energy—energy that seemed focused on her. "I have quite enough information now, thanks to you." She smiled at the white-haired founder and ignored Dane completely.

"There're a couple of details that . . . need to be discussed." Dane brought her wary gaze back to his own, chiding himself at the same time. Why couldn't he let her go? What was he doing pursuing a woman with a family?

He didn't need the complication in his life, especially when the woman in question felt like silk in his hands. Last night when he had explored her softer-than-a-butterfly skin, they had nearly taken flight together. They had been caught by a rare breeze as her arms had wound tightly around his neck.

"No, I don't have any more business with Mr. Scott," she said.

"Fine. I'll leave you in his capable hands. It was very nice meeting you, Miss Moore. And Scottie, you will take very good care of this lovely lady?"

"Yes, sir. Absolutely," Dane promised, knowing that Auggie's hearing aid was on the fritz again.

"You're a good man," Auggie concluded before he turned away. Dane merely smiled and nodded.

For an instant, panic filled her. She couldn't be alone with Dane—not again. She inhaled deeply and decided to walk on by him as though he weren't there.

"You're to be in my hands, Ms Moore." He gently caught her wrist as she skirted by him. His thumb skimmed over the satiny cloth of her jacket to find the velvet skin of her inner wrist scented with lilac. He pictured erotic warm nights before she retrieved her hand.

"Everything is in my report."

Was she trembling?

"You can read my final presentation to the FCC tomorrow." Her arched pink lips formed every letter carefully and her arched brow told him she wanted nothing more to do with him. "I'll send you the final copy."

"Tildie—"

"I told you I don't want or need complications in my life."

"Somehow last night things were simple," he said, watching the kaleidoscope of emotions in her eyes. "It was just a man and a woman; you and me together, alone...."

"About last night," she started inadequately. "It was...ah..."

"Terrific?"

"A fluke. An accident that should never have happened," she said, continuing up the hall. "One that won't happen again."

"I swear your feet left the ground for a moment last night, counselor."

"I hardly think so." Not practical down-to-business Matilda Moore. It must have been another woman, sighing in his arms last night. "I specialize in keeping both feet on the ground." His one arched brow showed his confident disbelief, which spurred her on. "I don't want you interrupting my life, my home—"

"Yeah, I had a terrible time, too." He nearly smiled at her instantaneous hurt expression. He pursed his lips but it was too late to hide the teasing smile in his eyes and the dimples in his cheeks.

"Lord save me from an aging boy-next-door." Tildie rolled her eyes as she huffed around the corner to yet another long hallway. It seemed the corridors were circular—or was it only her mind that was going in circles? "Do you think everyone falls in love with you?"

"I have a certain boyish charm."

"Let's just say I'm the one person who can resist it."

"Aren't you even mildly curious about why I left NASA?"

"I forgot all about that," she reminded him.

"The Matilda Moore I know wouldn't have," he stated. "Not the one who wants to ship pizzas to the world's starving."

"You're making fun of me."

"No. I envy you. You care, Tildie. And I believe maybe someday you could even care for me."

"You think I'm attracted to you, but I'm not."

"The hell you aren't. Why can't you admit it? What's so terrible?"

"Would you stop following me?"

"We just happen to be going in the same direction." He shrugged, then continued, "We just happen to have had a very nice time together last night. There's no crime in that. You act as if it meant the end of civilization as we know it. I don't—"

"Perhaps it would mean the end of my world as I know it," she said, showing more passion than she'd intended. "I'm finished with my business here, so I'm not going to see you again." As angry as she was, the blunt statement made her swallow hard and her steps slow.

"Wait a minute, you can't say something like that then walk away. What's going on? What does it have to do with the kids? I don't understand." He wanted to stop her. He wanted to say "Don't walk out of my life." But his logical mind wouldn't let him go that far.

"Goodbye, Mr. Scott." She stood in front of him now; she wanted to move on, but she rocked back on one heel a moment. "I think it only fair to tell you that you were right about Nigel and Associates; they are in it for the money." It was he who had made her decide to stand up to the senior partners of the firm on the SynTech case and she longed to tell him so. "You really did leave NASA as a protest, didn't you?"

"Does it matter?"

"Yes." Her voice was barely above a whisper.

He smiled as he brushed his thumb over her cheek. "There are qualities that I like about you very much, counselor."

That truth set butterflies darting in her middle.

"I want to continue to see you," he said.

"No." Again she wondered if she should tell him about the custody suit, but she knew if she did, she'd only complicate things for herself. It was better to let him think she simply didn't want a relationship.

He wanted to clear his senses of her perfume, to leave her and think things over, but instead he said, "I'm going to continue to see Micki and Jer." God, he loved the way her lips parted and her breath caught. He understood her reaction. His words had surprised him just as much as they'd apparently surprised her. "They're good kids. Open and honest. You could learn from them." His eyes focused on the wide blue eyes that flinched at his words.

"My presentation for the FCC is in this very briefcase." She spoke as if she had completely dismissed his pledge to see the kids. "If I don't hurry, I'll miss my four o'clock appointment to file the complaint at the Federal Building. My, look at the time." Lord, she was looking at the wrist without her watch. The man confused her so much and she was juggling so many feelings in her heart that she thought she was going to explode on the spot. Why was he insisting on seeing her kids again? "And from there my presentation will be on its way to the chairman of the Federal Communications Commission in Washington—"

"Tildie, I mean it. I'm going to see Micki and Jer as long as they want to see me." His boy-next-door aura had slipped a bit. His steel gray eyes held the determination of a traveler destined to reach his destination, no matter how distant. His eyes sparkled despite the deep creases below them that hinted of a sleepless night. "If that means we'll be . . . bumping into each other from time to time, we'll just have to make the best of it."

The best thing of all would be to wrap her arms around his neck and press her body into his, she thought suddenly.

"So we understand each other?" His half smile and warm, roaming gaze made her think that he'd read her mind. Sexy, heart-melting dimples appeared in his lean, tanned cheeks.

"You don't understand. You can't see the kids again, and you won't if you care at all." She made it by him, but couldn't forego one last look. "This is goodbye." She offered her hand, which was a mistake. Because when he took it, their hands felt so natural, so promising together. "Goodbye." From his curious searching expression she guessed he felt her shaking in her high-heeled shoes. He freed her hand and she turned and walked down the hall. One more corner and she'd be out of his sight, she thought firmly, emotion knotting in her throat. Her eyes were blurred and she nearly bumped into Bert Tundry.

"Mr. Scott makes quite an impression, doesn't he?" Bert said quietly.

He must have overheard at least part of their conversation, she thought. "I hadn't noticed." She continued to walk down the hall. She could feel the advertising executive's disbelieving eyes on her.

"It's strange how circumstances and professional choices put people in each other's paths," Bert said, following her.

"Only briefly."

"Sometimes we don't have a choice." It seemed she didn't have any power to keep Dane Scott out of her thoughts. She marched along, anxious to be rid of the former astronaut, Fun Design, and this hypertensive soothsayer.

"Mr. Scott is deceiving. He seems like just a charmer—"

"A clown, you mean." She should be glad that she'd never see him again.

"Yes." Mr. Tundry looked away. "I heard you were finishing up your business with us today."

"I'm going to the Federal Building today to file my presentation and they'll be sending it on."

"I'm sorry to hear you'll be leaving us." The man made Tildie uncomfortable, but she couldn't decide if it was because he was so nervous or if she just wanted to be away from Fun Design. "We decided to give you something to remember your times here at the company. It's the fun capital of the world, you know." He thrust an oblong bundle, carelessly wrapped in white paper and string into her hands.

"I've heard," Tildie said, trying to give back the package. "Please, that's really not necessary." How could she forget her days here?

"It's from all of us. Dane, too, of course." His darting eyes noted her expression as she swallowed.

"I can't accept this."

"Mr. Scott insisted. It's a small token really. You'll make my job a whole lot easier; he'll blame me if you leave without it. Put it in your briefcase." He nudged her arm that carried her new leather case. "And don't even think about it until later."

She realized from his insistence that the quickest way out of the plant was to take the bundle, and with a small sigh, she put it into her briefcase.

"It's a toy," he said, smiling. "I'm so glad I caught you. I contacted your office earlier and they said you were flying to Cleveland this afternoon."

"My schedule has been changed." That was the one bright spot in Tildie's day. "Someone else is handling the case in Cleveland now." Tildie had taken Dane Scott's tale about why he had walked away from NASA to heart. He had protested. He had stood up and had said his piece. She had, too, this very morning. She had tried once again to convince Arthur Hillenbrand into settling out of court on the SynTech class-action suit. But he had taken her off the case instead.

"You're not going to Cleveland at all?" Bert Tundry's skin turned almost white, from the top of his shiny head on down. Even his gesturing hands seemed to pale. "You're not going to—"

"I was taken off that case." She almost laughed with the relief she felt, despite the fact that her job was possibly in jeopardy. Aggressive firms like Nigel and Associates didn't keep associates on board just to handle the *gratis* cases.

"But you had a three o'clock flight." Bert Tundry's mouth hung open.

"Right now I have a four o'clock appointment at the Federal Building." She was relieved that her presentation would be filed and on its way to the commission on children's programing soon. She could put Fun Design and Dane Scott out of her mind. She knew she should never see him again. She had taken a stand on the SynTech case and she had Dane Scott to thank for that. At least something was going right, she thought. She paused before heading off down the hall. "I do appreciate all the assistance from your company, Mr. Tundry. Good day."

BERT TUNDRY SNATCHED the wrapping paper from a package of green antacid tablets. His fingers were shaking. He had a pain in his abdomen that was backing up all the way into his throat. He didn't want to call, but he had to let Tech Toys know the plan was down the tubes. This was to have been an auxiliary plan to bugging the drafting room, since that hadn't worked. The woman was to have been a courier, unbeknownst to her. She traveled from company to company, and it was perfect, or so Marcus Deevers had said. It was supposed to have been so simple, so clean. Now Bert's future job with Tech Toys and his fifteen-year tenure with

Fun Design was down the tubes. Why had he gotten himself into this? He must have been mad.

He remembered the casual dinner he'd had with the vice-president of advertising at Tech Toys after he'd sent the company his résumé. Marcus Deevers had expressed great interest in him, and before he knew it they were discussing new products that were in the works at Fun Design. He had made less-than-subtle inquiries about Dane Scott's plans for the Christmas line. The Tech Toys executive had made it clear that even Dane Scott's most insignificant doodlings could prove valuable. Bert knew that to be true after having watched the designer work for eighteen months. His hometown Midwestern charm hid a keen mind that never quit questioning, experimenting, or solving. His energy and curiosity levels were apparently boundless.

Mrs. Tundry's stupid son, Bert, had gotten himself caught in the middle. Why hadn't he seen it coming? Scottie would have never let himself be sucked into a mess like this, but then he was a lot smarter. Bert swallowed hard; guilt had been a steady part of his diet lately, along with chalky antacid tablets. *How do you spell relief? O-U-T,* he thought hysterically. He wanted out of this mess, now. Soon, he was on the phone with Marcus Deevers.

"Is the package on its way?" Deevers asked.

"I gave it to Ms Moore like you wanted me to." Bert winced from the pain in his midsection. "It's wrapped in plain white paper, tied with string. She stuck it in her briefcase, like you said she would."

"Good." There was relief in his voice. "So she should be boarding that plane soon. It won't be hard to retrieve it from her briefcase when she's at our head office. She'll never know she was a courier."

"One problem. She's not going to SynTech today. You told me she'd be going there. You said this would be very clean and simple." Bert popped another tablet into his mouth. "Someone else is taking over the SynTech case. That's what she told me. I don't know why, only that she has an appointment here in town today."

"You let her out of your plant with the model? You didn't stop her?"

"I didn't know what to say." Bert frowned. "I just gave it to her."

"You have to get it back," Deevers insisted.

"I don't like this. You said it would be simple. You said I wouldn't have to do anything. I want out of it," Bert insisted.

"There's no way out now, Bert. You planted the bugs and you copped the model. Someone is going to find out about it."

"Soon. The prototypes were scheduled to go down to production today. Remember I told you? I also told you this wouldn't work."

"Stop whining, Tundry. I hate it when you whine." His voice was cold and unsympathetic. "Get the prototype back from the lawyer."

"How?"

"Steal it again if you have to."

"She'd recognize me."

"Use your imagination, Bert. But remember this: I'm sending someone down to get that model from you tonight and they won't be regular Tech Toys employees—they'll be specialists. And they won't take any excuses."

"You never really intended to give me a job with your company, did you?" Bert felt his chest explode with pain and his heart pound. "You just wanted to find a sucker to do an inside job for you."

"It's a little late to be asking questions like that, isn't it, Bert?" There was a short silence on the line. "Have the model ready for the boys tonight. Don't mess up again, and you may have that job yet.''

But Bert hardly heard him. How could he get the prototype back from Matilda Moore, he was thinking, panicked. How could he get to the Federal Building before she did?

TILDIE SAT BACK in the seat as the taxi driver floored the pedal and the red-and-white cab spurted into the passing lane on Interstate 71. She glanced down at the briefcase on the stained seat beside her, remembering her parting gift from Fun Design. A toy; just a little something to remember the designer by. How very fitting, she thought, a touch angrily. Dane Scott had toyed with her emotions.

She steamed, recalling how she had responded to Dane's touch last night, how she had wanted to toss restraint to the wind and make love with him in the foyer. Had she ever acted so depraved in her entire life? There was something about the man, as nonchalant as he seemed, that kindled passion in her. Within the same few moments the man could irritate her no end and then make her laugh. He had said he would see her children again. He couldn't just walk into her life and into the lives of her children. Or could he? He'd certainly done a good job of that so far. He had just happened to show up at the baseball game, invite them out for dinner and then casually start to make love to her by the front door as if he not only had the power, but the right to do so.

The cab darted onto the Broad Street exit, the driver taking the direct route downtown. With a glance out the window, she knew where she was going and that she was on schedule. It felt good to be in control of something. All her life had been carefully planned, first by her father, then her husband. Then the need to support herself and her family had dictated her jobs and her career direction. And she'd been making it, until she'd gotten the letter in the mail telling her that Paul intended to sue for custody of Jer. Now she felt vulnerable again. But the former astronaut had inadvertently helped her see her best case against Paul, and had given her the courage to speak her mind about the purely monetary attitude of her law firm. Inside she felt stronger. Then why had she nearly fallen apart when he'd touched her today?

Tildie remained so embroiled in her own shifting emotions that she nearly forgot her date to meet Jer at Fryman's clothing store—Jer needed to look good for his eighth-grade graduation. But then the cab rolled by the Columbus Museum of Science and Industry, jogging her memory. Her kids loved the place; there was always something there to fascinate them.

She checked her watch. She'd scolded, commanded, pleaded and had finally sandwiched her appointments around her thirteen-year-old's baseball practice. Lord, what if the judge awarded custody of Jer to his father? But did her son need a man to guide him? Was she falling in love with Dane Scott? Impossible; a definite skew of a brainwave, she reprimanded herself. She wouldn't—couldn't—meet someone and fall in love in a few days, not a smart, careful woman like Matilda Moore. Not the conscientious homemaker who folded towels precisely before she put them back in the closet. Not the attorney who sewed up every detail before a deposition left her hands.

After the cab pulled into the curb, Tildie ran the final few yards to Fryman's. Tildie's father had purchased suits from Oscar Fryman for years, and now his son, Osky, ran the business. Once she was inside and had greeted her son, the fun part began. Jer sulkily stared at the choices that Tildie and Osky had collaborated on earlier in the week, while his mother made friendly "how's the family" talk with the store owner as she bustled between the racks and the fitting room.

"Mom, you brought your briefcase with you," Jer said curiously.

"I know. I didn't have time to go home after this morning's business, and I have to go to a meeting this afternoon." Tildie's patience was short. "Please, choose a suit."

"Guys don't wear suits."

"Any guy over the age of twelve wears a suit."

"I bet Dane Scott wasn't wearing a suit today. Do you know that he was on his own, away from home by the time he was seventeen?" Jer informed her with authority. "NASA and the military both wanted him, but he chose NASA. I read about him," Jer explained to his mother's amazed face.

"In a book?"

"Yeah, well, he's the first person I've ever known that I could find in an encyclopedia. How could I pass that up?"

Tildie nodded. Dane Scott had performed yet another miracle: getting Jer to read about something other than baseball.

"You saw Dane today, didn't you?"

"Yes." Her stomach flipped at the mention of his name. Was she . . . falling in love? An adult did not fall in love in five days. *Especially not a responsible adult who doesn't want to risk the custody of her only son,* she reminded herself firmly. "I'm not going to see him again, Jer."

"He said he'd be at my next game."

"Don't count on it." She hated Jer's look of disappointment. Did she feel let down, too? "I said goodbye to him today, just a little while ago." Tildie didn't meet Jer's eye. "I met him at Fun Design because of this case I'm working on, and this afternoon my part of it will be over, until the actual hearing in Washington several weeks from now. So..."

"So I read the stuff for nothing."

"No. Definitely for something."

"Micki is going to be really disappointed," he said, trying to mask his own feelings.

"It wouldn't work out."

"You like him."

"We're opposites. He's just too..."

"He makes you laugh. He even got you to go out on a school night. I hate to think what might happen if he were around more often!"

Tildie smiled at his humor.

"Mom, do you realize what just happened? You laughed at my joke."

"I wouldn't go so far as to say I laughed."

"I really think Dane is a good influence on you. Maybe we should keep him around a while. What do you think?"

"I think you think he'll get you out of homework."

"The man's a wizard, mom. What would a few math problems be to a guy like him?" Jer grinned. "And besides, you might decide you like him, maybe even love him."

"We just met. Things like that just don't happen."

"How do you know if you're in love or not?"

"You just know, that's all," she said, copping out. This wasn't the wisdom she had hoped to impart to her son. What made the answer even more banal was that she remembered her mother telling her the very same thing. Could it be that her mother had never been in love? Never hopelessly, madly, passionately in love? Tildie suddenly felt very sad. Didn't everyone deserve one wonderful love in their life? She swallowed hard. "Now, can we pick out a suit?" She stepped back, and when she bumped into her briefcase, she remembered the package. "Dane sent you something that might cheer you up."

"Nothing could cheer me up about wearing a suit." He gave his mother a grimace that suddenly became a wicked grin. "Unless I got to wear a pair of new baseball spikes to go with it?"

She pulled the white bundle from her briefcase and decided a little lie would not go amiss. "Mr. Scott wanted you to have this, and he told me to tell you to do what your mother says because she loves you." The boy's face softened into a grin.

"That doesn't sound like something Dane would say."

"I took the liberty to translate."

"Uh-huh." Jer lifted his chin and considered his mother in a new light. "You do like him, don't you?"

"Open it up." Tildie tried to hide the rich, rosy color on her cheeks. "It's a toy."

"Are you sure this isn't for Micki?"

"Maybe it's for both of you."

Jer opened the package quickly.

"He wanted me to have this? I've never seen anything like it before, mom. Micki doesn't have anything like this. It's new." He turned the multifaceted object over and over in his hands studying its unique angles and curves. Tildie hadn't seen anything like it either, but thanks to her parents and her sister, Micki had a closet full of strange space vehicles. She marveled again at how the designer wasted his obvious talent and abundant creativity on toys.

"It's all yours." Tildie smiled, amazed but thankful at the miracle the toymaker had performed on her son, turning a surly teenager into an amiable kid again. "Now, about the suit..."

CHAPTER NINE

THE CAB SQUEALED to a stop beside the hydrant at the corner of Fourth and Cherry. Tildie checked her watch. She had thirty seconds to run around the corner into the Federal Building and catch an elevator up to the sixth floor. Seeing Jer look so grown up and handsome in the sports jacket and slacks had been worth the delay. She'd even agreed to let him stop at Chip's house on the way home to shag some fly balls, as long as he called Micki to tell her to go to Aunt Sally's and went to meet her there later.

As she clambered out of the taxi, she suddenly remembered the ride in Dane's sports car, remembered how close the four travelers had been in the streamlined vehicle and how Jer had looked at Cynthia Edgars in the pizza place. She thought about Jer's question: how *did* you know if you were in love? She forced the question from her mind because it led to Dane Scott. She had said goodbye to him forever. She had it all under control with twenty-five seconds to make her meeting. She carried the presentation for the FCC in her briefcase, she knew where her children were, and she hadn't thought about Dane Scott again for nearly five seconds. *You're going to make it yet, Tildie Moore.*

Even the sight of a white-faced clown with a fright wig strolling along the street didn't phase her as she hurried toward the Federal Building. Theater and music students from the university often performed downtown near the Federal Building during the summer for book and beer money. This one was a little off the beat, since the entertainers were usually mimes and musicians, not circus clowns. Even so, the difference barely registered until she noticed that his wide, painted smile and quick, choppy stride were aimed directly at her. She smiled until she realized that he was coming toward her too quickly to stop. She darted, but his determined white-gloved hand hooked her briefcase.

"No!" She arm wrestled for the briefcase. "What are you doing!" She used her free hand to tear at the bright red-and-yellow wig he wore. But before she could pull it off, he jerked the strap of her shoulder bag down her arm. "Stop it! Help!" The clown spun her around in a circle, and the centrifugal force caused her to fall. "Stop! Thief!" She got to her feet and ran after him on her narrow-heeled shoes. "Those are my papers! My case!" She chased him past the Federal Building and up Fourth Street until she saw him jump into a car parked at the curb and drive away.

"My case! My first good briefcase." She swallowed hard as she stood on the curb, watching the car speed out of sight.

"Tildie, what's wrong?" Suddenly, just when she needed someone most, Dane Scott stood beside her. It felt wonderful to see a friendly face and hear a familiar voice—and to flow naturally into his strong, embracing arms. She pressed her trembling body against his broad chest as his hands glided over her shoulders in soothing circles. "It's okay," he breathed. "Everything will work out." His voice quietly soothed her.

"I can't believe this is happening." Instinctively, she wrapped her arms tightly around him.

"I was afraid I wouldn't find you again," Dane said. "It's okay now."

"Did you see him?" she asked, exhaling in blessed relief.

"I saw you running. Are you all right?"

"No!" she cried. She pressed her brow near his ear and her lips lightly grazed his neck, which smelled of reassuring leather and old-fashioned spice. "My dress is torn, I have runs in my stockings, I was accosted on the street by a clown, who stole my briefcase with all my papers—"

"Hey, hey," he whispered, "slow down—"

"I can't. He drove away in a car with my notes.... Oh, you feel so good!" She hugged him harder, seeking every ounce of safety and security from his sturdy, compact body. He was there for her when she needed somebody—needed him.

"I'm here." His lips smiled and nuzzled her earlobe and temple while his thumb brushed a tear from her cheek. At that very instant she decided she couldn't possibly love anyone more.

"I'm glad." She lowered her lashes, embarrassed that he could probably read her thoughts with the gold-flecked radar in his eyes.

"Feeling better?"

"Dane, it was like he was waiting for me. Like he knew I was coming." She shuddered and he held her tighter. "I don't believe it—I got mugged by a clown."

"I, for one, will never go to a circus again." He put a protective arm around her and said to some curious bystanders, "She's all right. I'm a friend."

"He spun me around and around. I fell down."

"You're all right now—that's what matters."

Finding herself back in his arms again, she could almost believe him. She could almost forget that someone had stolen her presentation—the presentation of the case that Fun Design didn't want presented.... She stiffened in his arms as the realization set in, and said abruptly, "Why are you here?"

"I'm a hero, remember? It's my job to be here for you."
His hand glided down her arm.

"You followed me to the Federal Building." Reluctantly
she eased out of his arms. "You knew when I'd be here."

"You're late, by the way."

"You hired him." She stared at him, her eyes wide and
disbelieving.

"What!"

"You hired the clown to steal my case!" she gasped, unable to catch her breath. "You didn't want me to work on
this case and you didn't want me to file the complaint, and
when other tactics didn't work, you stole it."

"Darling, I came down here to stop you from making a
big mistake."

"What? Saying goodbye to you?"

"For one," he agreed, nodding.

"And to keep me from filing the presentation and sending it on to Washington?" She drew herself up in a huff.
"Taking it from me and then pretending to help me. Holding me in your arms . . ."

"You weren't complaining a minute ago," he said evenly.

"You're despicable."

"Who jumped into whose arms here?" His stormy eyes
reminded her of how she had clung to him. "Don't try to tell
me you weren't glad to see me."

"That'll be the day," she retorted.

"Like the day you walk off with a million-dollar model?"

"What are you talking about?"

"I actually thought you were trembling today when I saw
you at Fun Design because you didn't want to say goodbye—"

"I certainly did want to say goodbye," she lied "I
couldn't wait to get away from you."

"Because you were afraid I'd find the model before you could sneak it out of the plant?" he asked.

"What *are* you talking about?" she repeated, her brow furrowing. Then she said, "You don't understand. I just can't date anyone right now. Which wasn't a problem until I met you. Now look at me." She felt tears pushing hard upon realizing his worst crime of all was stealing her heart. "I even imagined that I was falling in love with you." She pivoted and walked down the street. Over her shoulder she called, "I bet your story about why you left NASA was as phony as the rest of you, pretending to want to cooperate on this project, pretending interest in my kids—"

"I wasn't pretending." He hurried to catch up with her and did. "Everyone tried to tell me about you. You should wear a warning label: Beware of warm, caring... Damn, I am looking into your eyes right now and I want to believe you had nothing to do with taking it. What kind of a fool does that make me?" They stood nearly eye-to-eye on the sidewalk.

"You were the only one," he went on, "who's been in and out of the plant since I checked on the new models in the safe. I don't know how you did it, but it went out with you. You carried off a model worth millions of dollars." His eyes penetrated hers.

"I did? You're accusing me? But I was the one who was robbed!"

"So was I! By you, and I'm the one who trusted you. I created the designs. I'm going to get it back and I'm going to stay with you until I do." His steely eyes held a determined light softened by emotion. "Where are you going?"

She stalked along the sidewalk. "To the police! You may not have taken my briefcase, but you know who did. You won't get away with this."

"The police? Fine, I'll take you. I hear stripes are in fashion this year, lucky for you."

"You'd say anything to talk me out of this, wouldn't you?" She was too angry to look at him.

"Give back the model and there'll be no questions asked."

"No questions asked! I still haven't the foggiest idea what you're talking about. It was you who had your clown thug steal my papers." They both hastened along the street, she, marching to an angry beat; he, gesticulating wildly and circling her.

"Are you sticking to that crazy story?" he demanded.

"Yes. Because it's the truth."

"I didn't see a clown."

"I told you he jumped into a car and drove away."

"With or without his big floppy shoes?"

"He was wearing black shoes," she said thoughtfully. "Wingtips."

"There were a lot of cars. What did that particular car look like?"

"I don't know. It was...boxy. Beige, tan, brown, I think."

"A fine eye for design and detail. Conveniently vague!"

"I was upset. He stole—my purse!" She stopped dead still.

"You can't even keep your story straight. I thought he stole your briefcase."

"My purse, too! With my paycheck." Tears came to her eyes. "Which may be my last." She shook her head. "This has been some day. I nearly lose my job, I get accosted by a clown in the street, my only money in the world is stolen and I thought you and I..." She choked as she cried large, salty tears.

He heaved a surrendering sigh. "What did you think about you and me?"

"Why would you care?"

"I care. Don't ever doubt that," he murmured, as he wiped one salty tear from her cheek and pressed her close enough that gravity pulled her the rest of the way into his arms. His hands curved in mesmerizing circles over her shoulders and back. She felt so good in his arms, yet he knew he couldn't afford the luxury. "Come on, I'll take you to the police station."

THREE HOURS LATER, she sank into the leather bucket seat of the Corwin Special and closed her eyes. "Thank you for not abandoning me to the police." Her brain was still swimming from all the questions and the frustration of waiting. Lumbering Lieutenant Kowalski had questioned them first together, then separately, before they were told to wait in a stuffy, institutional gray room. Then, a generic three-piecer named Inspector Coleson had questioned them again. The only bright spot of the evening had been when she was able to call Sally to check on the kids. Finally she had asked the police if she were being detained. She wasn't sure what Dane Scott had told them, for they were questioned separately—he hadn't implicated her when they'd been together—but they made no charges. She strongly suspected that he hadn't accused her of anything. Was something really missing from his company? How could one toy model be worth a million dollars? The only one she remembered seeing was the Sky Lab model on Dane's desk and a few models on Auggie Klopperman's desk. But she didn't want to think anymore.

"I'm glad that's over and I'm glad you stayed with me," she said to Dane, the man she couldn't wait to get away from earlier in the day.

"Sure. I mean, do I know how to entertain a girl or what? The first time I have you to myself we spend three hours getting grilled at the local precinct."

"Please, don't tease me. Just take me home, please."

"Exhausted?" His one word held a world of empathy and concern.

"Have you ever tried to convince three skeptical cops that a man wearing a Bozo the Clown fright wig, Raggedy Ann tights and bright green pantaloons robbed me on a busy street in downtown Columbus and no one else saw him?"

"You certainly had me intrigued."

"I know it's unbelievable. So why would I make up a story like that?"

His sparkling eyes met hers. "The evening's not a total loss. We haven't had dinner yet. You can't refuse a comrade in arms."

"I can't go anywhere looking like this."

"I know just the place." Soon, Dane was pulling into the parking lot at Al's Spoon, a fifties-style dog-and-burger joint near the university campus; he flashed his lights for in-car service.

Tildie felt her energy level rise after several bites of the deluxe burger he'd ordered for her; she remembered she'd been too busy to eat lunch. Between mouthfuls she asked, "So why didn't you add to my misery and tell them about the missing company model you say I stole?"

"I had a couple of good reasons. Why didn't you tell them that you thought I was the culprit who engineered your mugging?" he questioned.

She searched her motives a moment. He hadn't accused her—that was a big one. They never would have believed her story in the second place. But most of all, she hadn't told them anything because he had stayed with her, and because he had deep, gold-flecked eyes that pored over her and energized her despite her fatigue.

"There was no use complicating . . . things." Her feelings for him were anything but simple. His extended kindness to her at the police station and earlier when he had held her had made her feel safe. What she wanted right now more than anything else in the world was to be in his arms with his hand stroking her back and hair and his sure, smooth voice telling her that everything would be all right. "I mean, they asked me so many questions. I couldn't remember the license number on the getaway car. I couldn't even remember the color of the purse I carried today, and I don't even know whether they'll look for it or not."

"It was shell white."

Dane Scott never ceased to amaze her.

"A little smile looks good on you," he said. "Can we go for a big one?"

She shook her head and took another sip of her soda. "Why didn't you report the model stolen from the company? Is it really true?"

"Yes. It's also true that you are the prime suspect. My logical brain says you were the only one to leave the plant and you were the one who had direct contact with our major competitor."

"Me?"

"You were in the head offices of Tech Toys just days before you came to Fun Design the first time. You were to go back to Cleveland today."

"I didn't go." They were sharing a bag of curly shoestring French fries with an easy give and take, as natural as their conversation.

"Obviously."

"No. I asked to be removed from that case. And I wasn't representing Tech Toys. I represented SynTech Chemicals.

It's a chemical plant in Parma, which, like Tech Toys belongs to the SynTech conglomerate." She looked at him. "Is that why you were so interested in my client in Cleveland?"

"Yes."

"Because of you, I finally got the courage to tell my senior partner that I wasn't going to work on that case anymore. It involved a class-action suit against SynTech, one of Nigel and Associates' biggest clients. The firm wanted to fight the case in court. Win or lose, Nigel and Associates stands to make a great deal of money. But all the depositions I took made SynTech appear negligent." She shook her head. "Fighting wasn't right, and it wasn't in the client's best interest. So I protested." She didn't want to meet his eye. "I don't know whether I still have a job. But I was right. The same as you were right when you walked out of NASA."

He didn't comment, just watched her.

"I figured if you had enough courage to protest against NASA and the military might of the United States, I could face my senior partners and SynTech. I know what you told me about why you left NASA was true, and I'm not going to forget it."

Dane sat uncharacteristically quiet. For once he had no quick remark or teasing expression. His silence nearly made her uncomfortable.

"You can deny that you did it," she went on, "but I know it's true. I can tell by your eyes. Your protests will make a difference down the road. What you did was right." She saw his Adam's apple bob as he swallowed. "You're a hero, Captain Starblazer. You may as well face it." She smiled at him, longing to reach across the car seat to touch his face and hair. She laughed self-consciously. "So, I'd like to take this moment to thank you. I thank you. My children thank you. The world thanks you."

He rolled his eyes and smiled.

"Let's face it, you *are* the Defender of the Planet." Her voice and her words were as light as she could make them. She wasn't at all used to him being so quiet and serious. His dimples were hidden and his eyes had darkened to a smoky softness. "Thank you for being there for me today and at the police station." His gaze promised always to be there for her and something else very sensual and private. She could feel the heat rising up between her breasts and flaming her cheeks. She laughed nervously. "And thank you for this burger. I was starving." She scrunched the wrapper playfully and handed it to him to put on the tray.

She could see the dimples emerge before he spoke. "Stick with me, kid." His voice was husky and low. "I'll take ya ta all the great joints."

She laughed for the first time in what seemed a very long while.

"I like the sound of that." Now his voice was ragged with emotion.

She smiled. At that very moment she knew that she loved Dane Scott. The truth of it was exciting, comfortable, overwhelming, and completely undeniable; it had to be love.

They finished the fries, sharing light conversation and an exhausted, happy silence. Then, somewhat reluctantly, Dane started the car and pulled out into the street. They went several blocks before he spoke. "Feeling better?"

"Yes."

"Feel like more questions about the incident today?"

She sighed. She hadn't wanted to think about it again.

"Was there anything about the man who stole your briefcase—I mean besides the clown outfit—that you remember?"

"I was so busy trying to get my briefcase back and he swung me around so hard. But I have the feeling that I've seen him before," she said thoughtfully, fascinated that the vivid picture came back to her.

"Do you want to go back to the police and expand your description?"

"No!" She sank back against the seat in exhaustion. "I can't remember where I've seen him." She sighed. "Tell me how a model can be worth a million dollars. Is it made of gold?"

"It's one of a kind, a secret model. It'll be used to make the mold for the Christmas line of toys. If another toy company got their hands on it, it could cost Fun Design millions in sales."

"That's why you were so worried about Tech Toys," she said. "But you didn't report it stolen."

He steered the shiny red car through pedestrian traffic near the Ohio State campus. "It's bad business to report stolen secrets. If they're ever found, they become evidence in a court case—"

"And public record in court." She sighed and slipped down a little lower in the seat. She didn't close her eyes all the way; she watched his leg work the pedals, his bare muscled forearm shift gears. She peeked at his turned-up nose and his burnished hair, which was alive with the lights of the setting sun and the neon of High Street. "What was your other reason? You said you had a couple."

"Two. Micki and Jer," he said, looking away self-consciously, as though he was mad at himself for letting too much out. "I wouldn't want them to think their mother was an industrial spy."

"Spy?" Her voice came out nearly a whisper—then she laughed. She couldn't help it.

"Oh, I know what you're thinking," he said, apparently pleased with his relaxation methods. "No one would ever believe that an intelligent, leggy, very healthy-looking attorney—"

"Thank you, I think."

"—would ever be a spy. Would *you* believe that?"

"No." She laughed. She felt relaxed and warm.

"That's the beauty of the disguise. In a minute you're caught up in her causes, her kids, and her sexy blue eyes instead of trying to guess what competitive toy company hired her to pose as a children's advocate."

"Do you really think my eyes are sexy?"

"They're the color of ocean water," he said, glancing at them again. "They remind me of home and family and…" He turned the car off High Street onto Lawrence and headed toward Upper Arlington into the red sunset.

"What else do they remind you of?"

"You want to play it to the end? Okay. They remind me of the time we kissed, and they're driving me crazy right now."

"I'm sorry." She smiled again and studied him unapologetically, thinking about asking him in when they got home and circling her arms around his neck. She stretched her arms and shoulders to erase the urge.

"Still tied up in knots?" He looked concerned and sympathetic. "I know a good relaxation method that we used in Sky Lab. Sit back in the seat," he instructed as he pressed a button on the dashboard so the back of her bucket seat could ease back. "Close your eyes." At her wary glance he assured her, "It's all right, I'll be right here. Picture vast oceans of blackness as far as your mind can see."

His quiet voice caused a peculiar warmth to move along her spine.

"Are you relaxed?"

"No. You're driving. I have an aversion to relaxing with a race driver at the wheel." Besides, how could she sneak peeks at him with her eyes closed?

He turned the car at the next block and pulled over to the side of the road when they were beside the country club golf course near the house on Upper Arlington.

"Close your eyes."

She took one last peek at his dented chin and furled brows before her lashes fluttered down. "The blackness seems bigger with the engines off," she said, exhaling slowly.

"Good."

"Is it legal to park here?"

"Relax. You want to be calm when you get home to see the kids, or they'll be worried about you."

"Okay. You did this when you were in Sky Lab?"

"Yes."

"How long were you up there?"

"Thirty-eight days."

"Could you shave?"

"No one's ever asked me that question before. I'd thought I'd heard them all. We shaved occasionally. Just often enough to feel comfortable in our helmets. Okay?"

"Umm." She nodded her head in appreciation.

"Close your eyes, counselor."

With little provocation she envisioned his smooth face roughed with a stubbly beard. She imagined its harshness against her tender skin, her throat, her breasts.

"Relax your breathing, counselor. No one's chasing you now. Easy," he said to her one open eye. "Breathe slowly. I'm right here."

The *Star Power* theme song eased into her mind. *Defender of the planet, he is always there....*

"You're safe, at peace. You don't have a care. As you breathe out, give yourself messages—whatever is going to make you relax. Remember as you breathe out, because that's the only time your body can truly relax."

She started to give herself messages with a gentle sigh. He is always there. Everything will work out fine. No robbery. No police interrogation. No custody suit. A happy home for the four of them. Black for as far as her eye could see. Peaceful. Relaxed. From a very long distance came a happy astronaut juggling little miniatures of Micki and Jer and Matilda in zero gravity. She smiled.

"That's very good," his voice soothed. "You're doing much better now." Those were the last words she remembered as she slid into the enveloping blackness.

CHAPTER TEN

SHE CUDDLED closer to him and flung an arm around his waist. Somehow, deep in the folds of her brain she felt cared for and warm.

His lips met hers and aroused her, but her lids remained too heavy to open. She sighed and glided her hand from his waist to the sturdy flat muscles of his chest. She was using his strong shoulder as a pillow, she needed it to lean on; it made her feel . . . safe—as if everything was all right.

"Tildie? It's Dane. Come in, space traveler." His voice was hazy, faraway.

"Don't leave me," she whispered. Her arm curled around the back of his neck and drew him to her and her lips found his rough cheek.

"I'm always here," he promised. "Always."

"Umm, my juggler. Love," she mumbled and smiled, as she nestled closer to his warm body.

"Yes," he whispered. His mouth tasted hers with the gentlest touch as his hand moved along the outside of her thigh, resting on her curved hip.

She felt assured and content as her fingertips toyed with the tangled hair on his chest. A vague notion of how her breasts would feel against it stirred her. Heat rose from her body and she wanted her clothes to float away into the darkness, the way they had in her dream last night. Yet they remained a constricting barrier around her breasts and thighs. Stretching and arching, she said with a lazy, sexy croon, "Make love to me." She pressed her breasts against him as she returned his kiss.

"Tildie...?" he breathed.

She smiled as she began to open her jacket and fumble with the buttons on her blouse. She longed to feel his touch, craved to feel his scratchy beard brush her nipples. He was tracing his fingers reverently along the line of her lacy bra. She took a breath and held it as he drew a fine, fiery line in the shadows between her breasts. She needed his gentleness and she wanted his touch; that was the way it would always be—she knew that. Her hands drew her blouse open and reached for the clasp at the front of her bra, but his hands stopped her. She moaned with disappointment. But he held her hands still with his sure ones; she didn't understand why.

What kind of a dream was this?

She heard her rapid breathing and pounding heart; she grew aware of her excited nipples aching for his touch, and noted the smell of real leather. She wasn't dreaming. Her bent knee met his hard thigh and her other foot contacted...a gearshift.

Her eyes popped open. Dane Scott hovered above her on the reclined car seat. His dark gaze glinted from a stray, reflected beam from the old-fashioned streetlight outside the car. She sensed his smile rather than saw it in the dark.

"Hello, counselor." She felt his all-knowing gaze on her astonished self. "Are you always so congenial?" he teased. "I could grow extremely fond of waking up beside you."

She glanced at the street lamp over his shoulder through the steamed-up windows. She remembered falling asleep, but how long had they been here? "What have I done?" She quickly buttoned up her open blouse and held her hand over her pounding chest.

"I'd say you've done everything right." He chuckled. "I'm certainly not complaining."

"I don't see any humor in this," she said, brushing her tousled hair away from her cheek, keenly aware that her body still felt taut and excited.

"Oh, I forgot. You're only interested in pure facts, details, right, Matilda?" he teased her.

How long had he watched her sleep? Lord, she had dreamed that she begged Dane Scott to make love to her.

"Actually, the cold hard fact is—and I'm willing to swear to this in any court—you talk in your sleep." She knew his taunt was accompanied by a smile.

"I didn't say anything!"

"You mumbled about your juggler, whom I presume is me—" he hesitated for a loaded moment, but she refused to ask "—and about love and about—"

"It hasn't crossed my mind," she lied.

"Careful. Your nose is getting longer, Tildie. Maybe in your dream you expressed what we've both been fighting for the past few days." He breathed out in frustration.

"I didn't express anything."

"Only because I woke you up too soon."

She had looked so beautiful, felt so right cuddled against him, he couldn't resist kissing her. She had asked him to make love to her and there wasn't anything in the world that he'd rather do, but he wanted her to be fully awake. And she had spoken of love, no matter how much she denied it. Hadn't he been fighting the same truth? He knew if he continued to make love to her tonight there would be no fighting it, ever.

"I like your long, pointed nose," he told her as he studied her profile, half-hidden in leafy shadows.

"My nose isn't pointed."

"It kind of—" his index finger traced the area from between her furrowed brows down, until he tweaked her nose "—turns up right here."

She lifted her chin.

"And I like the way it flares when you're excited, like now."

"I'm not excited, I'm angry."

"Guess again, Tildie." He certainly hadn't intended to fall in love with Matilda Moore, but now that he had he wasn't going to let it be any easier on her than it was on him.

"We've acted like a couple of irresponsible teenagers." She straightened her skirt and pulled her satiny jacket back onto her shoulders.

"Yeah. Isn't it great?" He heaved a poignant sigh as he leaned back in the driver's seat.

"I wouldn't know. I was dreaming, asleep. I didn't know it was you."

He smirked in rhythm with her excuses.

"It was a terrible mistake."

"See? That's where we're really opposite." He leaned toward her. "I don't think we made a mistake at all. I think we belong together." He could nearly hear her gasp. "I know what you're thinking, how could a laid-back rocket scientist find true happiness with an uptight attorney with a ready-made family? I have a theory about that, but it defies all logic."

"We can't see each other again."

"There's a chemical term for it, but what it amounts to is, we drive each other a little crazy, but we'd be crazier apart."

"Please take me home."

"I only know that I'm a very happy man, because you come alive in my arms and I love the way your voice sounds when you're just waking up—kind of airy and sexy."

"Don't say any more."

"'Make love to me, Dane darling,'" he intoned in a breathy whisper.

"I didn't call you 'Dane darling.'"

One of his brows arched higher than the other. "Maybe you were more awake than I thought," he speculated with a grin.

"Don't look at me that way," she said, averting her eyes. "Please take me home before someone sees me out here."

"No one's going to see us. There's no one around."

A tap on the window nearly startled her out of her skin.

"All right," he conceded. "You're right about this one thing, but I'm right about everything else."

Metal tapped against his window again.

"Don't open it. It could be a detective hired to watch me."

"What?"

"Please don't," she whispered.

"Or it could be someone after the toy."

"What toy?"

The tap was more persistent. "This is the police. Open your window, sir." A flashlight beam could be seen through the steamy glass.

"Lord, we're going to get a parking ticket."

"Hey, that's very good." He grinned. "You almost made a joke."

The window glided down electronically. Tildie hid behind Dane's shoulder to avoid the searching beam of light.

"Do you know that the golf course is closed after dark?"

"No, I didn't know that, officer."

"You are Mr. Dane Scott?"

"Yes, I am."

"And is Ms Matilda Moore with you?"

Tildie's heart sank.

"Yes."

"Are you all right, ma'am?"

"Yes, I'm fine." If she'd felt any finer in Dane Scott's arms the officer would have found them making love. Tildie collected her wits. "May I ask what this is about?"

"There's an APB out on you, ma'am," he said.

"Why?" she stammered.

"Your stolen property has been recovered, ma'am. As nearly as can be determined from the articles you had listed, everything was found intact in your briefcase and your pocketbook."

"That's wonderful!"

"Why would they steal it if they didn't take anything?" Dane's curiosity took over.

"In this business it usually means one of two things: either they couldn't use, hock or fence what they stole, which evidently wasn't the case here. There was money and plastic in the purse, and the briefcase itself would have brought a few bucks. Or then there's another theory, more likely in this case, it seems. They didn't find what they were after, so they dumped it."

"Thank you for the information."

"Since it's so late, I think it would be all right to pick up your things at the station house in the morning."

"Thank you, Officer Webster," Tildie said, reading the name tag on his uniform.

"Does that mean I can take the lady home now?" Dane asked.

"Actually, I should give you a ticket for being in this park after hours, but...I could be convinced to let it go this time. Especially if you could sign an autograph for my youngest son," the cop said. "He wants to to be an astronaut someday. I know he'd get a kick out of it."

"Sure." Dane took the pen and paper offered to him.

"Thanks. And, ah, you might want to wipe the lipstick off your cheek, sir."

"Yes. My intentions exactly. Thank you." Even in the dark, Tildie could see his cheeks darken to a ruddy tone.

Dane pressed a button to zip the window up. He reached across her thigh to pull a cloth from a compartment in her door. She watched him as he vigorously wiped the window so he could see to drive. She couldn't help but giggle.

"No one's around." She mimicked his earlier prediction.

"Now she laughs," he complained under his breath.

"Why, Mr. Scott, I do believe you're blushing," she said between chuckles. It was a treat to see the man nearly speechless.

"Give me a break, lady." He tried to retain his gruff manner, but he stifled a laugh.

She pulled another cloth from the same compartment and, capturing his chin, turned his head so she could wipe his cheek. "Yep. Officer Webster was right. It's pink lipstick, all right." She scrubbed his cheek vigorously.

"Did anyone ever tell you that you have a wicked sense of humor?"

She tried to hold in laughter, but she couldn't. "There's some on your neck, too," she sputtered.

"I can't help it. I had a vixen on my hands," he teased, and then his gray eyes turned to elusive smoke. He brought his firm lips over hers and she was lost again in pleasure as he slowly leaned her back onto her reclined seat.

"You are a totally dangerous man," she breathed.

"Only because you love me."

"I—"

He put a finger to her lips to stop her words. "Don't deny it, Tildie. Enjoy it," he whispered before he kissed her lips again. A flashing blue-and-white light behind the car reminded him of his orders from the police.

He cursed softly as he released her from his arms and moved behind the wheel to start the engine.

She laughed away her tension. "Let's pick up the kids and go home," she said without thinking while bringing her seat back up into place.

"That sounds good to me." He put the car in gear and drove away.

"On second thought, I'll go home and pick up the kids. Better yet, just stop the car and let me out here and I'll walk the rest of the way. You're a sweet brave man, but I don't want you to pull up in front of the house."

"What is that about? You think you have detectives watching your house?"

"Yes. That's why we aren't going to see each other again."

"Why? Why are they watching? Charlie Patrick ran checks on you, but he didn't watch the house."

"This doesn't have anything to do with Fun Design."

"What then—a jealous husband?" He was joking, but he realized that he'd hit a nerve. "What does Paul Moore have to do with this?"

"Tomorrow morning I'll go to the police and pick up my papers; then I'll file the report, and you and Fun Design will be out of my life," she said, choosing not to answer his direct question.

"I can't do that," he said at last. "I was serious about the thief still being after that model. If I concluded that you took the model out of the plant, other people are going to think the same thing. You heard what the police officer said: the reason the thief dropped everything is because he didn't find what he wanted. That means he's still looking."

"You're just saying that to frighten me."

"Tildie, you think nothing can happen to you because you have the might of the law on your side."

She lifted her chin.

"Thieves don't pay any attention to the law," Dane reasoned.

"Just drop me off at the corner. It's only a block to the house," she insisted. "Stop the car, please. What can happen in a block?"

"I'm going to take you to your front door," he promised as she felt for the door switch that would lift the hatch-style doors. She found it just as the car reached the stop sign at the corner. The door lifted like a wing ready to free her from its protection. An unfriendly blast of warm, humid air hit her as she hurriedly stepped out.

"Good night . . . no, goodbye," she corrected, memorizing his face and the tense set of his shoulders as both of his hands held tight to the steering wheel. The rest of his compact body was hidden in the dark.

"I'm going to see the kids again," he vowed.

"Please don't," she said, as she stepped onto the curb.

He brought the door down, and then squealing tires and the smell of burnt rubber filled the still night, as he took off around the corner, leaving her standing in a blue cloud. As she stood in the lonely vacuum that followed the wake of the red racer, she regretted sending him away. But keeping her family together was worth an aching heart. How could she feel so wonderful and on top of the world and so crushed in the same hour? Love indeed was a joyous and terrible thing.

She had only walked a few yards at a quick pace before she felt it. Eyes watching her. She scanned the street, the lawns, the porches, searching in the shadows that the old-fashioned street lamps couldn't reach. The sound of her high heels hitting the concrete walk knifed through the quiet night sounds of crickets and croaking frogs. Dane had succeeded in scaring her, but she reminded herself that the "eyes" were probably only those of a detective hired by

Paul's attorneys. At least she had beat him at the game by sending Dane away. That was her only consolation.

She had the right to feel paranoid, after having been robbed once today—by a clown. And she thought—or felt—that she'd seen that clown before.

Thinking she saw something reflect light on the sidewalk ahead of her, she stopped to listen, but everything was silent. She walked on, knowing that a detective wouldn't bother her. She wished Dane hadn't scared her again. She figured that she'd see that gaping, painted smile in her sleep. She knew she'd seen him before—on a wall, in a picture. Was that a shadow moving near the trees along the sidewalk ahead? She hesitated again and decided that her imagination was getting the best of her. But it took all her courage to walk between two hulking maples on either side of the walk.

"Where have you been?" Dane asked from the shadows.

Despite the familiar voice, Tildie gasped and jumped.

"I'm sorry I couldn't let you go it on your own, kid."

"How did you get here so quickly?" She took his arm gratefully.

"I'm a race driver, remember?" He smiled, then checked her eyes. "I'm sorry, I didn't mean to frighten you."

She had no argument when his strong arms went around her and he guided her to the house.

"That settles it. You're stuck with me until this model is found. I'm not leaving you again for a minute," he vowed, leading her to the front door. He took the key from her and unlocked the door.

"It's probably only the detective Paul's lawyer hired to watch me."

"Why?"

She stepped into the dining room from the foyer, quickly glanced through the oak spindling up the open stair, scanned the rococo Chippendale chairs around the massive dining table, and peered into the formal living room.

"Something's not right," she said.

"What's the matter?"

"I don't know." She stepped into the living room and flipped a switch that lit several lamps. "I sense that someone's been in the house while we were gone. I know that's impossible but I just feel it. I'm probably just paranoid because I've already been robbed once today."

"It could tend to get on one's nerves. Why would your ex-husband hire a detective?"

"Paul's attorney would hire one." She decided to tell him the whole ugly tale. "Paul is suing me for Jer's custody."

"He can't take Jer away from you."

"He would if he could prove or at least convince a judge that I was an unfit mother on moral grounds," she said.

"That's why you don't want any man around?"

"Yes."

Dane drew in a deep breath and let it out slowly. "You can't lose Jer. I wouldn't want to cause that."

"If the judge decides that Jer would be better off with a man to guide him through his teen years, he could award him to Paul." She threw up her hands in frustration. "And maybe he'd be right. What do I know about being a teen-age boy?"

"You know Jer; you've raised him. He's a good kid. You've done a great job."

She gave him a tiny grateful smile before she answered. "But it'll be up to the judge. And I'm sure Paul's lawyer would love to hang a morality charge on me before the hearing so the judge will think I'm a bad influence."

"You? Miss Propriety?"

"Walking the straight and narrow was never a problem until I met you," she said, walking to stand in the archway to the living room.

"Why? Because you found yourself in a steamy parked car with me?" He almost smiled. "It's hard to be perfect all the time, Tildie." She squared her shoulders to confront him, but he appeared temporarily distracted.

Perfection. That was the word that tipped him off as he looked around the room. It was more a feeling than anything specific. One lamp shade wasn't sitting on the base as it should have been, and the large picture book on one of the end tables hung over the edge slightly. It wasn't much, but in a house that Matilda Moore kept to perfection, it was enough to give him an uneasy feeling. Every picture frame was at right angles and every book sat precisely on the shelf as though it had been filed. Perfection, except for those two little details. Had someone been in the house? Had someone other than himself entered the perfect sheltered world?

"You can't stay here," she said, breezing from the living room through the dining room and into the kitchen.

He pursued her. "I'm not leaving until the model stolen from Fun Design is—"

"Fun Design! That's it! On the wall in the lobby. I stared at it for half an hour my first day at Fun Design—the day I met you," she said as if a revelation had come to her. "That's where I've seen that clown before."

"What? Tildie, why are you turning on every light in the house?"

"Because it makes me feel better, all right? Would you please leave! I'm home, I'm safe now. I know that a person dressed in the costume of the Fun Design logo robbed me today." She already regretted telling him about the custody suit. She didn't need the complications. She had to make it clear that she wanted him to leave.

"The clown suit has been in mothballs for several years."

"Maybe that was what the funny smell was," she said, continuing to move through the house turning on lights. "Would you please leave now?"

"Why would someone from Fun Design rob you?"

"To get the presentation," she said, heading into the kitchen once more.

"The thief didn't take that."

"Then to...I don't know why!" She walked to the patio door.

"Where are you going?"

"You won't leave, so I will. I'm going to get the kids."

"Wait. You can't go like that, with the tear in your skirt. You'll frighten them."

"You're right about that," she conceded, then clarified, "but I'm right about everything else. You really should go."

"No way, lady. You're stuck with me," Dane stated resolutely. "I'm not leaving until the model is found and I know you're safe."

"Maybe that's what the clown from Fun Design was after, too?"

He followed her as she started up the stairs.

"Will you give up on the clown, Tildie?"

"Would you please leave?" With each step she debated why she wasn't arguing more heatedly with him. Was it because she was frightened about who might be watching the house, or because she wanted him to stay?

"I know what this is about. You don't trust yourself to be alone with me." He put his hand on the square newel post and watched her hips sway as she went up each step. At his words, she stopped.

"That's not it at all," she argued. "We aren't good for each other."

"That's not true. We balance each other."

"We get on each other's nerves. We're opposites." She continued up the stairs and into the hallway.

"Let me get this straight." He took the stairs two at a time to catch up with her. "Are you worried that someone may see us together and assume that we're having an affair or—"

She stepped into her pale pink bedroom, flicked on the light, and stood staunchly in the doorway. Dane relaxed against the wall and looked beyond her shoulder to see a rose-colored Tiffany lamp on a nightstand beside a wide bed with an inviting pink satin coverlet and ruffled pillows. He could imagine her bare creamy skin against the satin. Perfection. When his eyes returned to her deep blue round ones, he suspected a little of her starch had wilted.

"—are you saying that if we had time alone together," he continued, allowing his gaze to flicker onto the satin bed again, "we would be making love?"

The gold-flecked gaze that weakened her knees and tugged at her insides indicated that he already knew what her answer would be. She wanted to take his hand and lead him into her bedroom, but she couldn't...wouldn't. In one smooth move she slammed the door in his face and locked it.

"I'm going to change my clothes now and I want you to be gone when I come out," she warned through the closed door.

Dane placed his palms flat on the door and leaned on them. There was so much tension in his body he thought he could fire like a retro-rocket. "Is that why you rushed to present your case on Fun Design—so you wouldn't have to work with me?" he asked, annoyed by the barrier between them when he wanted to hold her.

"I don't think you're listening," she said, tossing her jacket on the bed. "We wouldn't work well together; we can't agree on anything." She unbuttoned her skirt and let it slide down over her silky slip. "We are opposites," she reminded him—and herself—as she unbuttoned her blouse, remembering his kisses and his tender touch.

"Yeah. I'm a man, you're a woman. It works out very well that way." He spoke through the door, listening to the sounds of her undressing, longing to touch her. "Do you know the problem with you?"

"No!" she snapped.

"You fall apart. You can't take it. You're plenty strong enough when the going is tough, but not when things go well. When I get close to you, when I hold you, you panic, because you know it could be very good for both of us."

"We aren't good for each other." *Not now,* she added mentally as she slipped a shell-white dress of soft linen over her head.

"That's a lie and you know it," he said, leaning his head against the wood. "I'm laid back and you're uptight. So what? So we aren't alike. I'd say we balanced each other out. Like the North and South Poles."

Tildie buttoned the dress she'd pulled from her closet. She didn't want to listen to his words, but his tone drew her in.

"If you extended a line through the Poles, you'd see that they aren't opposite at all; they work jointly to hold this little speck together."

She wrapped a long, narrow leather belt around her waist twice and slipped on a pair of sandals. She tried not to think about the two of them together.

"Where on that line of infinity do north and south meet and become one? That's where we are, Tildie, at that very place." He heard the door unlock and open.

He smelled fresh lilacs and saw Pacific blue eyes filled with stars. The skirt of the light linen shirt dress looked as though it should have been caught by an ocean breeze. His gaze moved from her curved lips down to the white sand-dollar necklace at her throat, to the dozens of buttons that held the front of her dress together, to her smooth thighs. She looked natural and free—beautiful. He wanted to make love with her. Afraid he'd been silent for too long, he said, "It's a little frightening when I become serious about something or someone." He smiled, embarrassed by his response to her beauty. She took his breath away. "The truth is you—"

She put her fingers to his lips to stop his words. "Let's just go get the kids," she whispered.

CHAPTER ELEVEN

THE ATTRACTIVE DARK-HAIRED WOMAN sat at a table on the patio near the floodlit pool and watched while Jer quietly swam laps; Micki was out of sight. Tildie walked toward her and accepted her concerned greetings.

"I'm sorry it's turned out to be so late, Sally," Tildie apologized as she kissed her sister's cheek.

"Mom and dad were here, too, but I sent them home and told them I would call," Sally said. "You know dad, he'd already called the police commissioner and the mayor with a complaint."

"I'm sorry everyone was so worried," Tildie said contritely.

"So? What happened and how did it go with the police?" asked Sally.

Dane watched Jer swim while Tildie told her sister what had happened without giving away all the details of the incident. Sally stole glances at him over Tildie's shoulder.

"The police found my briefcase and purse, and nothing was taken. I can pick them up in the morning," Tildie finished.

"She's leaving out a few interesting things," Dane told Sally, whose arched brows indicated she'd guessed as much.

"Sally, this man who insists on following me is Dane Scott," she introduced.

"Of course, the astronaut-turned-executive who wears tennis shoes." Sally smiled and extended her hand. "I've heard a lot of things about you."

"Some good, I hope," Dane said as he took her hand.

"A few." Sally smiled.

"Thank you for staying with Tildie, Mr. Scott. Sometimes my sister is a little too zealous and doesn't realize there's danger out there."

"That's why I plan to stay with her a while longer tonight in case the incident isn't over yet," Dane said to Sally above Tildie's objections. "I'm not leaving her or the kids until I know they're safe," he insisted once more.

"You can't stay." Tildie's determined blue eyes engaged his. Those glittering stars were his new frontier; he had to reach them so he could bask in their beauty forever.

"Tildie, you should listen to this guy. If there's still danger—"

"Thanks for keeping the kids," Tildie said, interrupting Sally's advice. "I'm sorry it's so late."

"You know it's all right. They've been worried though, much quieter than usual. I told Jer to swim laps because I knew he'd fidget away otherwise. Micki is still awake, over by the steps."

Dane caught Tildie's gaze, and with only an instant's communication, each moved off toward the children, Tildie to Micki and Dane to Jer. When he finished his lap, Jer crossed his arms and hooked them over the edge of the pool at Dane's feet.

"Hi." Dane sat on his haunches to get closer to the boy. "I'm sorry I kept your mom out so late."

"If I'd known she was with you, I wouldn't have worried."

Dane smiled at the vote of confidence. "The mugger knocked her down, but she's all right." He wanted to be honest with the boy. "Your mother, champion of justice, tried to save her purse." Dane shook his head at the possible consequences. "She was lucky. The mugger just sort of spun her around, and she fell."

"Did the cops get him?"

"He wore a disguise, so she couldn't identify him." Dane remembered how she had flown into his arms right there on the street, how her body had shuddered. He recalled his own terror as he'd gently brushed her hair away from her cheeks and eyes to see if she were hurt. "She was a little shaken, mostly scared. But she's all right. That's what counts."

"Right."

"But, uh, I'm going to stick around for a while tonight, okay?"

Jer frowned with concern.

"Nothing to worry about; just to be safe," Dane said quickly. They talked for a few more minutes about swimming, baseball practice and the next game coming up. Finally Dane said, "Your mom and sister told me there's a dance coming up for the eighth-graders. Have you asked her yet?"

"Who?"

"That golden-haired beauty who was in the Pizza Circus the other night. Remember her? The one you stared at most of the evening?"

"Oh, her." Jer tried to sound nonchalant.

"I can understand why you were so interested. She's very pretty. Are you going to ask her?

"Cynthia Edgars, I believe is her name?"

"That's right." Jer slipped below the surface.

When he resurfaced, Dane said again, "Well, have you asked her?"

"She doesn't know I'm alive."

"Oh, I don't know. I detected quite an interest on her part—"

"So she likes pizza."

"An interest in *you*," Dane clarified. "Your mother thought so, too, and she's a woman, so she knows about these things."

Jer looked hopeful for a moment. Then he muttered, "I don't want to go to the dance anyway."

"You're saying that you wouldn't like to hold Cynthia Edgars in your arms?" Dane questioned. "Stranger things have been known to happen than for a beautiful girl like Cynthia to talk to a quality person like yourself."

"Sure. And the Indians could win the pennant."

Dane could understand the boy's defensive posture. Hadn't he been numb and uncaring until Tildie had waltzed into his life?

"When you open yourself up a little, there's more of a chance for something good and unexpected to happen. Maybe not quite as good as winning a World Series, but very close." Dane smiled. He hadn't really expected to care about Jer and Micki and their uptight mom in the beginning, but now he felt stronger, wiser and richer than he ever had in his life.

"Who wants to dance anyway?" Jer defended.

"Right. Who'd want to hold a pretty girl in his arms and smell the perfume in her hair?" Dane knew he wanted to touch Tildie, hold her, kiss her. He longed to make love with her until her body surrendered in his arms, melting her last ounce of fight until every care, every worry, every argument was forgotten.

"All right, I would like to do that, but I can't."

"Do you have an old prom injury?" Dane crossed his arms over his chest.

"No." Jer laughed. "It just wouldn't work out. We're opposites."

"Oh." Dane looked off toward the house. Where had he heard that argument before? *Women,* he thought, as he looked back at Jer, who was sulking, with his chin resting on crossed arms. They got to a guy every time.

He allowed his gaze to follow Tildie as she walked back over to Sally. He watched the reflection from the outside lights scatter over the skirt of her dress. He wanted to dance with her now, while the shimmering lights and the moonbeams were turning her hair to white gold.

"Why don't you ask mom out?"

Dane shrugged, wondering if his thoughts were so damned apparent that a thirteen-year-old boy could read them. "She might turn me down."

Jer looked up sheepishly, as though he'd spilled his guts. "How did you know I was afraid to ask Cynthia Edgars to the dance?"

"Oh, it's a little thing called experience." Dane grinned. Tildie had tuned him in to people again, had made him vulnerable, and now she was trying to send him away. "You just have to decide whether she's worth the effort and the chance of a broken heart. But not feeling anything is a lot worse than feeling bad for a little while." Dane decided that he wouldn't go back to his numb world any more than he would let Tildie chase him off tonight when she could be in danger. He'd stay. Besides, how else would he know whether Jer was going to ask Cynthia to the dance? Dane smiled. "You can dance, can't you?"

"Sure. Mom taught me. She said I'd want to know someday."

"See how smart your mom is?" If only he could get her to wise up about how they belonged together. Why couldn't she see that? Didn't she know that he would never allow Jer to be sent to Chicago, away from Micki and his mother? "Trust your mother's judgment in these things. She wanted you to dance or she wouldn't have taught you," Dane said, remembering Tildie's sexy voice asking him to make love to her. "Cynthia seems to be a very nice girl." He waited for Jer's agreement. "So ask her to the dance." Jer slipped below the surface to cool off. "You ask Cynthia, I'll ask your mom? If we strike out we'll both swim laps. Deal? Is it a deal, home-run king?" Dane nudged the reluctant boy's arm. "She was watching you in the restaurant. I saw her blush and smile, which is a definite sign of interest."

"Do you think so?"

"Do rockets fly?"

"I'll do it. Thanks." Jer's face brightened.

"We'll stick together on this one." Dane smiled. "I may need your help sometimes. And your mom and sister may need us both."

"Sure thing. And, uh, something else: don't think I'm crazy, but earlier I thought I saw someone in our house," Jer said. "I mean I thought I saw lights." His eyes narrowed. "Was there someone?"

"It's very possible. But let's don't mention it to Micki or your mom. They've had enough for one day." Dane remembered Tildie's feelings and his own suspicions that someone had been in the house.

"What's going on?"

"I'm afraid it might involve some secrets stolen from Fun Design. But between you and me we'll make sure everything is all right when we get back to the house."

Jer bit down on his lower lip.

"Hey, with your muscles and my brains, what could go wrong?" Dane grinned. "And I'm also going to ask your mother out right now. Then it'll be your turn to ask Cynthia to the dance."

As Dane circled the pool to reach Tildie, she turned her back, blocking him from her sight as she talked with Sally. For two cents he'd forget about her and the toy model. But he knew that was impossible. Stepping closer, he saw that a spotlight illuminating the house was backlighting her dress. He could see the exact shape of her hips and breasts. It was exciting. He wanted to carry her off to her pink satin bed and make love to her.

"Well, I'll go check on my kumquats." Sally excused herself semi-gracefully and drifted away. Dane smiled at his newfound ally. When Tildie turned toward him, the stars were still shining in her eyes.

"If you want to save your son's social life, you'll smile and say yes," he said seriously. "If you don't, he'll probably never ask a girl to a dance for the rest of his life."

Tildie glanced beyond his shoulder to see Jer's pensive expression. "How can I refuse, even if I haven't the vaguest idea what you're talking about?"

He memorized the gentle slope of her nose, her determined chin and the hair behind her ear, and breathed in her clear summery scent as she tried to ignore his gaze.

"You can't. Do you want to whisper it in my ear?" he teased, leaning toward her. For an instant her soft hair, smelling like fresh strawberries, caught and clung to the stubble of beard on his chin. Her lips parted, her blue eyes softened, and he longed to kiss her and to touch her.

"What will my 'yes' mean?" she asked.

He fantasized about laying her body down on the soft satin and unfastening her lightweight dress, one button at a time, until her creamy breasts glowed in the pale moonlight. He said, "It means Jer will ask Cynthia Edgars to the eighth-grade dance—" she smiled and nodded her head "—because you just agreed to go out with me tomorrow night." He couldn't curb a smile or resist sliding an arm around her waist. "We have to make this look good for Jer."

"But I don't even want you here now."

"Why don't you look me in the eye and tell me that, counselor?"

Her glittering eyes met his. "I don't want you making pacts with my son," she said, holding her chin stubbornly high.

"You can't say it, can you?"

"Don't be ridiculous. I'm concerned about Jer."

"Don't look at him." He laughed gently. "Thirteen-year-olds never like to have their mothers watch them. Relax, mom. Show him that asking for a date can be an enjoyable experience, for the dater—and the datee."

She smiled.

"You're looking again."

A chortle bubbled in her throat as she snatched her curious gaze away from Jer and focused all her attention on Dane.

"That's much better," he said. At that moment he had the crazy, powerful feeling that she'd always look at him with that same mysterious wonder. "Where would you like to go tomorrow night?"

"We can't go out then, or ever."

"Wrong answer."

"It's the only one I can give you."

"What if there weren't a custody suit—then what would your answer be?"

"That's academic."

"Do you have any idea how badly I'd like to make love with you, on that pink satin bed of yours?" He pulled her closer for an instant to prove his point.

"It can't be," she said, insisting on a proper distance between them.

He nodded his head thoughtfully. "He may never tell you, but trust me, Jer thanks you for saying yes and for teaching him how to dance. And Cynthia Edgars thanks you."

Her lively eyes lit up. "They're both welcome."

He loved to see her smile.

"Do you know that your smile lights up your whole face?"

She glanced away, embarrassed.

"It does. I like it," he stated simply. He also didn't want to be without it ever again, but he didn't say that. "How's Micki?"

"I'm not sure. Would you talk with her?" Tildie asked hesitantly.

"Sure. Anytime."

"She's feeling blue and I can't cheer her up." She smiled at his unconditional willingness. "She's sitting over there on the bench."

"All by herself? It must be serious."

Tildie studied the troubled little soul swinging her crossed ankles as she perched on the old-fashioned park bench tucked in among the sleeping day lilies. "I'll go inside and say good-night to Sally." As she moved away, she asked, "Was Jer afraid to ask Cynthia?"

"Same old story," he affirmed quickly before they parted.

"She is very pretty."

"You have to admit the kid has good taste. I think it's from watching his mom," Dane whispered dramatically. He turned away and began to walk over to Micki.

"Hey, where's my Star Cadet?" he called.

Micki didn't look up as Dane folded his body to sit on the bench beside her.

"Hey," he said brightly, "I'm sorry I kept your mom away so long. The police had a lot of questions."

"If I'd known she was with you, I wouldn't have worried at all." She contemplated the toes she was wriggling in her sandals. "I know you'd protect her, just like the Captain protects the Princess of the Sercerian moon."

"I'd do my best. I'd watch out for you, too." He put his arm around the blue pack she carried on her back, but she moved away from him as though he had offended her. "Are you angry with me?" he asked, surprised.

"No." She remained stiff and alert.

"What's in the backpack?" He gently tugged on it, trying to jump start the conversation that had died.

She swung her body so that the pack was farther away from him. "Nothing—dolls."

He'd never seen the precocious child play with dolls—only her Star Power toys. "Are you feeling all right?" he asked.

"No. I'm tired. I'm just a kid and it's past my bedtime," she said, asserting her power. "I want to go home."

"Sure. We'll head home as soon as Jer has his clothes rounded up."

"You're coming, too?" The little girl brightened a moment.

"Sure. You," he said, gently tapping the end of her nose, "are one of my three most favorite people in the world and—"

"Really?"

"Absolutely. And I want to make sure that you, your brother and your mom are safe, okay?" Without a word, she gave him a hug and he gently wrapped his arms around her and her backpack. To care about someone and have them care back felt like winning a lottery. He bent down and kissed her hair. "Ready to go?" Her chin nodded against his chest. He squeezed her again. He knew that not only did he have to protect this family, he had to keep them together. He'd never let anyone take either of the two kids away from Tildie. "Will you try to smile so your mom won't worry?" She nodded again, not letting him go. They sat and held each other, listening to the frogs in a nearby creek and the water rippling off Jer as he pulled himself out of the pool. "Your hugs make me feel very good and very special," Dane said at last. Then they sat quietly listening, as if they had all the time in the world together.

"I love you, Micki. No matter where you go or what you do, I want you to remember that. Will you remember?" She nodded again and he could feel wet tears on his shirt. "I know you can do anything you want, be anything you want when you grow up—grow up more," he corrected so she wouldn't be offended. She didn't say anything, but he could hear her sniff. "Are you ready to tell me what's wrong?" She shook her pigtails. "Will you tell me someday?" She nodded and gave him another squeeze. "Okay. I'll wait. Just remember. I love you and you'll always be my girl." The little girl sniffed again.

He didn't know how long she'd been standing there, but Tildie was smiling down at both of them. "Are we about ready?"

"Your mom wanted me to cheer you up. I'm not doing too well," Dane said to Micki.

"Yes, you are." Micki kissed his cheek. "Women cry sometimes for no reason," she said, moving away as she rubbed her eyes and wiped her nose on her arm.

He really did love this plucky little kid.

"Don't they, mom?"

Tildie swallowed the lump in her throat. "Sure." She thought she was controlling the swell of tears pushing behind her eyes quite well. It moved her to see this man cuddling her daughter so naturally. Why did a man always look so sexy and strong when he held a child? Tildie couldn't imagine Paul having the patience to hold Micki like that. *Dane Scott may be short of stature,* she thought, *but he's very big of heart.* She fell in love with him even more in that instant. He squeezed Micki again, tugging on her mother's heartstrings.

Tildie's eyes were beginning to blur now, but she could only expect so much; she turned to jelly watching old reruns of "Donna Reed" and "Leave It to Beaver." A close family: wasn't that what she'd always wanted, first as a kid, then as an adult? A perfect family. And when she didn't get that, she'd made everything else as close to perfect as possible so she wouldn't lack the closeness, the love. "Let's go home." She spoke without thinking, then saw Dane's pleased expression. "Kids, before you go ahead, say goodbye to Dane. I'm sure since it's so late—"

"Mom, Dane should come home with us because the house is scary." Micki saw a monster behind every tree, Tildie knew. "He should come with us in case there's a ghost or something."

"There are no such things as ghosts."

"It's the 'or something' I'm worried about," the normally practical Jer confessed.

"I promised them I'd stay with you for a while," Dane said simply, knowing Tildie would never allow a promise to be broken. Micki grabbed his hand as he spoke and he turned to her. "Do you really think I'd let you face all those dark shadows alone?" he teased, as they started the short walk home.

"We don't need your help." Tildie tried to sound brave.

"Yes, we do," Micki said. "The monster is still there. I can see it through the trees."

"Micki, please. You're just imagining things."

"No, it's there under the streetlight in the Wilsons' driveway." They squinted between houses and across the street. "It's been there since the morning."

"Micki, that's a van," Jer said.

"A dark gray one with black stripes. It looks sneaky in the night and anyway, the Wilsons don't have a van."

"They aren't back from Florida yet, either," Jer said slowly. "They just sent word for me to mow their lawn."

Tildie remembered the strange feeling she'd had that someone had been watching her and the house. Her heart sank as she wondered if Paul's detective had enough information already to scuttle her chances in the custody suit.

"Mom, please. Dane can stay with us tonight, can't he? Then I won't be afraid. I promise," Micki pleaded and Dane patted her back.

"How 'bout if I tuck you into bed?" Dane appeased the spooked girl.

"Okay." She stepped closer to him.

Dane cautiously unlocked the back door and prepared to enter the house....

CHAPTER TWELVE

DANE WALKED from room to room with Jer on his heels until he was satisfied with how the house looked and felt.

"I'm not scared anymore now that I know Dane will be staying." Micki was smiling as she sat at the kitchen table with her mother.

Dane, who was returning to the kitchen, heard Micki's remark and caught sight of Tildie's panicked eyes.

"Will you take me upstairs, Dane?" Micki asked.

"I promised, didn't I?"

"Promise you'll stay all night or I won't be able to sleep." The child was an expert. Before she knew it, Tildie had agreed that Dane could stay until morning. They left the kitchen, Micki chattering excitedly to Dane about the Sercerian council that was planning an attack on Cyclon.

"Jer, go right to sleep; no radio tonight," Tildie reminded her son quietly.

"Yeah."

"Did you thank Dane for the toy he gave you?"

"No." Jer avoided his mother's eyes. "I lost it."

"Jeremy!" Tildie whispered.

"I had it and then I didn't. I've looked everywhere. I thought I had it at Aunt Sally's, but I couldn't find it. I'm sorry." Jer shook his head. "That's why I haven't said anything."

"We'll find it," she said. As he headed for the stairway, she wondered if thoughts of girls were what was befuddling her usually dependable son.

On her way up the stairs, she heard Micki explain to Dane in a pseudo-sophisticated tone that he could marry her mother now, "because mom says, 'only dads stay overnight with moms.'"

"That's nice to know," he said, quickly arching a brow Tildie's way. She groaned silently and went back downstairs.

When Dane joined her a few minutes later, Tildie pitched a blanket and pillow in his face.

"Was it something I said?" He laughed. "You've got a very funny daughter. She refused to take off her backpack—she's sleeping with it on."

"It's probably a phase. Of course that's what I thought about the letters she wrote to you, and look where that's led."

"Where *has* that led, Tildie?" She looked up at his sparkling eyes and impish smile. "There's no use in either of us resisting, you know; the kid wishes on stars. We don't have a chance of staying apart."

"You'll sleep in here tonight." She tried to keep her voice businesslike and detached as she led him into the den. "I think we can pretty well assume that Paul's detective is watching the house. That's why I'm putting you in this room—far from mine."

"Should I wave good-night to them and always keep one foot on the floor?"

"You don't take anything seriously, do you?"

"Some things." The expression on his face when he said it was the one she liked best, the one that put a flurry of butterflies into her stomach. She hated that he obviously knew how he affected her, but she wasn't going to let him have the satisfaction of her giving in to him again. "Don't get any ideas from what my daughter said."

"About moms and dads?" He shrugged. "Naw." A smile lurked at the corners of his mouth that soon broke out into a wide grin. "It had a nice ring to it though, didn't you think? 'Only dads stay overnight with moms....'" He cleverly manipulated the innocent words to sound more erotic than domestic.

"I just want to remind you that I've already tried the family thing and it didn't work," Tildie snapped.

"Maybe it was the right idea, just the wrong man."

"We had the perfect wedding," Tildie said defensively.

"Let me guess: you wore white and your father was marrying you off to a handpicked groom."

"Uncanny guess." She avoided his gaze.

"And the lovely bride had silken, wheat-colored hair nearly to her waist and you wore a flower about here," he said, fingering a few strands of hair near her cheek. "Sorry I missed it," he said, looking into her questioning eyes. "Micki had an old photograph that she showed me, though."

"So you could see what a picture-perfect family we made. My husband was very successful, I kept a home from the pages of *Home Beautiful*, and we had two children—the appropriate number for the perfect family."

"But you didn't love him."

Was it really so simple? She'd worked for years to keep the family together, yet she'd watched it crack and get chipped away, a day, a month, a year at a time.

"You can't plan love, Tildie. Believe me I've tried. It doesn't work. It doesn't fit into launch schedules." He nearly smiled at the memories of some of his stilted relationships, none as passionate or exciting as what he had with this fighter.

"I've been down on people since I walked out of NASA. I swore I wouldn't care about anything or anybody again in my life. I figured, hell, there wasn't much time left for anybody." He shook his head. "Then I got a letter in the mail asking me if I wanted to have a daughter. Me, a workaholic who had always put his career above all else. But I didn't have a career anymore...." He looked away from her eyes. "Micki puts her arms around me and I feel ten feet tall. That's stretching it, I know." He laughed at himself.

He couldn't have said anything more endearing except for his next words.

"That little kid loves me." The flecks in his eyes glowed. "I don't know why. And that makes it all the more incredible."

She wanted to speak, but words stuck in her throat.

"Whatever happens between you and me may not be picture perfect, but whatever it is, it's going to be real."

"I'll say good-night now," she said. "I think it would be best if you left, after all. I'll tell Micki that you left very early in the morning."

"I'm not leaving, not until I know—"

"I didn't ask for your help," she argued, wondering who was going to protect her against her own heart.

"You're trying to start a fight, aren't you?"

"With you it comes naturally." She turned to march away.

He stepped into her path.

"Someone was in this house tonight," he said, at her startled expression. "This isn't just games anymore, Tildie. It could be dangerous."

"You're saying this to frighten me, and I don't like it." Her eyes showed fear as she glanced toward the window that faced the street, but she talked bravely. "No one could have been in the house without the police knowing. We have a burglar alarm that automatically alerts the station. Now would you please leave.''

"I'm not leaving," he said stubbornly, following her out into the dim, quiet hallway. "I'm also going to convince you that we're very right for each other."

"I don't know whether you've noticed, but we don't do anything but argue." She lifted her pointed chin and pursed her pink lips.

"Yes, I have. Micki calls it sexual frustration." He lifted an expressive golden brow. "I think she's right."

Her eyes narrowed furiously.

"You have to admit," he continued, "it boggles the mind to consider what we'd do if we ever stopped fighting."

"Don't say any more. Stop before you completely infuriate me."

"Infuriate or ignite? You can't deny your very sexy and very willing response to me earlier this evening."

"I didn't know what I was doing."

"Is that your defense, Ms Attorney?"

"Yes."

"Do you know what you're doing now?"

"Yes. I'm throwing you out on your ear. I know that we don't belong together. We're opposites. We don't even know each other." She was nearly pleading. "And there is someone parked outside watching this house—"

"No one can see us here," he told her firmly.

"Stay away from me," she breathed as he moved closer.

"What's the matter, Tildie? Are you afraid of your own feelings?" He breathed the words near her cheek.

"I only let you stay this long because Micki was frightened."

"That's not the only reason, Tildie." He leaned closer and kissed her forehead, then her temple, then the long column of her throat.

She could feel her pulse surge and her blood flow as her protest grew fainter. "We're opposites...." Why didn't she push him away? Why did she sigh as his mouth gently nibbled along her throat?

"Yes, isn't it wonderful? I'm a man, you're a woman." His hand eased up over her ribs. "It works out nicely." He smiled as his nose nuzzled hers, and as he spoke, he nearly touched her sweetly curved lips. "A little yin, a little yang?"

His mouth met hers in a gentle caress until she couldn't recall any longer why she had objected to the pleasure. Yes, they were opposites. He was relaxed, confident, loving, while she vibrated with a tormenting tension down to her toes.

Seeking relief, she slid deeper into his embrace and wrapped her own arms around his neck. Her breasts flattened against his chest and her thighs moved against the hardness of his legs as he kissed her again. No argument, no matter how logical, could overcome the powerful current that surged through her at that moment.

She kissed him with a sweet vengeance. She wanted to make love with him until he lay breathless on the floor, until she had unraveled his cool, comfortable edges to reveal raw nerves. She wanted his body to vibrate with need for her. Tildie celebrated when he moaned, and her hand ruffled the hair at his nape, then eased over the flat muscles of his back and down his spine. Their mouths gently opened to each other to share, to give pleasure, and all she heard was the rush of her desire roaring through her veins. She wanted him to unbutton her dress, to touch her breasts, to make love to her.... Yet suddenly he was pushing her way.

"Whoa, Tildie," he whispered. Did his voice tremble the slightest bit? "Tildie, do you want me to answer it?"

"What?"

"The phone. It's ringing."

Finally she heard a clamoring ring over her pulse. She rushed by him, humiliated that she had been breathing too heavily to hear the phone.

"Hello," she said, trying hard to sound normal. "It's for you," she called to Dane, holding her hand over the mouthpiece. "How many people know you're here? How many people other than the detective outside will testify at the hearing?" She handed him the receiver and fled the room.

Dane wanted to run after her, but he knew she wasn't ready to listen. "This better be damned important," Dane said into the receiver. With sharp movements he unbuttoned his shirt.

"They're after it." The voice was slurred.

"Who is this?" He pulled his shirt off over his head and threw it down into a chair near the phone, then put the receiver back to his ear.

"Scottie, don't hang up. It's me, Bert!" He took a quick breath. "They're after it."

"Bert, have you had too much to drink?" It took a moment for Dane's love-fogged brain to clear.

"No. A couple of thugs from Cleveland just tried to rearrange my face. They're mean guys, Scottie."

"Bert, what are you talking about?" Dane winced at the obvious pain in his co-worker's voice. "Are you all right?"

"I'm afraid they're going to come after Matilda Moore."

"This is about the model, isn't it?"

"Yes. I did something really stupid. I got mixed up with Tech Toys. They said they would make me a vice-president."

Dane couldn't suppress a moan.

"I know, I know. I was really stupid."

"You took the model from the safe, planted the bugs, and dressed up like a clown to steal Tildie's briefcase—"

"Yes. She had the model."

"You could have hurt her," Dane accused, angry.

"No. I wouldn't. You know that, Dane."

"She swore she never had the model," Dane said. "I believe her."

"She didn't know. She thought it was just a toy. When I gave it to her I told her it was from you." Bert breathed in sharply. "But she didn't have it with her when I snatched her purse and case, so what did she do with it?"

That was the answer that Dane intended to wheedle from the gorgeous woman he'd just been holding in his arms. "I'll find out," he said to Bert. Visions of him seducing the answer from Tildie as he unfastened her dress one button at a time came to his mind. Memories of her velvet-smooth skin haunted him. "How badly hurt are you?" Dane asked.

"A couple of fractured ribs and a broken nose. Ah! Ooh! I never liked it anyway."

"Sounds like you need a doctor. Who's after the toy?"

"Some characters with the names of towns: Frisco Eddie or Reno Jack, I don't know. Just find the model and get the lawyer and her kids out of the house, Scottie."

"Are you going to be all right?"

"Yeah, I'm going to hide out. Scottie, I'm sorry they got her address out of me. But you should have about forty minutes."

"Thanks, Bert. You're a jerk, you know."

"Yeah." The dismal caller hung up. But before Dane replaced the receiver he heard three tiny clicks. He stared at the phone, remembering warnings from Charlie Patrick about bugs. This one was tapped, he was sure. By whom? Was it the thugs working for Tech Toys, or a sleazy detective trying to make a case for taking Jer from his mother? It was time for Dane to put his renowned steel-trap mind to work, and all he could do was worry about Tildie and the kids.

He rushed to his briefcase and pulled out a transmitter locater. He walked around several rooms, swinging it randomly until it lit when he was pointing at a lamp and a picture frame. That was all the proof he needed to know that this wasn't a nickel-and-dime operation. This was fancy stuff, compact and sophisticated. He figured the first step was to get the kids out of the house—except the first thing he really wanted to do was tell Tildie he loved her. He took the steps two at a time and found her coming out of the bathroom. She wore what looked like a man's shirt, and it was nearly dropping off her shoulders and clinging to her body in wonderful places that weren't quite dry. She smelled of soap and of soft, feminine skin. She was about to speak, so he put his fingers to her mouth, moved her back through the bathroom door, closed it, and turned on the shower full blast. Only then did he let her speak.

"You should be gone by now," she started. Despite her cold shower, despite all her efforts to wash him out of her mind, the sight of his bare torso excited her more than she wanted to admit. "Do you always stay where you're not wanted?"

"Absolutely not." His eyes more than hinted that he was fully aware she wanted him to stay the night, wanted him to make love to her. The room quickly filled with steam from the hot shower, exacerbating her own desire.

"You are a swine." She brushed by him to go out, but he held the door closed. His gaze searched her vast blue eyes so deeply she felt as if part of her was being transferred to him.

"I'm trying to keep you from getting hurt."

"Then stay away from me." She noticed beads of moisture gathering on the rough stubble on his cheek and a healthy sheen glistened beneath the curled mat on his golden chest. "Because of you I could lose my job. I could lose my son." *I could lose my sanity,* she thought, too, wanting more than ever to feel her naked flesh against his hard, compact body.

"There is someone watching the house."

"I've been trying to tell you—"

"They also have listening devices planted all over the house." He spoke clearly. "In order to do that, they had to bypass all the sophisticated security alarms you said were on the house."

"I don't believe you."

"This is not the work of an ordinary gumshoe," he insisted.

"What are you saying?"

"This isn't about the custody suit. These people mean business, Tildie. They want something that you have."

"You're saying all this cloak-and-dagger stuff to frighten me back into your arms. It's not going to work," she said, meaning to push by him.

Catching her arm he said, "I need some straight answers from you." His eyes glittered.

"I hate you! Is that straight enough?" she hissed wildly above the rush of the shower spray. She blamed him for the terrible raw emotions that loving him had exposed within her—frightening, losing-control feelings that she'd never experienced before. She loved him despite the fact that being with him could jeopardize her custody of Jer. That was impossible. Lifting her chin, she said, "You won't ever find me in your arms again." She could feel her cotton shirt sticking to her in the steamy room, clinging to her breasts, sucking in at the small of her back and dipping into her navel.

"Lady—" his voice was low and husky "—you're looking at a man who's solved problems like how to orbit Mars and how to land men on the moon. I'm up for challenges, Tildie." He hesitated a moment as his eyes briefly roamed her face. "And I'm aiming high right now. Someday I will reach those stars in your eyes."

Her ocean-blue gaze questioned, but she didn't resist as his mouth dipped to brush kisses along the column of her throat. His lips lingered there, tasted her soft skin, nuzzled her ear. "Then I'll know what it is about you," he whispered as his hand pressed into the small of her back and easily guided her hips to his body, "that makes me want to..." His mouth covered hers, tested and tenderly explored.

Very deliberately, his index finger traced a V in the deep opening of her shirt, deftly unfastening the top button and then the next. "You don't hate me," he assured her. He purposefully brushed the limp fabric aside until the shirt slipped from her shoulder. His thumb touched the velvety lower curve of one breast, and he lifted its full weight as his other hand skimmed over her lace panties.

"I hate you," she swallowed, trying to keep her voice steady instead of breathy and jagged. She wanted to hate him, wanted to fight the pleasure that rushed over her, but she stood expectantly still as clouds of steam billowed around them.

He shook his head. "If you hated me, it would be easy," he breathed, as he dropped a trail of kisses down her neck. "I'd be finished with the uptight, uptown lawyer who sends rockets off in my head every time she looks my way."

Tildie held his gaze as his hand followed the globelike curve of her breast.

"No, you don't hate me," he whispered. His fingers flirted with the tip of her nipple, taking her breath away.

Did she see *his* smooth edges frayed with desire? The hope consoled her body, which was burning with a delirious fever. She studied his honest eyes and the sexy creases around them that gave his boyish face character and credibility.

She'd believe anything he said. If he told her now that he loved her, she'd know it was true.

"Where's the model, Tildie?" He knew he should be getting her and the children to safety, and all he could think about was making love to her.

She clutched at her shirt and pulled it up on her shoulders. She was too angry to remember that it was unbuttoned, and that soft curved flesh showed through the opening.

"All this was for the model?" She put her hands on her hips in irritation, opening her shirt wider to show the graceful valley between her breasts. He wanted to make love to her more than ever; he wanted to make her forget everything but the feel of their bodies together.

Instead he asked, "Where is it?" It took all the willpower he had not to pull her into his arms.

Her breasts swayed with natural ease under the shirt as she hissed, "I told you—I never had it." She leaned with her back against the door, breathing hard. He could still see her soft flesh under her shirt.

"Where's the toy that Bert gave you?"

"Bert Tundry?" she said wonderingly. "I don't understand."

"I told you that your house is bugged. I wasn't kidding. That's why the shower is on—to muffle our conversation," Dane said to her puzzled expression. "There are also a couple of gorillas hired by Tech Toys headed this way right now to do us bodily harm if we don't—"

"I don't believe you."

He took the "pen" from his pants pocket, clicked the top and pointed it around the room.

"What are you doing?"

"Looking for bugs," he whispered.

"With a ballpoint pen? I think you're supposed to use a can of Raid," she said with acidic skepticism.

"Cute. I'm trying to save your life and you suddenly adopt a sense of humor."

"Maybe it's the playful company I keep," she countered.

A red light on the pen flashed as Dane waved it near the medicine cabinet. He quietly opened the mirrored door and spotted the device taped to the inside metal wall. He pointed it out to Tildie.

"Who? Why?"

"They're after the toy Bert gave you."

"He said it was from you."

"He lied. It was the top-secret model toy. He also tried to steal it from you. You were right; it was a Fun Design clown."

"I don't understand."

"That was Bert who called to warn us."

"Why did he take it?"

"He thought he was going to get a high-level job with Tech Toys, and instead they conned him into stealing the model from the safe."

"You mean the million-dollar model looks just like a toy? A little blue toy?"

"That's it! Where is it?"

"I..." She closed her eyes for an instant. "I don't know."

"This is a poor time to make jokes."

"I was so angry with you, I never wanted to see you or the toy again, so I gave it away because I didn't want to think about you," she said, then paused. "I gave it to Jer."

"Let's get it."

"He lost it. He doesn't know where it is. He told me that earlier and I believe him."

"These guys aren't going to take no for an answer." Dane glanced at the ceiling for guidance. "We have to get out of the house, all of us."

She looked more frightened. "The kids?"

"We'll send them back to Sally's. They'll be safe there." His breathing was nearly back to normal now.

"I'll call her."

"No. The phone's tapped too. We don't want anyone to know where the kids will be."

Her cheeks paled.

"Get them dressed in something dark," Dane said. "With hats to cover their light hair. We want them invisible in the dark."

"They'll be so frightened."

"We'll make a game of it. You'll see."

"What will we do?" she asked.

"We'll find the toy."

"What if we can't find it?"

"Hey, someday when we're old and gray we'll laugh about this." He tried to picture her hair being gray instead of blond, and attempted to imagine the lines around her eyes and mouth. He knew her eyes would never lose their captivating color or the stars in them; he knew she would always be beautiful to him.

"Promise?"

"I promise." He smiled. "Get Micki ready," he whispered. "I'll roust Jer."

CHAPTER THIRTEEN

"IT'S OKAY, JER." The boy's eyes opened wide; his body jerked. Dane hated to startle him. He clamped a hand tightly over his mouth, so he didn't make a sound. "It's okay, Jer. It's Dane. I need your help," he explained. After he thought the boy could hear over his pounding heart, he asked, "Do you remember the toy your mom gave you?"

Jer nodded. "It was neat." His voice was scratchy and thick from sleep.

"Do you have it?"

"No." His eyes were closing again. "I lost it."

"Jer, wake up." Dane jiggled his shoulder.

"I don't know how I lost it. I had it at Chip's and I thought I took it to Aunt Sally's, but I couldn't find it," he mumbled.

"Could it still be at Chip's?"

"Maybe, I don't know."

"We need to get it back to Fun Design."

"That's what was stolen?"

"Yes."

"Mom didn't take it," Jer said, defending her.

"No, someone gave it to her to take out of the plant and told her it was from me," Dane explained. "She didn't know it was stolen when she gave it to you." Dane looked at him solemnly. "A lot of people are trying to get their hands on that toy."

"Why?"

"It's the model of a new toy we were hoping to introduce soon. If another company gets hold of it, we could lose millions of dollars' worth of business."

"I'm sorry. I—"

"We'll find it." Dane moved off the edge of the bed. "But it's important that you and Micki get out of the house before anyone comes looking for it."

"Who?"

"Get dressed now. Put on dark clothes."

"I can't." The boy held the sheet to his chest.

"Jer. I'm counting on you to watch out for your sister. I'll take care of your mom. We're a team."

"I can't get out of bed." The boy didn't budge but clamped the sheet tighter around his neck.

"Aren't you wearing anything?" From Jer's sheepish shrug came a world of understanding. "It seems part of our team needs to suit up." Dane tried not to smile. "It's okay, I'll turn my back and you can dress." As he turned, Dane looked out the window at the striped van parked two driveways down. The Wilsons were still in Florida, so who the hell did that truck belong to? He glanced back at Jer, who was tucking a dark brown shirt into a pair of jeans. Jeremy Moore was a strong boy, but could he do a man's job? Dane was counting on it. As Jer joined him at the window, Dane said, "Once we leave this room we mustn't speak until we get to Micki's room. There aren't any listening devices in these rooms."

"Bugs!" he whispered. "What's going on?"

"I'm not sure what or who is involved, but it has to do with the model." Dane put his hand on the boy's shoulder and squeezed gently. "Once you leave Micki's room, you mustn't be heard or seen. You'll go out the patio door and walk to Aunt Sally's garage and—"

"There's an alarm on her garage. But we could go to the change room near the pool."

"Good. Stay there until morning and then go in to the house and stay with Aunt Sally. You'll be safe there. When you get to the change room, flash the outside light twice, so your mom and I will know you're all right."

"What about mom?"

"We agreed. You take care of Micki. I'll watch out for your mom." He put a hand on Jer's shoulder. His pale blue eyes held courage, like his mother's. "We'll find the model before they do, but we want you two kids safe first. Do you understand what you have to do?"

Jer nodded.

The two men shook hands.

MICKI WAS CLINGING to her mother as Dane and Jer walked into Micki's bedroom. Even in the dim light from a flashlight it was obvious an unspoken pact had passed between the two males. Feelings of complete responsibility that he'd never felt before rushed through Dane as he moved toward the mother and child huddled together on the bed. The new emotions were at once a terrible weight and a powerful strengthening agent. He knew he'd protect them with his life if he had to, and he wanted an exclusive on the job for a very long time. What a feeling for a man who had sworn he'd never care about anything or anyone again.

"This is your chance to be a real hero," Dane said as he brushed his knuckles gently over Micki's cheeks. She looked like a pint-sized, teary-eyed second-story man, with her wheat-colored pigtails crunched under a dark stocking cap. She wore an old black Capital University sweatshirt, blue jeans, and black Mary Janes, her darkest shoes. "This is your chance to be a genuine Star Cadet. I'm counting on you." His smile and words, which were meant to encourage her, only made her dissolve into a fit of racking tears.

"Hey, what's wrong?" He stroked her back and met Tildie's gaze, which was as surprised and confused as his own. "Micki, as soon as we find the toy and get it back to Fun Design where it belongs, everything will be okay," he said, sitting down on the bed beside her.

Tildie welcomed his help. She had the feeling that something other than the imminent escape was bothering her little girl, but she had no idea what it was. She intuitively sensed that if anyone could find out, it was Captain Starblazer.

"What's the matter, Star Cadet?" Dane's voice held a concerned note. "Hey, Micki," he whispered. "How's my girl?"

The little girl climbed into his lap and held on to him, plainly heartbroken.

"Are you ready to tell me what's bothering you now?"

She nodded and sniffed against his chest. "All this trouble is my fault." Huge tears rolled down her cheeks. "Because I broke it," she choked.

"What do you mean?"

"I broke...the toy...everyone...is looking for," she confessed between sobs.

"Honey, do you have it?" Dane asked, nearly jubilant.

She nodded and pointed to the pack on her back. Tildie dug down gingerly and pulled the valuable prize from the blue nylon bag.

"There's another piece, too," Micki squeaked.

"It's the landing platform," Dane said, assessing the damage.

"I only meant to look at it," Micki cried again, "and it snapped in my fingers."

"Micki, honey, it's all right," Dane said, rocking her. "I made the model. I can fix it."

"Really?"

"Didn't you know that I'm the world's best toymaker and fixer?"

Micki sniffed involuntarily, watching his face.

"It'll be all right."

"But am I still your girl?" she asked, scratching her leg with the hard sole of her shoe.

"Absolutely. My best one." He gathered Micki in the most enormous, gentlest hug that Tildie had ever seen, a picture that brought tears to her eyes. "But next time will you tell me what's wrong instead of keeping it all in here?" He pointed to her heart. "Will you do that? Do you promise?"

"Yes." She nodded solemnly.

"Good. And I promise that as soon as I get the model fixed I'll send it to Roy—he's a friend of mine at Fun Design—and he'll make it into a toy made of tougher stuff that a kid can really play with—stuff that won't break, okay?"

She nodded and smiled.

"Good. That's better." He hugged her and rubbed her shoulders to reassure her.

Micki did need a father and no matter what the adults decided, the child had chosen Dane Scott. If there was ever a shred of doubt in Tildie's mind, just the sight of this unconditional bond between him and her daughter left no question in Tildie's mind that she irrevocably loved Dane Scott.

"Micki, your mom and I need your help." Dane moved his gaze from Micki to check with Tildie. His questioning double take and smile upon seeing her face made Tildie realize that her feelings must show in her eyes, in her expression. "Your mom and I want you and Jer to be safe, and we also need to have the toy safe. You've done a good job hiding the model so far, so would you keep it with you now?"

"Really?"

"Yes. I know you can do it. Jer's going to keep watch and you're going to keep the model in your pack, okay?"

"Do you think I can?"

"Is there only one Sercerian moon?" he asked, smiling at her.

"Absolutely." She grinned.

"We're counting on both of you," Tildie said, placing her hands on Jer's shoulders. "Do your best."

"Now you have to hurry to your aunt's. When it's safe we'll call you and tell you where to meet us." Dane looked up at Jer. "Remember the light."

Jer nodded.

"I'm ready." Micki swallowed. "I've got my communicator. And mom, you take this." She handed Tildie her blue Star badge that Dane had given her for her birthday, her most prized possession. "It'll bring you good luck. Always let the stars guide you, mom," she said seriously.

"Thank you, I will," Tildie said, accepting the treasure and slipping it into the back pocket of her jeans. "Everything will be all right very soon and I'll send for you."

"Will you stay with mom?" Micki looked to Dane for confirmation.

"I promise," he said. "I won't let her out of my sight."

"Are you going to be my dad?"

That question seemed to take the confident Captain by surprise.

"I think you'd make a terrific daughter," he replied, sidestepping the question. He playfully tweaked her nose. "Hurry now. But don't say another word outside this room." He guided her to the door.

"Love you, baby," Tildie said as she kissed Micki's cheek. Jer wouldn't hold still for a kiss, but his mother took hold of his cheeks with her fingers and met him square in the eye. "Lord, you've grown another inch," she said and swallowed. "I love you, Jer. Take care of yourself and your little sister."

Moments later at the patio door, she let them go—Micki, dragging her pack with the model tucked in it and a doll's head peeking out, and Jer, who towed his kid sister by the hand. For a heartbreaking moment Micki turned back toward the house one last time before they disappeared in the dark.

Tildie prayed for the stars to guide them and for God to keep them safe.

In the dark, Tildie squeezed Dane's hand as she led him to the formal dining room, where they could see Sally's house through the trees. She bumped into the hutch around the corner, and when she recovered her composure, they continued on to the large, leaded dining-room window at the back of the house, where they waited for the light to come on in the change room. Tildie wondered who else might be watching the back of Sally's house. She held Dane's hand, needing a friend; sending her children off into the dark had been the hardest thing she'd had to do in her life. She swallowed.

She stared so hard that shadows began to move. At last the small cabana light flashed once, twice, then went out. The kids were safe. Tildie leaned against Dane's shoulder, thankful that he was there. He turned and eased her into his arms, slowly rubbing her back. He knew what she needed. His mouth touched hers and she returned his kiss gratefully, naturally. They were no longer at odds, but together. They were partners protecting the children from thieves in the night. At this moment, being in his arms felt so right, so comforting, so much like forever. She heard her dark nylon jacket rustle as she wrapped her arms around his neck and kissed harder. His hands slipped below the jacket to search for her warm skin. She felt light-hearted from his tender caress and his trail of kisses to her right ear.

"We have to go," he whispered, his lips brushing over her earlobe. "We're running out of time."

"I'd say you just ran out," a voice said in the darkness.

Tildie turned her head so quickly to locate the strange voice she thought her neck would snap. It came from the shadow near the dining-room door.

"This is your jealous ex-husband, I hope," Dane said as he eased Tildie out of his arms to face the man moving slowly toward them. Evidently he had made his way into the kitchen through the patio door. The children had gotten away just in time, thank God. The strength drained out of Tildie's knees instantly.

"I forgot to—"

"Reset the alarm," Dane finished for her.

"I appreciate your making it easier for me," the gruff voice said. "But tell me, yous weren't tryin' to go somewhere?" The question came from a bulky silhouette of a man standing before the bay window at the front of the house. "You aren't going anywhere." For the first time Tildie caught a glimpse of the gun he carried in his hand.

Tildie's voice lurched, then stuck in her throat when she tried to speak.

"So this is the lady who decided to go into business for herself?" The man walked to the far end of the long oblong table and put one hand on a high-backed Chippendale chair. "I got plans like that myself. When I find it, I'm going to sell that toy to the highest bidder. So how 'bout let's save ourselves all a lot of time and pain, and tell me where it is."

"I don't have it," Tildie said.

"I just rearranged someone's face who told me that. I'd hate to do that to you, lady." He hesitated. "I'd hate to, but I would."

"I don't have it," she said more calmly, forcing her voice to be low and slow.

"You wouldn't try to lie to ole Frisco Eddie, now would ya?"

"No. She's very big on honesty," Dane said, while Tildie tried to catch her breath. "She really doesn't know anything about it—Bert involved her in this. It's all a mistake, you should let her go and—"

"You're Dane Scott, the astronaut," the man said conversationally, pointing at Dane with his gun.

"That's right."

"Yeah, I heard you was smart," Frisco Eddie said. "Maybe if we can't come up with the toy, I could get some bucks for you. Maybe your toy company would pay to get you back, since you're so smart."

"No, he's not," Tildie said firmly.

"What can I say? She doesn't appreciate me," Dane said, giving Tildie a quick glance. "Get lost, lady!" Dane said sharply to her. "Take a hike! Eddie and I can do the talking—" he turned to him "—or do you prefer to be called Mr. Frisco?" he asked, giving Tildie a shove toward the front door. "You remind me of a fellow I worked with once, down in Houston at the Space Center."

"Oh, yeah?" the man said, interested, "I've always wanted to see one of those suckers takin' off, ya know."

"It's a thrill," Dane agreed. "Nothing like it in the world." He looked Frisco Eddie in the eye as he spoke, taking note of the man's oddly cherubic features and praying Tildie could make it to the door.

"Not so fast, lady. Get back there," Frisco Eddie snarled.

"You don't need her," Dane reminded him. "You have me."

"I'd say we got both of you." Tildie could hear Frisco Eddie's snicker. "Cover 'em, Reno."

Just then Tildie noticed a thinner shadow coming out of the kitchen.

"Where the hell have you been?" Frisco demanded.

"I stepped in a flower bed and messed up my shoes," the thinner man complained.

"Do ya got 'em covered?"

"Yeah, yeah," he grumbled.

Tildie had returned to Dane's side, and now Frisco moved toward them. "Sit. Sit. You in this chair." He directed Dane to the heavy Chippendale at the end of the table and Tildie to the chair around the corner from his. "He was trying to make me think he was angry with her, but I found them in a very friendly lip lock when I came in here."

Tildie flinched as he quickly tore off the satiny, braided rope ties from the draperies. "We'll just continue with this romantic evening," the intruder said, then flicked a cigarette lighter very near Tildie's ear, which made her jump. He reached across her and lit two candles on the table. "Put your hands behind your back, on the outside of the chair," he ordered. He tied her wrists tightly, then moved on to Dane.

After he'd bound Dane, Frisco Eddie looked at Tildie and said, "Now that we're all cozy, where's the toy? We know that you took it from the company. That was the deal. You were supposed to come to Cleveland, but you messed up. That made the man from Tech Toys angry. But it was better for us, right, Reno?"

Reno Jack laughed his agreement.

"We can sell it to whoever we want. Maybe Fun Design would buy it back for more money. How much would you pay to save your toy and this pretty lady here, Mr. Astronaut?''

Tildie tried not to meet Dane's eyes, but she couldn't help it. Each light gray iris held a tight black center between narrowed lids.

"You have me or the toy to sell, not the lady." Dane's voice remained even as he mentally checklisted his options.

"Are you going to tell us where it is or do we have to trash the house looking for it?"

"No! Please listen to me. It's not here!" wailed Tildie.

Reno Jack turned to her. "Lady, we just about separated a guy from his face tonight to find out that you still got it." His face looked gaunt and mean in the flickering candlelight. "Where is it?"

She avoided the hoodlum's eyes as he circled around the table.

"I don't know."

"Maybe weez going 'bout this all wrong, Frisco."

"Shaddap. Maybe we just need a little more light on the subject," he said, flicking on his lighter again and moving it closer and closer to Dane's throat. "Now will you tell me where it is?"

"This reminds me of the time the cooling unit went out on Sky Lab," Dane said, calmly craning his neck away from the flame. "It must have been 150 degrees in the capsule..."

Tildie couldn't listen; she could only see the flame getting closer to his bobbing Adam's apple. "Stop! Stop, please! I'll tell you!" she cried out.

Dane exhaled slowly and swallowed as he met her eye.

"Tell me now!"

"Don't listen to her," said Dane. "She's in love with me and wants to save my neck." Dane spoke to them, but swung his gaze to Tildie with a hopeful expression on his face. "Do you love me, Tildie?"

"Yes! No!" This hardly seemed the time or place to discuss her feelings for him.

"Which is it, lady? The suspense is killin' me."

"We've only known each other for a few days," she explained to Frisco Eddie.

He nodded, almost as though he were sympathetic.

"You love me, Tildie, don't you?" Dane persisted.

"Come on, tell him, lady," Reno Jack urged. "I get all sentimental. You know what I mean?"

"What do yous think this is, the friggin' 'Dating Game'?" Frisco Eddie shouted. "Where's the damn toy?"

"Tell me you love me," Dane ordered.

"Stop it! I can't think!" she shouted at them both, Dane and Eddie, her emotions ricocheting from elation to cold fear.

"Tell us where the toy is or your loverboy astronaut gets sent into permanent orbit."

"I threw it away!" she shouted. "Bert told me that the toy was from Dane. And at the time we were having a quarrel. I was so angry with him that I threw it away the first chance I had. I didn't want anything that would remind me of him. You can understand that—a quarrel and all?"

"She was crazy about me even then," Dane said.

"I was so angry at him that I drove out behind the Fun Design factory and threw it in the Dumpster. It's probably still there."

"In a Dumpster? Because you didn't want to be reminded of him? That's your story?"

"What can I say? The woman is mad about me," Dane said in an exaggeratedly modest tone.

"Reno, go out to the kitchen and turn on the stove."

"It's dark in there," the man complained.

"Switch on a light."

"What are you going to do?" Tildie swallowed.

"Don't ask," Dane said, shaking his head.

"We're going to fry us up a little something, honey, starting with your astronaut here," Eddie threatened, his cherubic face suddenly looking quite frightening.

"I told you not to ask," Dane said upon seeing Tildie's devastated expression.

"Reno, get the burner red hot and put a pair of tongs or a knife on it."

"What can I tell you? She's a terrible liar." Dane shrugged. "But this just proves that she was telling the truth before."

"Tongs or a knife?" Reno called from the kitchen.

"Either one, dummy! Just do it!" To Tildie he said, "We'll give you some time to come up with a better story. The truth this time. You have three minutes," he said, going into the kitchen after his partner.

Tildie, bound with satin rope, sat trembling in the heavy rococo chair. Her eyes clamped shut, she tried to assess their situation. It looked hopeless.

"Have I ever told you how beautiful you look by candle-light?" Dane murmured.

She shot daggers at him as she wriggled to free the bindings on her wrist. "Will you be serious for a moment," she said, exasperated.

"I'd rather not, because when I am, searing pain keeps coming to mind," he said. "I'd rather think of you."

"What are we going to do?"

"I think it's obvious. We're going to get married, raise the kids, maybe have a couple of our own if you can fit them in around your law cases—"

"This is not the time to talk about that. Those two hoods are going to come back in here to brand us any minute now!"

"Thanks for the pep talk, coach," Dane breathed. "It's good that you're trying to keep my mind occupied. At least tell me you love me—"

"What good would it do?" she almost shouted. "Even if we get out of this mess, I can't see you. There's the custody suit to think of. I can't risk losing Jer by having a relationship with you. There are the hearings, too. We shouldn't see each other."

"As soon as you admit that you love me, we can start working things out—together."

"How?"

"Trust me."

"There's nothing to work out."

"Tell me you love me, Tildie. Let me be a happy tortured man. Don't fight me now," he whispered.

She fought down the lump in her throat. "You're protecting my children." She looked away from his understanding eyes. "You were so sweet and understanding with Micki tonight—so wise..."

"That's what fathers are for."

"She loves you very much."

He smiled. "I know she's captured me for a lifetime," he admitted. "So has her mother."

Tildie's heart melted.

"Tell me, Tildie."

"I don't want you hurt."

He raised his brow expectantly.

"All right, I believe I'm falling in love with you."

"Huh-uh. Not good enough. I won't buy that falling-in-love stuff. That allows for the possibility that you could fall out of love." He shook his head. "No way. You have to love me."

"All right. I love you." She caught his small, victorious smile, noticed the droplets of sweat glistening on his face. "This is under duress, you know. It wouldn't hold up in court."

"You love me," he said, grinning.

"Heaven only knows why," she grumbled. "We're total opposites. We even argue about—"

"Not about this." He shook his head slowly, watching her eyes carefully. "You love me."

"Now what do we do?"

"What I'd like to do is kiss you," he said.

"I'm sorry. I'm a little tied up right now," she said, trying not to smile.

"Yeah—" he nodded "—okay. The kids are safe, we know that. All we need to do is save our own hides, because I'm going to hold you to what you said. Hell, I just want to hold you." He smiled slightly. "'I threw a million-dollar model in a Dumpster.'" He shook his head incredulously.

"It stalled them, didn't it?"

"Just long enough for them to heat up the tongs." He winced at the thought.

"We're arguing again! It's time to come up with a brilliant idea, Captain. Maybe you could ask your on-board computer or—"

"You just gave me an idea, counselor." His voice reflected his enthusiasm. "But you'll have to at least meet me halfway for the plan to work," he said. "Hop your chair around here. Do it," he said to her skeptical eyes.

"What is...this about?" She talked between efforts to lift her weight and the heavy chair off the floor.

"Do you still have the Star Cadet badge Micki gave you?" he asked, hopping his chair toward hers.

"Yes." Squirming in her chair, she tried to reach into her back pocket for it.

"You do that so well." He smiled.

"I can't reach it."

"Shift closer and I'll get it."

She did, and then he lifted his chair slightly, reaching his hand around the back of the baroque chair. "We can use the 'unsafe killer pin' on it to shred this loosely bound cord. It doesn't have a great cutting edge, but it might do."

He fished for a few seconds longer in the pocket of her jeans and at last slid the Star badge out.

"Give it to me. I'll shred your rope first," she suggested, knowing he'd be able to pull harder against the rope. After the badge carefully changed hands she began to scrape the sharp end of the pin over the satiny fibers. The pin bent, but the rope continued to shred. "I may have to check into this safety approved pin. It could be dangerous." She scratched deeper.

"You never give up, do you, counselor?" he said, pulling the cord.

"No." She scraped harder, stretching and tangling the fibers. She could hear him work the rope, straining himself to the limit.

"I think I can—" He slipped one hand free and turned in his chair to untie the other until finally he was rid of the chair. Standing, he lifted her chin. "You're looking good, sweetheart," he said as he quickly released the binding on her wrists. "I'm going to hold you to what you said," he added as he led her toward the door.

"Hey, what's going on in there?" Frisco Eddie shouted.

Dane picked up a Chippendale and crashed the curved legs into the leaded window. Glass shattered everywhere. He

grabbed Tildie's hand and they jumped through the gaping
hole. They hotfooted it over crunching shards, dodging
whizzing bullets that ripped through the rhododendrons.
They dashed around a bank of lilac bushes and slipped
through a hedge into a neighbor's rock garden. They could
hear Frisco Eddie puffing and Reno Jack cursing the dirt on
his shoes. Tildie's heart pounded, but she ran to keep up
with her partner, who didn't abandon her hand as they
charged into the next yard. Her legs were beginning to feel
like lead and her lungs ached. As they rounded a fence, Tildie stopped, trying to catch her breath.

"You can't stop now," he rasped, tugging on her arm.
"You aren't going to get out of loving me that easily. Come
on." He jerked her out of her rest.

"There they are!" The voices of their pursuers were much
too close.

Dane dragged her farther, and they circled a bank of
bushes, then slipped behind a fence until they were suddenly penned in by an army of wooden stakes. As Frisco
Eddie came around the fence, Dane pulled Tildie down to
the ground. They lay face to face between rows of shiny fo-
liage and fence. She couldn't hear anything but her bumping heart and she felt Dane's breath on her cheek. A shadow
crossed the end of the row only a few feet away. Dane put a
finger to her lips and she inhaled quietly and held her
breath.

"Do ya see 'em, Eddie? I don't see nothin'."

"How are we gonna get that toy without 'em? I don't hear
nothin' neither. They're prob'ly off this block by now." He
paused a moment. "They could've caught a bus, maybe to
his apartment. We got that address, right?"

"I say we boost the car. And forget the toy."

"It's a one-of-a-kind car. The cops'd pick us up in a
minute."

"I liked the astronaut's car, Eddie." Their voices faded as they walked farther away.

"They're gone," Tildie whispered, gently leaning her forehead against Dane's chin. Neither of them moved for what seemed like a long while. Their bodies sank into the soft soil and molded to each other, feeling very warm after their run. Involuntarily she pressed her body even closer to his for assurance and safety.

"I told you you weren't going to get out of loving me," he said, smiling.

He had also told her they would get out of their fix alive and they had. He'd protected her and her kids. He loved her. She sighed. He squeezed her tighter to him. The feel of his scratchy beard against her cheek, the warm friendly smell of him and the scent of damp leaves filled her. Her breasts were crushed against him and her thighs met his, stirring a tropical heat between their bodies. His smooth lips first touched her ear, then her flushed cheek and then the corner of her mouth. She answered his caress with a soft kiss of her own. He groaned, then reluctantly pulled away from her.

"We have to find a safer place," he rasped.

"What are we going to do?" she whispered, thinking she'd picked a poor moment to decide she had fallen in love with him.

"I think it's time that we . . . caught a bus," he said.

CHAPTER FOURTEEN

THEY RAN THROUGH BACKYARDS, dodged barking dogs, and jogged across the golf course. They connected with a late crosstown bus and then hiked the remaining mile to Fun Design. Dane opened his office door and Tildie collapsed on the modern divan.

"Why are we here?" She looked around and took in the photograph of Earth on the wall and the lamp by the chair, which was the shape and shade of the glowing moon, complete with craters.

"No one would ever look for us at the scene of the crime, right?" He smiled. "I can draw a set of fake designs for a toy," he explained while Tildie marveled at the fact that he was maintaining his easy calm. "If we run into Frisco and Reno again, it may trade us out of some trouble."

"That's assuming they'll listen first and shoot later."

"Dad always warned me about associating with men named after cities."

"Your father is a wise man," Tildie said, rubbing and bending her stiff neck.

"He was."

Tildie looked up, regretting that she knew so little about his family. "I'm sorry," she said.

"So am I," he responded. Then, abruptly changing moods, he grinned and said, "You look great by candle-light. When I promise my girl a never-to-be-forgotten evening, I'm not kidding." He shuffled through a few letters on his desk.

"I can't be as cool about this whole situation as you."

"It's my astronaut training," he said casually. "If something went wrong we were trained to go through the checklist of possible solutions. If X doesn't work, try Y."

"Are you that way about everything?"

"We escaped, didn't we? Even if we did have to use plan Z, but that was far preferable to being rounded up and branded."

She shuddered. "What if plan Z hadn't worked?"

"We could have gone back to plan A," he said. "We couldn't have given up after having come that far." She sensed that he spoke of other, more personal matters. "Why don't you get a little sleep," he said, heading toward the door.

"Where are you going?"

"To draw up that toy design."

"Don't leave!"

"I'll be right down the hall," he said soothingly, "just three doors away."

Her expression said that was much too far.

"It won't take me long," he assured her. "I'll use the computer in the drafting room. I can make a bogus toy design good enough to fool the Bobbsey Twins." He hoped his last words would cheer her up, but she wasn't responding. Dane pushed his nose to the side and spoke roughly, "Whadayasay, yous guys?" He waited for her to smile, then said, "That's better."

She averted her gaze from his, then said, "Would you sit with me for just a little while?" There was plenty of room for two on the free-form suede divan. She patted it with her palm in invitation.

"Sure. I mean, it'll feel funny, both of us not being tied up, but we could give it a try." He gave her a smile, expecting her to return it, but she didn't.

"I don't want to be alone—not now." She moved closer to him when he settled beside her.

"Tildie—" he gave her a doubtful look "—I really should go do the drawing." If he got any closer to her there was no guarantee that he would ever tear himself away. How long had he wanted her to look at him with her welcoming blue eyes, the way she was doing now?

"I know if *you* didn't want to be alone, I would stay right by *your* side," she said playfully. "Please, stay now," she pleaded, amazed that she had grown to need the assurance of having him by her side. She didn't want to think about tomorrow, when they had to part.

"Ya got me there, Frisco," Dane said, mimicking Reno Jack.

"Oh, shaddap," Tildie replied, then laughed and shook her head. "How can you make me laugh after all we've been through tonight? How can I feel so happy?"

He pursed his lips to hold off a knowing smile. "Because you know the kids are safe. Because no matter what, you care—because it's right to care."

"And you don't?"

"Oh, yeah," he whispered, "I care very much. Don't ever doubt that." He took a deep breath and let it out slowly. "You've made a believer out of me, lady." He studied her ocean-blue eyes, her high cheeks and her proud, delicate chin. "We're doing the right thing because we both believe in justice, and the kids toys are made for, and all the good things in life." He cocked his head as though he were marveling at a mystery. "You're very special, Tildie." He nodded his head as if to emphasize that fact. "You were able to make me believe in people again, to care about things again." He shrugged. "But I still don't know whether to thank you or curse you. The truth is I'd about written off the human race until I bumped into you. You took my whole life by surprise, you and Micki."

"You, too," she sighed, appreciating his warmth and strength near her. "You're very good for her."

"Do you think so?"

"False modesty does not become you," she teased.

"You should have seen my father and my sister, Annie, together." His thoughts were inward, his expression thoughtful. "When she was little, she and my father were very close." He shook his head. "I never really understood my father. He was a brilliant man, you know, but what I remember most about him was that he was so patient."

"And you don't know any other man like that?" she said, checking his honest, questioning eyes. "You were wonderful with Micki tonight." She remembered choking back tears as he talked to her daughter with such strength and gentleness.

"When Micki hugged me tonight, I realized for the first time how successful and rich my father really was." Tildie enjoyed hearing the low timbre of emotion in his voice. It made her feel warm and comfortable. "He was a geologist. He could have had a high-paying job with one of the big oil companies—he had offers. But he chose to be a high-school science teacher, so that he'd see more of his family."

"I'd say he was very successful because he loved your mother and both of you." She added simply, "He was a hero."

"When I was holding Micki tonight, I realized that he really had it all," Dane said. "A family, love."

"Sounds like a very lucky man."

"Yeah," he breathed. "For the first time in my life, I'm understanding what I've missed. What he had. When he

died in an automobile accident, Annie was about Jer's age."
Tildie instinctively moved closer to him. "He was 45. I'm
almost forty-five. I've done and accomplished a lot, but I
don't have what he had—the important things. Holding you
in my arms, I feel I have them within reach." His expression and his eyes held naked emotion, and he quickly looked
away. "Micki is a sweet little kid who gives me hugs for no
reason at all. Do you know how great she makes me feel?"

Tildie remembered the little girl crawling into his lap tonight, looking as though she felt thoroughly safe there. He
was, after all, Captain Starblazer, Defender of the Planet....

Tildie knew that Dane had cared enough to walk away
from a job he loved in order not to be party to forces that
threatened the Earth. He had also protected Micki tonight
with his silence. Tildie loved him and his kind heroic heart.
He didn't have to do either of those things. "We—Micki,
Jer and I—turned your life around, is that it?"

"Would I hang around to be shot at and branded if that
weren't true?"

"I guess not." She carefully took his hand in hers,
studying its squareness, the creases near his knuckles, and
the fabric burns on his wrists from trying to loosen the rope.
These were the hands that had freed them tonight, that
comforted her, that could make her feel wonderful. Yet incredibly, they could also design vehicles that traveled into
space and—"Will you juggle for me again someday?" She
felt silly requesting it, considering all the knowledge he carried in his mind, yet his juggling act seemed to make him
most accessible.

"Anytime you say." His voice was soothing—low and
quiet.

She liked his capable hands so much, she decided, lacing
her fingers through his. They fit together well, she thought,
her eyes following the vein at his wrist to his sturdy fore-

arm. He had been there for her and for her kids. She shuddered to think that he could have been hurt, protecting her children. "Dane, thank you for—"

"I told you," he interjected gently, "you don't need to thank me for anything."

"Dane, I can't think of anyone that I'd rather—"

"Share a foxhole with?"

"Yes." She laughed.

"I feel the same about you." He smiled. "I think we've learned a lot about each other in our short time together. I mean, we've seen each other under fire tonight—literally. How many couples can say that?" He studied her lips and cheeks. "When the chips are down, we do pretty well together. You're a trooper, Tildie. I don't know of anyone I'd rather argue or agree with—for the next fifty or sixty years." His honest gray gaze searched her eyes with a private urgency. "I want to make love with you very much."

Her heart thumped in her chest.

"That's why I should work on that drawing now."

"We both know nothing has really changed," she said, even though she felt as if the Earth's foundation had slipped a few giddy inches. How else could she have met and fallen hopelessly in love with this wonderful man in a few days "The custody hearings are still coming up and we shouldn't associate—"

"Commiserate or fraternize." He nodded. "I had a feeling you'd remind me of those details again."

"While the suit is still pending, I really can't afford to risk—"

"I know." He swallowed. "I wouldn't want you to. Jer belongs with you and Micki."

"So what do we do now?"

"Well . . ." His loving gaze reminded her of intimate moments they could share. "I'd like to do something like this...." His warm, firm mouth touched her soft lips, tenderly at first. "Or this." His lips slanted across the corner of her mouth, tasting, testing.

Tildie murmured her pleasure, enjoying the delicate magic he was weaving over her.

"Tildie," he whispered, easing her back on the divan with a caress that lightened her head and filled her heart with longing. For the first time in her life she knew she was in love—from her head to her toes. For the first time in her life she'd found a man with whom everything felt right. Must she deprive herself of a beautiful love because it was the wrong time in her life? Not tonight. Not after what they had been through together, not after he had protected her children. But she felt more for him than gratitude; she loved him. She didn't want to deny it tonight. She'd let her body and her mind celebrate her happiness. Tomorrow would be too soon to be cautious. Tonight she'd love him as though there were no tomorrow.

"I'd better go now and work on the drawing."

"Stay, please," she said as she started to explore his face. "Don't go," she whispered. The tip of her little finger rimmed his sexy mouth; her thumbs traced his golden brows. His face was so familiar, as though she'd known it for many years. He wasn't breathtakingly handsome, she decided, but he was definitely attractive, comfortable and extremely nice. He was the carefree boy-next-door, grown older now, with lines near his eyes and across his brow that gave his face maturity and depth; she loved his face. She exhaled contentedly, and as her fingers trailed over his temples and into his tousled, burnished hair, she could almost imagine him experimenting in his basement: the dreamer, the thinker, the one no one took seriously until he designed a spacecraft that landed on the moon. Her fingertips brushed over his lean cheeks, his dimples and chin, all roughened by stubble. She longed to feel that scratchiness on the creamy flesh of her breasts. She kissed his cheek, allowing her lips to linger against the harshness.

"That was very nice," he whispered.

She kissed him again, her lips catching the corner of his mouth, her tongue gently testing. It had been forever since she'd felt so right with a man.

"If you keep this up—" he arched his neck against her fingers that toyed with curled hair at the nape of his neck "—I may not be able to..."

For the first time tonight Dane Scott seemed a bit frayed, unnerved. She reached for his mouth again and... Did she only imagine that he trembled when he pulled himself away?

"The drawings, I'll work up...some..."

The thought that she was exciting the always calm designer to the point of unraveling his NASA-trained control made her feel wicked and wonderful. "Is it warm in here?" she asked. She purposefully undid her black jacket. After all, she figured, their clothes wouldn't float away like they did in her dreams. She slowly unzipped the dark jacket he wore, then slipped a hand inside his shirt and commenced a stroking motion down his ribs.

"Are you seducing me, by any chance?" His voice was jagged.

"Am I doing a poor job?" she said as she unfastened the buttons on his shirt.

"Not at all!" he said, breathing heavily.

"Would you like me to stop?"

"Maybe in about forty years, but I doubt it."

She smiled as he held a breath while her fingertips edged along the waistband of his slacks.

"Are you sure you want to do this?" he asked.

"I only want to think about the two of us together in this room now," she replied. "I don't want to think about tomorrow, just tonight." Her eyes invited, pleaded.

"What if I want more?" He put his arms around her and gently lowered her on the divan.

"Only tonight," she whispered. "Agreed?"

"You know we never agree on anything," he said, smiling, bending low to tug gently with his teeth on her vulnerable lower lip. His eyes glittered in the light of the moon-shaped lamp as he slowly unfastened the buttons of her dark blouse. He caressed her long throat and trailed a line of tiny kisses along the hollow of her collar bone. As if executing some erotic ritual, he solemnly, slowly, took off her jacket and blouse.

"You're very beautiful." His words caught in a ragged breath. Dane felt inadequate saying them, because there was more than beauty behind the stars in her eyes; he wanted to know what fueled that glow. He also wanted to make love with her until they both fell into an exhausted heap. He felt extraordinarily strong as blood surged through him. Yet at the same time, her delicate hand trailing over his ribs made him feel shaky and weak. Her warm body and her eagerness were causing an unbearable tension in him. He wanted to lustily devour her soft curves, but he also longed to cherish every touch, every sigh.

Slowly he kissed the pulse in the hollow of her throat, nibbled on the exposed skin of first one breast, then the other. His chin brushed over her breasts and she arched her back, lifting her fullness higher.

Tildie was bare, except for her wispy vanilla lace bra that molded her breasts into globes. His rough chin nudged into her cleavage while he sucked curved flesh into his mouth again and again, sending shivers down to the base of her spine and to the tips of her breasts. His sandpaper cheek sensually grazed her velvet flesh and the harsh contrast aroused her body and her senses until she moaned from the tormenting pleasure.

She'd dreamed of making love with him, but a dream would no longer do. She needed him. She drew in a breath as she watched his index finger pull down the lacy edge of her bra and gently circle her left nipple. His finger flirted over the tip, then easily rolled the tender pink bud this way and that, shooting sensations through her body.

Dane loved the way her body responded to his every caress, to his every breath against her skin. With his index finger he folded down the soft silky lace of her panties that were riding low on her hips, until he found the light cloud of soft hair, which he parted gently with his fingertip. He'd never in his life had his senses and his mind so completely filled with a woman. His whole body vibrated with a need that whipped up a fierce, almost unbearable tension within him as he tasted and nibbled his way back to her breasts.

He unhooked the clasp of her bra and enjoyed the shaky catch in her throat as he unveiled her pale breasts that glowed creamy white in the cool lamplight. The valley widened between each round globe and he explored her perfect, excited peaks, then her long flat belly, the navel that dipped into a sensual rosy shadow, and her hips, which flared to promise more treasures. He knew he wanted to spend a lifetime learning her body, finding every spot that could please her. Reverently he bent over her, and she rolled slightly to offer her breast. He nibbled the tender place where her breast met her ribs, while her hands toured over his back, his buttocks and his thighs, sapping his strength and flushing him with power in the same instant. He knew he was a lost man. This woman owned him; her hot, unrestrained passion had captured his body and her compassionate heart had possessed his soul. He sucked each champagne-pink nipple into his mouth, flicking the sensitive tips with his tongue.

Gracefully she rolled her shoulders, raking each nipple over his cheek and into his mouth over and over until both lovers groaned with excitement. Freed by his thrilling hands, she reached above her head, clutching the end of the divan, and offered her body without reservation, totally trusting his mouth and his hands as they pored over every inch of her. She opened naturally to him as his hands gently played over her abdomen and between her thighs. She'd never truly given herself to anyone, except for this one man, whom she had trusted with her life, and now with her love.

Dane drew one tight nipple into his mouth, and rolled the other under his thumb, making her hum with tiny contractions within, causing her to whisper, "Make love to me." Her fingers stroked over his thighs and his ribs, exploring and arousing as they trailed over him. He moved carefully between her thighs, never taking his eyes from hers.

Slowly he began to enter her as her nails trailed over his back, his buttocks, and down his thighs. Bending to kiss her parted lips, he moved inside her, gently at first, then harder, until she tilted her hips up and wrapped her legs and arms around him, enveloping him with her body and her love. She couldn't want or love him more. She'd never felt so free, so natural than she did while moving with him, moaning her pleasure through parted lips.

Her partially closed eyes opened wide, and he saw it—the glow turn to a dark fire as her body freely circled and enveloped his own. She loved him—that was what had fueled the flame. She loved him. That was what made her the most exciting woman he'd ever met and that was why her beautiful body opened to him completely, unconditionally, until he thought he'd lose his mind from the pleasure and love she gave him. She was giving herself as a wonderful gift, free and clear, with no bottom line, no regrets, no misgivings. A terrible tension gripped his body as he thrust deeper into her. They moved their hips against each other in the ancient sexual rhythm of give and give and give. She loved him and he loved her!

She clung to him with her knees and wrapped her ankles at his back as he thrust deeper until he vibrated and convulsed within her. She hugged him to her tightly, not wanting to let him go, needing to feel his hard body against her soft, accepting one. Kissing his ear and neck, she let her hands stroke his hot skin as he filled her, loved her.

It was a long time before they could put their feelings into words.

"I'm not going to let you go, Tildie." He lay beside her and held her so tenderly she wanted to cry.

She turned to face him. "I don't want to think about tomorrow," she whispered, desperately wanting to hold off reality awhile longer.

"I didn't agree to love you only tonight," he said, propping himself up on his elbow so he could gaze down at her. "We should always be together." He dipped his head and nestled a kiss in the valley between her breasts. There were patchy flaws of red skin on the creamy white, where his rough beard had scratched her. He soothed the tortured velvet with his knuckles, drawing her nipples into hard peaks again.

"We enjoy each other very much." His gray eyes grew more confident and a dimple marked his cheek because of her undeniable response. "What—no argument, counselor?" he asked as he skimmed his fingers over the tender outside curve of her breast.

She blushed from his knowing smile and from her own shivery reaction to his touch. She'd just made passionate love with the man, had shamelessly offered herself to him and had stroked his body in hot passion, and yet he could still make fire come to her cheeks.

"I could get very fond of waking up next to you in the morning," he said, knowing that he didn't want to wake up without her. He wanted to return to the paradise they'd shared again and again.

"We're opposites," she said.

"Yeah," he whispered, slowly circling his thumb around the sensual target. "Aren't we lucky," he murmured, dragging his thumb over her nipple, bending the tip with a precise pressure that caused her to reach her arm above her head to lift herself closer to him.

The erotic torment triggered an ache within her to make love again. His hardness that strained against her soft curves had brought her to wanton desire once more. Thank heaven they were opposites! They rubbed and convulsed against each other until they could no longer bear the torment. It was only supposed to have been one time, one night. But she knew that it wouldn't be nearly enough. Still, she said, "We agreed, only tonight..." Her words faded out as he continued to caress her. "I want to make love with you again, but I'm too sleepy. You certainly know how to wear a girl out." She sighed. Her body was willing, but she felt heavy and slow, as though she'd been overcome with a drug of passion.

"We must be doing something right." He smiled. "Don't worry, we'll have a lifetime to love each other." He cuddled and kissed her for long wonderful moments and she nestled nearer to him, soaking up his tenderness and love.

"We agreed not to—"

"I can't let you go, Tildie." He drew her close despite the fact that she had turned her back on him. However, he felt encouraged when she couldn't bring herself to move completely out of his arms, so he tucked her rounded fanny snugly against his hips and warmed her satin-smooth back with his chest. "We fit so well together. We're very compatible." He smiled as he reached over her to cradle a breast in his palm. "Very nice," he breathed.

"Yes, Dane darling," she murmured, snuggling closer to his strength and warmth.

"Micki got us together with all her wishing, and I'm not letting her go either," he said, and his tone turned more serious when he added, "I know that until now I've missed the best and I refuse to give it up now that I've seen it. Tildie, I saw it in your eyes—you love me."

"I can't," Tildie said. "We shouldn't be together now."

"I know it's bad timing for you. I know it has all gone too fast, but I love you." He held her closer. She loved the feel of her body next to his. "I'm not going to let you or Micki or Jer go."

"Dane...the custody suit." She turned in his arms to face him to quiet his wonderful flow of words. "We shouldn't..." She loved his face, she decided: the boyish nose and the quick dimples and the honest gray eyes flecked with love.

"I'm not talking about an affair, Tildie, I'm talking about love and marriage." He held her tighter. "I know that Jer belongs with you. No one has the right to take him away," he said. "I won't let that happen."

"The judge decides."

"I'll think of a way."

"Starting with plan A?"

"It's a place to start," he said. "You'll see. It'll work out. I've been doing the impossible for years." He smiled. "That's another way we're different. I dream dreams and then I figure out a way to make them come true. You don't dream at all because you're afraid they can't come true.

Believe this one, Tildie." He squeezed her gently. "It'll happen."

Hadn't he made her, the uptight crusader, feel like the most relaxed woman in the world? Dane held her closer, making her feel toasty, comfortable, sleepy. She couldn't remember ever being so content and satisfied.

"I wish I could believe you," she said sleepily. She wished they could stay hidden away in this room, safe and cuddled together forever.

"You can." Using his thumb and forefinger, he tipped her chin up. "Pick any of those stars over there and make a wish, Tildie. I'll just make a wish on the stars I see in your eyes." He smiled. "Very powerful stuff, wishes."

Her blinks became longer and longer as she stared at the mural on the wall, a painting of a moon and stars, while she sank deeper into his arms.

"We made love with the lights on," she whispered.

"Only the moonlight," he teased. "You've very beautiful." He kissed the end of her nose.

The passion they had shared had mellowed her into a state of pleasant exhaustion. "But after this is over, we have to go our separate ways," she mumbled. "We agreed."

"When have we ever agreed on anything, counselor—except for a few moments ago? We were wonderful together," he said, brushing back silky hair that had fallen over her cheek.

"Uh-huh," she murmured.

"You love me very much, don't you?"

"Uh-huh."

"You can't live without me, can you?"

"I'm asleep, so you can't believe a word I say," she muttered. A tiny contented smile curved her lips as he kissed her shoulder, which responded by moving in a graceful circle. Even in her sleep she loved him.

CHAPTER FIFTEEN

TILDIE SEARCHED FOR HIS WARMTH, stretching her arm across the divan, smoothing a hand over the suede. But Dane was gone. Her eyes popped open to find him, but she was alone in the round room. The moon lamp still glowed and a soft, lightweight cotton blanket covered her naked body and soothed her skin, still tender from their lovemaking. Maybe the uninhibited eagerness that she'd showed the night before had scared him away, she thought worriedly.

Even though her mind had pretended it was for one night, her heart and body had loved him as if it were to be forever. That could definitely have made a man think twice. Or three times, since he'd triple his responsibilities with her and her ready-made family. She sighed, then stretched her long body and stared at the ceiling. She had never felt more loved and complete than she had last night. Maybe there was something to his theory that opposites fit together to make a whole, like the North and South Poles. They had certainly come together last night. As she remembered how her body had felt under the weight of his, a tug deep in her feminine core reminded her that she longed to make love with Dane Scott again and again. She wanted to feel that content, whole feeling again—a dangerous notion for a woman who had a family to keep together. She sat up to clear her love-clouded brain and deny her lust-filled body. She should call the children. How could she have slept so late? When she heard the doorknob rattle behind her she instinctively pulled the blanket up to cover her chest and looked back over her shoulder.

"Good morning," Dane said simply, his dimples showing momentarily in beard-shadowed cheeks.

"Good morning," she said, her voice holding a hopeful note. Could he hear how eager she was to know whether he had enjoyed last night, whether he...? *A wise woman shouldn't speculate beyond today, this minute,* she told herself. "Early riser?"

He pursed his lips for an instant. "I went down the hall to use the computer." He motioned toward the drafting room, but he didn't take his gaze from her. How long had he wanted her to wake up and say good morning to him? It had seemed like forever, but it had definitely been worth the wait. She was more beautiful than ever in the morning. "I can draw faster on the computer." He walked toward his desk, realizing he was studying her too closely.

"Oh." She nodded.

"We have a drawing now, in case we need a bargaining chip," he explained, trying to sound unconcerned. He'd never seen anything so enticing in his life as the elegant lines of her bare back. He wanted to stroke the sensual column that curved into the small of her back and down to her perfectly rounded bottom. He longed to trace her flared hips and kiss the delicate angles of her shoulder blades.

"I see," she said. This senseless conversation wasn't the one she'd wanted to have at all. Why wasn't he saying anything about last night? Why wasn't he holding her and promising that as soon as the custody suit was over, as soon as they could be together, he would be at her side?

"It may not work, but...it's a way out."

"I see." Is that what he wanted, an easy way out of an entanglement with her?

"So..." He wanted to make love with her again so badly he could taste it. That was an unwise desire for a man who needed to start a plan rolling to return the model to the factory. So he stood like a statue near his desk, afraid to go any closer to her for fear that he would be lost in the glory of her velvet skin, the smell of her cornsilk hair.

"Well," she said, not knowing quite what to say. She had had virtually no experience with morning-after conversation, but somehow, she'd never expected it would be like this. She had never figured that she would be the only one to fall in love. But she shouldn't be disappointed, she reasoned, because that was what she had wanted all along: to be left alone so that her family unit wouldn't be endangered. Alone was suddenly a very ugly word.

In the silence that fell between them she brushed her hair from her cheek with her hand. The tiny movement sent graceful waves over her back. Dane wanted to make love to her until she moaned and gave herself to him like she had last night. For a few glorious moments he had totally possessed her. He hadn't had to share her with any other person, commitment or responsibility; she had been his. He hungered for the same miracle to happen again.

"Well," he said, looking away from her, moving the drawing he carried to his other hand, which already held a pair of glasses.

"Do you wear glasses?" She was pleased that she had correctly guessed that about him. But how many other details about this man would she be cheated from ever discovering? She swallowed more disappointment; she wanted to know him, to see him work and play, to watch him teach Jer how to juggle and—

"What?" he said absently, then answered, "Yes. I have a pair for the computer and a pair for reading." He exhaled slowly, not wanting to talk about mundane things like reading glasses. He wanted to sweep her into his arms and make her promise to marry him. "Get dressed, okay? I'll make some coffee." He tried to shake the frustration from his voice. Damn, he wanted to make love, not coffee. This was the woman who had made him care about people again, and most importantly, she had made him feel right about himself.

She hesitated for a moment, sitting on the edge of the divan, wanting to say something. But at last she got up to gather her clothes. She tried to wrap the blanket around her, but he caught glimpses of her heart-shaped bottom and the shadowed cleavage between her breasts when she bent down to fetch her clothes from the floor.

It wasn't fair for her to look so beautiful, he thought, fumbling with the coffee maker as if he'd never seen the machine before.

She looked at him self-consciously, holding her bundle of clothes to her chest, and he turned his back to give her privacy. The woman who loved him last night would have dropped the blanket and walked slowly toward him to seduce him again. But this morning Tildie was inhibited. All was quiet except for the sound of her getting dressed and the trickle of boiling water through the coffee maker.

"I'm going to call the children," she said, straightening the collar of her blouse.

"Good," he said, facing her too soon. She hadn't buttoned her shirt yet, and her shirttails still hung down below the waistband of her jeans. He could see the lacy bra molding the soft creamy mounds of her breasts, holding them invitingly high. Her electric blue eyes met his, nearly challenging him, daring him to peel off her clothes and to make love to her. Or was that what he wanted to see? Before she looked away he didn't have time to check for the glow her eyes had held last night. She slowly buttoned her shirt, torturing him. He couldn't bear to see her reserved this morning after all the glorious freedom she'd showed in his arms last night. "We'd better hurry," he said.

"Yes, we wouldn't want to waste any more time."

Her voice, her actions, her posture, held tight restraint. He hated it. He raked his fingers through his hair. "We can call the kids and ask them to meet us in a safe public place, some place they know well," he said.

"Then as soon as you get the toy, we all go our separate ways?" she asked.

His eyes flinched at her businesslike tone. He didn't want to go anywhere without her and the kids ever again. But that was what she wanted. Was it really fair to try to persuade her otherwise? "It might be safer that way."

"I'll call." She numbly picked up the phone and started to dial. He was right. It would be better if they parted. As soon as they made sure that the children were safe, as soon as they returned the model, it would be over. How bad could a broken heart be? When she and Paul had separated, she had experienced stress from the change in life-style and had been shaken up, but she hadn't suffered a real loss of love. How could she miss something she had never had—until last night?

"Where are we going to meet?"

"I don't know." She wanted to get this over with; she wanted to be away from him.

After she'd dialed, she hoped the children would answer quickly so she could hear the voice of someone who loved her before tears came to her eyes.

"Tildie, we need a place—" Dane started to say.

The phone was answered, and Micki's voice sounded strong and wonderful.

"Hi, honey." Tildie was joyful with relief. "It's great to hear your voice. Are you both all right?"

"We're fine. Are you? Is Dane with you?"

"Yes." She glanced at Dane, who was watching her closely.

"Did Dane stay with you all night?" Micki asked bluntly.

Color immediately tinted Tildie's cheeks. "Yes," she answered cautiously, turning her back on Dane, trying to keep any emotion from her voice.

"And?" Micki evidently couldn't tolerate the suspense or the silence. "He's a nice person. He'd make a great dad," she tried again.

"Yes." Tildie wetted her lips.

"Mom? Are you all right?"

"Yes." *No,* she thought to herself. Her heart, body and mind missed the man already. She hated him for making her feel so miserable this morning, but loved him for having made her feel so wonderful and complete last night.

"You love him, don't you?" Micki added squeals of excitement when her mother didn't deny it or argue. "You love him, you do! Or you would have—"

"Micki, could I speak with Jer?" Tildie cut the youngster short. What good did love do now? Dane Scott had given her her first real taste of love and passion, but this morning he would barely look her way.

"Mom?" Jer's voice asked more for confirmation than identification.

"We need to meet with you to get the model," Tildie said.

"Micki won't let me get away without her. She's determined to be in this to the end." Jer clued her in above Micki's clamoring.

"Let me talk with him," Dane said, taking the phone. "Jer, we need a busy public place that you know well," he explained.

"COSI," Tildie said over his shoulder. "The Museum of Science and Industry. The children go there a lot in the summer."

"Your mom suggested COSI. What is Micki so excited about? What is she saying?"

"My tweetie bird sister is bouncing up and down singing that mom loves you."

"Oh? That sounds interesting," Dane said, attempting to meet Matilda's eye.

She knew instinctively what Jer had told Dane, and she faced Dane with her hands on her hips. "Are you going to believe what a nine-year-old child says?"

Dane could feel an argument coming on and decided he was up for a fight if there was any chance at all that he could have her love. "I might," he said. He considered Tildie's anger and the fire in her eyes. Could that light change back into a loving glow?

" . . . so?" Jer was saying. "So should we meet you at the museum?"

"Yes, as soon as you can." Dane got back to business as he watched Tildie pace. "As soon as we hang up, take the crosstown bus to COSI and we'll meet . . . Where should we meet?"

"Near the Presidents display on the third floor," Tildie supplied.

"I heard that," Jer said. "So?" He hesitated for a moment. "Do you love my mom?"

Dane studied the woman beside him carefully. "Yes," he answered. "But I may have to argue it out with your mom. You know how she is?"

"Yeah." Dane could envision Jer's grin.

"No, how is his mother?" Tildie asked, annoyed by the apparent conspiracy.

When Dane mouthed the words "very sexy," she pivoted in a huff. Dane couldn't keep the crinkly lines near his eyes from deepening or the joy out of his voice. "It's all going to work out," he said into the mouthpiece. "We all have to travel across town, so we should get there about the same time. When we see you at the museum, you'll pass the model to me, then you and Micki will go back to where you're safe. Understood?" When Dane received the affirmation they said their goodbyes. He felt great—until he heard three tiny clicks after Jer hung up. He had been so distracted by Tildie that he'd forgotten to check the phone or the room for listening devices.

He whispered a curse. "This phone is tapped, too," he said, hating himself for having been so careless. "Dial them again," he insisted, shoving the receiver at Tildie. "Maybe we can catch them before they leave."

Tildie met Dane's eyes. "Frisco Eddie and Reno Jack wouldn't recognize the children," Matilda said hopefully as she dialed.

"This is too sophisticated for the guys from Cleveland. Who could it be?"

"The van!" they both answered together.

"They've seen the kids. They'd recognize them!" The phone rang five, six, then seven times. "Micki and Jer are on their way!"

Dane grabbed Tildie's hand and hurried for the door. "We've got to get to the kids before the people who are listening do."

They ran hand in hand down the hall and through the deserted stamping room with its stationary assembly line coiled like a giant sleeping dragon.

"We'll take a company car!" Dane said, pulling her, bursting through yet another door and hurrying toward the shipping department.

"What car?" Tildie asked, panting as they stared at the fleet of Fun Design delivery trucks. Our Business Is Putting Fun in Your Life was printed on the side of each truck.

"All the cars are out," he said. "The only alternative is one of those rigs." Dane sifted through the box of keys in the dispatch office and pulled out a set for the truck closest to the large bay door.

"We can't get there in this."

"Hey, when I promise a girl a fun time, it's first class. Come on!" Dane said, jerking her hand to tow her along.

"Can you drive one of these things?"

"I've piloted a spaceship around the earth and I race Corwin Specials on weekends," he said, opening the door and stepping up to take the driver's seat.

"That's not what I asked," she said as she climbed up into the passenger seat.

"Hang on to your briefs, counselor," Dane said grimly. "We're ready for blast-off."

He stepped hard on the accelerator and raced the truck toward the main entrance of the fenced-in parking lot. Small stones on the blacktop bounced against the bottom of the vehicle, and Tildie held on to her seat for dear life.

"When we meet the kids, we'll have to have a plan," Dane said.

"If we make it!" Tildie said through gritted teeth.

"Have I ever let you down?" He shifted gears.

When the truck nearly reached the open main gate, a tan-colored sedan drove in through the opening and headed for them.

"It's them!" Tildie recognized the two men in the front seat of the sedan gesturing with handguns. "It's Reno Jack and Frisco Eddie!"

"Hold on!" Dane shouted as he braked the truck and turned the wheel to steer clear of their path. As the truck

swerved and turned a tight circle in the vacant lot, the centrifugal force threw Tildie toward the door. Before she hit
it, Dane lunged for her and drew her in close to him, holding a strong arm around her waist.

"Thank you," she panted as she braced her back against
the seat.

"You aren't going to get away, love," he said. "Not until I get some answers." Dane drove the truck in a larger arc
until he knew the sedan was following, and then he raced for
the gate. The truck slipped through the entrance and
squealed rubber as it turned onto the street. "Is Micki right?
Are you in love with me?" he asked bluntly, feeling that he
didn't have time to beat around the bush.

"The sedan is right behind us. I really don't think this is
the time to talk about that," she said, trying to spot the
robbers in the side mirror. "Can this thing go any faster?"

"It isn't exactly aerodynamic," he said, glancing at her
profile. "I think Micki's right. I think you do love me." He
took an instant to check her expression as he guided the vehicle down the industrial park road, whizzing by utility poles
and under high-tension wires.

"You can think what you like, but that doesn't make it
so," she said.

"I saw love in your eyes last night."

"Maybe I changed my mind," she said, knowing it was
useless to deny that she had enjoyed making love with him.
"One of us did, anyway," she said under her breath. Dane
Scott had loved her completely last night, but this morning
he'd refused to look at her.

"What do you mean?"

"You weren't the one who woke up alone this morning,"
she said, hating herself for reliving the emptiness. She didn't
want to be alone now, or ever again. "They're gaining on
us."

"We'll lose them when we get into traffic."

"We won't exactly blend in with this thing," she said, troubled by more than their present situation.

"You were angry because you woke up alone this morning?"

"I don't want to talk about it." She crossed her arms over her chest, but when the truck swerved she hung on to her seat again. Angrily, she noted his confounded smile—so smug, so knowing, so sexy.

"You thought I had changed my mind?"

"We don't have time to discuss it now."

"Why not? We've only got a couple of thugs from Cleveland chasing us and—"

"And a dark van that could be gray," Tildie informed him after checking in the mirror again. As she spoke, the truck took another corner. "They're turning, too. It's gray. It's probably the one that was parked across from the house."

"At least we're ahead of them," Dane said. "But who are they?"

"Turn right at the next corner. It'll get us to the expressway quicker," she said.

"Or I could stay on the streets and try to lose them in traffic," he said.

"We're going for speed," she argued, and stared at him when he barreled the truck through the intersection.

"We can't outrun them on the straightaway in this buggy," he countered.

"It's amazing. We can't even agree on how to drive across town." She shook her head.

"That's not what your hostility is about," he declared as he threaded the cumbersome truck through the slow traffic. "You woke up on the wrong side of bed this morning because it was empty."

"You aren't going to let this alone, are you?" she said, checking on the trailing car and van.

"Not a chance."

"When I woke up you were gone." She hated to sound so accusing, and added quickly, "I can understand. The idea of taking on a ready-made family can be very sobering when morning comes."

"I went to make the drawings—"

"It's very understandable that a man would want to pull away to review the situation."

"Would you stop thinking so much, counselor? Don't try to analyze everything," Dane said.

"The fact still remains that we're opposites."

"Stop trying to make sense out of you and me. Just enjoy it. We may argue some, but I know we were in complete agreement last night when we made love, and we also agree on two other very important points."

She looked at him with raised brows.

"Micki and Jer," he answered. "Why do you think I'm driving like a maniac to get to them? I want them safe and happy." He checked the sedan, which was close to his bumper, as he spoke. "I fell in love with Micki before I loved you." He spoke quietly, trying to figure out why she doubted. "And Jer...he's *your* son, Tildie, not Paul's," Dane said. "I won't let anyone take him away from you."

When Tildie glanced up at him, his one hand on the wheel and the other shifting the transmission, she knew she could believe him. She knew he'd do whatever needed to be done to keep the three of them together....

"I want the four of us to be together," he said. "What made you doubt that for a minute?"

"When you returned to your office, you could hardly stand the sight of me," she said tentatively.

"Because when I saw you sitting on that divan, I wanted to take you in my arms and start making love to you all over again," he said. "But I knew that if I touched you or kissed you, we wouldn't get to the kids until much, much later."

"You didn't change your mind?"

"Not a chance." He gave her a quick grin. "But I won't do anything that'll jeopardize your custody of Jer," Dane said. "I want to help." He paused for a moment. "We could get married right away." He looked for traffic before he pulled the truck into the intersection, slipping past vehicles with blasting horns. "Then a judge couldn't possibly take Jer away." The maneuver delayed the sedan and van behind them, giving them a three-block lead.

When Tildie had recovered from her shock at his words, she said, "How stable will he think the marriage is when he finds out we've only known each other for a week and a half and that we argue all the time?"

"Last night when we made love we agreed perfectly and you trusted me completely. That's the way it should be for married people." He didn't allow her to object. "It's in the stars for us, Tildie." He smiled. "Micki has been wishing and wishing. And I for one don't want to let her down."

"We can't rush into anything. That wouldn't be fair to any of us."

"If the judge decides that Jer needs counsel from a man, I can do it." Dane turned the van onto Broad Street, only a few blocks from the museum. "Why would a judge give that privilege to Paul Moore? I've talked to Jer more in the past few days than he has in the past six years." He swerved the truck around a slower car. "And what kind of father is he, who doesn't even call on his daughter's birthday?"

Tildie saw the unflappable Dane Scott upset for the first time, and it was because he cared about her son, and her daughter—and her. She smiled inside and didn't worry when the truck screeched into the driveway at the museum parking lot.

"We'll try the side door first." Dane steered the truck across the driveway and stopped it, blocking both lanes before he jumped out. Tildie scrambled to meet him at the front of the truck. Finding that door locked, they ran for the front entrance. The four-story glass facade didn't hide them when they hurried up the sloping ramps inside. The aisles were clogged with a living sea of green: hundreds of Girl Scouts were touring the museum, giggling and trying the hands-on exhibits. They all carried knapsacks and rolled-up sleeping bags. Dane held Tildie's hand as they weaved their way through the group. They were nearly to the replica of the Gemini spacecraft on the second level when they saw Frisco and Reno walk through the front door into the huge glass atrium and look in all directions. Dane pushed Tildie into the spacecraft and crawled in beside her. "Wait for the den mothers to catch up and we'll try to blend in with them," he said, squeezing in next to her. "I certainly wish you could've been with me in Sky Lab," he teased.

"Can't you be serious?"

"Yes. We're going to be fine," he assured her.

"I know," she whispered. She wanted to kiss him but a little blond Girl Scout scowled at them.

"We'll get to the kids." He glanced at the entrance. It seemed Frisco and Reno couldn't decide which way to go. "The chaperons are coming, but we have a minute."

For an instant it looked to Tildie as though he was going to kiss her, but then he breathed out heavily. She wasn't sure whether it was because of the run, the danger, or being close to her. It was all three, she decided, noting her own pounding heart. "You didn't tell me why you and Paul broke up."

"He chose to leave." She fiddled with some of the dials on the control panel of the mock spacecraft because she didn't want to look at him.

"I know you, Tildie. You would have done anything to keep your family together." He looked at her, loving her with his eyes. "Didn't he want the kids? Is that why you're doubting me now?"

"You're wonderful with Micki and Jer."

"Why did he leave?" he asked.

"Here are the chaperons." Tildie nudged him. Quietly they climbed out and mingled as best they could. Dane snatched a Girl Scout hat from a knapsack and popped it on his head. Tildie hunched down to blend in with the girls as they moved along. They allowed the busy Girl Scout leaders to talk around them and over their heads.

"Are you ever going to tell me why he left?" Dane whispered.

"I don't want to talk about it," she replied, noting that the girls around them were beginning to notice them.

"Why don't you tell me," Dane whispered. Before she could argue, he tugged on her shirttail and pointed at the tinted glass facade: the dark gray van was parked in front of the museum. Tildie craned her neck to see if she could spot its owner walking on the lower level of the atrium. Then she heard a familiar voice say, "There they are! They're with the Girl Scouts," followed by a deep, "Shaddap!"

At the sound of the voices, Tildie glanced over her shoulder. From the corner of her eye she spied round-faced Frisco pushing his way past the little girls and Reno tripping on a sleeping bag.

"It's been a pleasure, ladies." Dane tipped his green cap and grabbed Tildie's hand. "If you'll excuse us." He used his arm to gently spread a wider path for them to hurry through, but it was Saturday morning, and clusters of children were crowded around every exhibit. In a glance, he saw the two thieves and two other men following them. He put an arm around Tildie's shoulders and moved her along to the museum's columned entryway. The door led into a high-ceilinged main lobby with tiny white tiles on the floor and a balcony with a wood railing that circled the second story above the large room. Dane slapped down money on the counter for their admittance, but didn't wait for his change.

"Wait, sir!" a museum attendant called.

They headed for the elevator in the corner of the lobby when they saw the doors open, but before they got there the doors of the small glass-walled car closed.

"Mom!" Micki called down from the balcony above.

"Stay out of sight," Dane yelled to her and Jer.

"What's wrong?"

"We'll be right up," Dane responded, checking the entrance to see if the thugs had spotted them. "But stay out of sight."

Meanwhile, a crowd had gathered around the huge silver ball that hung from the ceiling. It assured the watchers that the world still turned, but Tildie thought she saw it lurch, and then she saw Frisco Eddie step up to the door and try to push his way ahead of others. Tildie took Dane's hand and together they jumped over the low rope that surrounded the display and dodged the huge silver ball as it swung near them. Tildie knew they'd never make it to the top before the thugs came. Still holding Dane's hand, she dodged behind a placard announcing a computer exhibit, and then zipped around a display of Ohio inventors. Dane faced her, keeping watch over her shoulder and the edge of the exhibit.

"They're going the other way."

"Toward the mineral display?"

"Yes."

"What about the others?"

"There're two guys, very serious types, in three-piece suits. They split up, but they're not coming our way."

"We'll give them a little more time and then we'll head for the stairs."

Dane looked into Tildie's eyes and brushed hair from her cheek. "You have a moment to tell me why Paul left," he said quietly. When he saw her stiff expression it suddenly came to him. "My God—another woman? Was that it?" She looked away in pain, and he shook his head incredulously. "The man was such a loser that he didn't realize when he had the best?"

His voice held a comforting sincerity. It was astonishing how Dane Scott could make her feel as though she and the children were the best things that had happened to him in his very accomplished life, Tildie thought wonderingly. Aloud, she said, "I told you Paul was very competitive. He always wanted what he couldn't have; he thrived on the challenge of the chase. At some point he decided that he wanted his secretary, that she was more challenging than a woman with two small children."

"How could he do that to you and the kids? I don't understand," Dane said.

She didn't want to meet his eye. "I had once been a challenge to him, too. Marrying me was more like a merger than a marriage. Cabe Fitzsimmmon's daughter." She shrugged. "We never really loved each other; we had expectations from each other. He wanted wealth and power. I wanted a family."

Dane studied her profile, trying to interpret the emotions that crossed her face.

"I wanted to have a happy, close family more than anything in the world. I still do. You've brought that dream alive in me again."

He smiled, turned her toward him and brushed his lips over hers. "Stick with me, kiddo, and you'll have the whole thing—all the togetherness you could possibly want with mama bear, papa bear and baby bear—or bears," he teased.

She laughed despite her breathlessness.

He looked into her eyes, "Promise you'll marry me, Tildie."

"Dane, we are running away from thugs and thieves."

"We're running for our lives, for you and me, and for the kids," Dane stated. "We love each other."

"Knowing you has made this the most exciting, confusing, frustrating time in my life, but—"

"Never a dull moment. I promise." He grinned at her.

"But what if what we feel right now isn't real? What if it's from the excitement of the chase, from the dangers we've faced together that we may still encounter?" She shook her head and met his honest gray eyes head on. "I want to believe. I want to—"

"You trust me with your life, then trust me with your love, Tildie." It was an earnest, simple appeal.

"We'd better go," she said, unable to give him an answer. "We'll make sure the children are safe and the model returned and then we'll have time to consider how we feel."

"I already know," he said.

"Please." She took his hand and they cautiously walked from their hiding place and headed toward the stairs once more. They were nearly halfway up the long staircase when they heard a gruff voice behind them.

"Hey, yous two," Reno Jack called. "Stop where you are!"

Instinctively they both stopped in their tracks and put their hands up.

"Put your hands down!" Frisco Eddie obviously had his fingers on a revolver in his windbreaker pocket.

"Do ya got 'em covered, Frisco?"

"We don't have the toy," Dane started.

"Shaddap."

A woman and her son started up the stairway. "This stairway is closed," Tildie called down to the woman, alarmed.

"Beat it, lady," Frisco Eddie said threateningly, frightening the woman and the little boy, who hustled away.

"Hand over that model now." Reno Jack looked nervous. "I don't like this, Frisco. Someone followed us in here. I don't see 'em now."

"They're after the model, too," Dane said, using his hand to silently urge Tildie back up the stairway.

"But we don't have the model," Tildie said convincingly, cautiously moving back one step at a time.

"I have it," Micki's little voice piped through the stairwell.

"Honey, stay back," Dane said. "Don't come out where they can see you."

"They have guns," Micki whined. "They'll hurt mom."

"Micki, do what Dane says," Tildie said. "Everything will be all right. This is too crowded a place for them to hurt anyone. Stay back, honey."

"I have the toy," she said again.

"Wait a minute." Reno Jack pulled his gun from his pocket and moved it from one to the other.

"Cover the kid."

"I don't see her." Reno was confused.

Dane took Tildie's hand as they slowly backed up the stairs away from the guns. He spoke calmly as they went. "This is a lot of trouble to go to for a toy. Dangerous, too. A lot of people around, a lot of kids." There were two in particular he was worried about. Curious onlookers began to gather at the sides of the open stairway to watch the drama unfold.

"We ain't gonna let you get away," Frisco Eddie said.

"Yeah, you think you can outsmart us," Jack added, waving the gun toward them.

"Don't hurt them," Micki cried and ran from her hiding place behind the post.

"No, honey," Tildie shouted. Jer tried to pull her back, but the determined little girl charged into her mother's arms.

"I tried to stop her," Jer said, looking bewildered and pale when he saw the guns for the first time.

"It's all right." Dane's voice remained calm as he glanced at the mother and daughter, knowing that it was just such a bond that made him strong. He stepped in between them and Frisco Eddie and Reno Jack.

"The kid's got the model, Frisco!"

"Shaddap."

"We'll give you the model, then you can let us go."

Reno Jack's eyes lit up.

"No," Micki protested. "It's not—"

"Honey, it's all right. You were very brave. You did your job well," Dane assured.

Dane brushed a hand over one cheek of Micki's upturned face. "But we should give them the model now."

"But it's not—"

"It's all right, honey," Dane said, easing the blue knapsack from her back. His clear gray eyes met Tildie's and a life's worth of communication passed between them—not only assurance of love, but protection and the knowledge that plan C was being put in motion, unbeknownst to the thugs on the stairway. "I'm going to toss the bag down to you. Then you'll let us go."

"Maybe we'll let *them* go," Frisco said, indicating Tildie and the kids, "but you could still be worth somethin'."

"Okay, me and the model in return for them."

"Okay."

"But Frisco—"

"Shaddap," Frisco Eddie said to his partner, exasperated. "We'll take him. Someone will pay. And besides, how else are we gonna get outta here? This place is crawlin' with cops by now."

"That's right. So it's me and the model for them," Dane insisted.

"That's very noble, Dr. Scott, but we can't let you do that." A voice at the bottom of the stairs dramatically interrupted the negotiations. A man quietly stepped up behind Reno Jack and trained a gun on him. Another covered Frisco Eddie.

"Who the hell are you?" Reno Jack asked.

"I presume you are the people with the fancy listening devices who have been following us and listening in?" Dane asked.

"That's right." The man stepped into view as he spoke. "We would have come to your rescue earlier, Mr. Scott, if you hadn't been so clever."

"You questioned us at the police station when I reported my briefcase stolen. You're Captain Coleson." Tildie searched her memory, fitting the slim, taciturn man wearing the three-piece suit in the right place in her mind. "You're with the police."

"Let's just say we're with the government," Coleson affirmed. "We've had you and Mr. Scott under surveillance since you came to the police station the other night. The local police were under orders to call us if anything unusual happened concerning Mr. Scott."

"Dane didn't do anything wrong," Micki defended.

"No, of course not," the man agreed. "We just wanted to make sure that no one was trying to do anything to him.

He knows things that could possibly jeopardize national security if told to the wrong people.''

"Kind of like when Cyclon tried to make Captain Starblazer reveal where the Firecon Anti Laser shield switch was located?" Micki asked.

The man coughed discreetly and raised a brow. "Yes, something like that." He seemed to have taken a shine to the little girl. "Your friend Mr. Scott is a very smart man. He's a vital national resource, so he must be protected."

"Kind of like an historical landmark?"

"Yes." Coleson almost smiled. "We would have brought him into custody before, but he got himself out of some pretty tight fixes. Kind of like Captain Starblazer," he said before the little girl could ask. "Perhaps someday he'd consider government work?"

"No, I don't think so. The toy business is dangerous enough for me," Dane said. Suddenly he remembered the knapsack he was still holding. "There's a prototype model of a toy in this pack," he said. "It's really what they're after, because it could be worth a lot of money if sold or ransomed to a competitive toy company."

"Or to the Russians," Coleson said. "Spies have taken microchip patterns from toys by the drove this year."

"Russians?" Reno Jack nearly shouted.

"Shaddap," Frisco Eddie responded, disgusted. "We don't know no Russians."

"I'm sure they don't," Dane said. "These are just a couple of hardworking Robin Hoods, trying to make a dishonest buck." He prepared to pass the knapsack to one of the government men.

"Dane," Micki said, tugging on Dane's shirt. "I hid the model in the echo chamber on the first floor. That's what I've been trying to tell you," she said.

"You hid the model?" Dane said. "You saved the day, Micki." He hugged her and laughed. "You're the best Star Cadet ever."

"Am I still your girl?"

"Always," he said, gathering her into his arms.

In a matter of moments there were museum security guards everywhere, holding back the curious. Newspaper photographers and reporters fought their way through the crowds and shouted questions at them. Dane bragged about Micki's cleverness and Jer's bravery until the kids' buttons nearly popped with pride. Tildie tried to piece all the information together for another reporter. Out of the corner of her eye she saw Dane mouth to Micki, "Your mom loves me," and then Micki break into a satisfied grin. Industrial espionage, a chase through Columbus streets and a showdown in a museum would be served up with the morning coffee in the *Dispatch*, and Tildie knew she wanted to hide in Dane's arms for the rest of the night.

"Mr. Scott, I'm going to have to insist that you come with me." Coleson remained detached and serious. "This story will make national news when the wire services get hold of it. Just in time for the six o'clock news. Every Russian spy in the nation will know where you are. An intolerable situation. It's a matter of national security, sir."

"But I..." Dane looked at Tildie, who stood too far away from him to hear the conversation.

"There are other agents present to make sure Ms Moore and the children are safe and that the toy is returned, sir."

"I want to say goodbye," Dane said.

"There's no time. You really should disappear for a while."

Tildie looked at Dane just in time to see Coleson leading him away. Their eyes met and she saw some emotion flicker in his eyes, but she couldn't read it.

He mouthed the words "Kiss the kids for me," before he smiled a goodbye.

She watched as the agents firmly parted a path for Dane, and in a matter of seconds he disappeared into the crowd.

CHAPTER SIXTEEN

Dear Captain Starblazer,
I don't know where you are, but I want you to know that you made me feel very brave at the museum the other day and I love you and I'll be a Star Cadet forever. We miss you very much.

Fun Design got their model back, and Reno and Frisco told the police about Mr. Tundry, mom, and Tech Toys. The law firm that mom worked for didn't like one of their associates saying that their biggest client tried to involve her in a crime, so mom lost her job. She says she did the right thing, but she's feeling bad because she's out of a job and the custody suit is coming up.

I'm trying, but I can't cheer mom up. I think she needs you. Don't forget that you promised you would marry her and be my dad. Now would be a good time, because she needs to be rescued like the Princess of the Sercerian moon. Captain Starblazer, please come home. Love always from your smart and brave future daughter,

Micki Moore

Seeing the familiar print on the wide ruled paper made Dane shake inside. "We miss you very much." The simple, direct words filled him with emotion. He had a family with a smart, brave little girl who adored him and a woman who loved him and could make his body vibrate with desire. He was the luckiest man in the world. Micki's letter was the first piece of correspondence he'd been allowed to see, and he read every word over and over. It had been more than a week since the CIA agents had spirited Dane out of Columbus to a quiet house on the coast of Maine. He was comfortable there, watching green breakers roll in and dissolve on the sand, but he had too much time to think, to remember talking to Jer, holding Micki, and making love to Tildie. He missed them so much that he ached.

Dane had paced in the house and jogged for miles along the beach to soothe his mind, but it hadn't helped. Coleson and the other agents assigned to protect him had insisted that more time was needed to throw any Russian spy off his trail. Frustrated, Dane had tried to explain that he needed to be with Tildie and the kids, especially when Paul Moore was making a legal bid for Jer's custody. The agents heard over and over that Chicago was too far from Jer's mother and sister. He asked them why a judge would turn the kid over to Paul Moore, who hadn't wanted Jer when he was small and probably wasn't any more faithful to his new wife than he was to Tildie. What kind of an example would that be for a teenaged boy? When Dane went off on these tangents, Coleson would quietly say, "It's all being taken care of, Mr. Scott. There's nothing to worry about."

Nothing, Dane thought bitterly, except he had a family at home and he wasn't with them when they needed him. Family. The very word conjured up warm feelings and memories of birthday barbecues. Thoughts of Tildie both soothed and tortured him. How could Nigel and Associates fire her for doing what was right? He was furious and worried at the same time. Would a judge give custody to a single parent who was unemployed?

Dane suddenly decided that he'd had it with protection, with national security, and he ranted at Coleson that he was going to see Tildie and there wasn't anything he could do to stop him.

"I understand you're not eating or sleeping," Coleson said in a flat, detached voice, as if he hadn't heard a word Dane had said. "I hear there's only one cure for that," he said, handing Dane a ticket for a flight to Washington. "Ms Moore will also be in the city on this date, at the FCC hearings, so you'll have a chance to speak with her. Immediately after you testify at the hearing you'll fly to Boston," he said, giving him an address of a house in Cambridge. "You'll teach aeronautic design classes—"

"Teach?"

"You'll instruct classes at Harvard." Evidently Mr. Coleson had friends in very high places. "This is a safe house, and will serve until you and Ms Moore can find other accommodations."

"I can't go to Cambridge. I can't just ask her to pack up the kids and move to Boston. She's fighting that custody suit—"

"Yes. This may help," Coleson said, handing him a video cassette tape. "Ms Moore's attorney will find this very useful in building a case against Paul Moore." He shrugged and said by way of explanation, "The kid should stay with you and his mother."

"A movie?"

"You were right. Moore isn't faithful to his wife. Names, times, dates and places are documented," Coleson said. "All that we ask in return is that if your country goes to war or if NASA gets into trouble you'll lend your unique talents to help the cause. Agreed?"

"I would have done that anyway," Dane said.

"I know. You're a good man, Mr. Scott," Coleson said it as though the compliment rarely passed his lips. "That's why I free-lanced my help." He gestured toward the tape and then wrote something down on a pad of paper. "This is a telephone number where I can be reached if you experience anything suspicious. However, if you promise to keep a low profile in Cambridge for a month or two, we probably won't see each other again," Coleson said, shaking Dane's hand.

Right now Dane didn't want to think of anything other than seeing Tildie again. With that in mind he packed his bag, flew to Washington, rode in a taxi through the snarl of traffic, and walked into the hearing room—just as his name was called.

Tildie stood behind a table reserved for the attorneys presenting the complaint, her long fingers pressing the smooth oak again. She wore a pale mauve, tailored suit, which hid her pleasant curves. Watching her face, with her lips slightly parted in surprise, her eyes questioning, all Dane could think about was pulling her into his arms, kissing her, loving her.

As his gaze met Tildie's across the room, her knees turned to jelly and she slowly sank back down into her chair. He looked handsome and scholarly in a suit that was a couple of shades lighter than his sun-toasted skin. Carrying his statement in one hand and his reading glasses in the other he looked more like a sensitive poet than a calculating aerospace scientist. This man never ceased to amaze her, this man she loved. She barely heard the first few questions put to him, nor his answers.

"Yes, I met Ms Moore when she came to the Fun Design plant." She looked beautiful, but tired. Had she not been able to sleep the past two weeks? He knew of a wonderful way to make her curl up in his arms and sleep like a babe....

Tildie could only drink in the sight of him. Together they had gone through plan A, B and Z, had run for their lives, had escaped in a delivery truck, had protected the children, and had made love. How she longed to make love with him again.

Soon, Dane was reading his prepared statement asking the toy companies to downplay the violence and the hard sell on their cartoon programs. With a few well-placed questions to the designer along with the descriptive statements, the Fun Design lawyer reviewed the events surrounding the stolen model and its rescue by Dane, Tildie and her children. With his line of questions the attorney planned to prove the point that the large toy companies faced more serious battles every day than the Nielsen ratings. Toys were a very competitive business.

Tildie tried to organize her own questions in her mind. Hadn't they been at odds most of the time? Weren't they opposites? Tense and laid back. Soft and hard. Silky and harsh. Tildie recalled the heat kindled between their bodies as they arched and pressed against each other. Now it seemed he was on her side all along. She didn't even want to bother cross-examining him. She only wanted to ask him where he had been, whether he still loved her, and if he was all right. He looked as if a lot of his energy had been drained away. She wanted to take him in her arms to revive him, but instead she forced herself to ask her questions. Their conversational voices gave the hearing a comfortable caring tone as they each expressed their concerns about the hard sell of toys.

They both conceded that the toy companies were fighting each other for the market dollars, and cautioned that the children should not become the battleground. Neither of them preached or scolded, but each understood and passed that understanding on to the listeners. She smiled graciously and thanked him when she had finished with her questions. His returning smile and pleased eyes conveyed how proud he was of her, and she felt as if she would melt down into her high-heeled shoes.

After the hearing was adjourned, Tildie stayed at the table talking with the other attorneys retained by Better Television for Children. She slowly packed her presentation into her briefcase, occasionally glancing over her shoulder to see if Dane had lingered to talk or if he'd been whisked away again by government agents. That day in the museum she had been relieved to discover that the people following them had been from the CIA, but when they had hurried Dane away so quickly she also realized that he was in a lot of danger, or the government wouldn't have sent people to protect him. She realized that the CIA was probably forcing him to stay out of sight, and though she wanted him safe, she missed him terribly—even if they had argued about everything. She even missed that, she realized, as the other BTC attorney agreed with her yet again.

"Four years from now, children's programing will be discussed again by the commission and we'll be there to make sure their suggestions go even further," the young attorney said.

"Better yet, go for more feminine role models," a pleasant tenor behind Tildie suggested.

She didn't have to turn to know that a dimpled smile and crinkled eyes accompanied the words.

"It seems that we can't agree on anything, Mr. Scott," she said, facing him.

The other attorneys and members of the BTC thanked him for his prepared statement and his testimony, and they invited him to join their group for drinks and dinner. He graciously declined, and Tildie promised to catch up with them later.

After Dane congratulated her on the FCC's reception to the BTC's complaint, Tildie said, "Hopefully the toy companies will actually regulate themselves on their advertising techniques as the commission suggested. At any rate I'll be back four years from now to make sure that they do."

"You sound very confident."

"It's a good cause."

"Yeah," he agreed, his voice fading to a whisper. "How are things going for you, counselor?" Dane asked after the others gathered in groups to leave the hearing room. "Micki sent me a letter about your job. You did the right thing."

"I know." She met his eyes. "If there hadn't been a conflict of interest, I would have had one new client," she said. "Bert Tundry asked me to defend him."

"Bert." Dane shook his head.

"Actually the picture isn't that dark for him," she said. "I convinced the District Attorney to give him immunity for his testimony against Tech Toys. That suited Auggie Klopperman, who's after Tech Toys, not his own employee."

"What about a job for you?"

"Some members of the BTC recommended me to a national group called the Caucus for Children's Rights."

"Terrific! Where are they located?"

"They have active chapters in several different metropolitan areas around the country," she explained. "I have an interview with them in a few days."

"They'd be lucky to have a crusader like you," he said, allowing his eyes to roam over her. "You did your job very well today."

"Thank you."

By now they had most of the room to themselves. "How are things going with the custody suit?"

"I received word this week that our court date is set for September 22," she told him. "It hasn't shaped up to be the greatest week." The worst of all was that she had had to face it alone.

"Would it help to have a cheering section in the peanut gallery?" he asked.

She smiled. "I don't think so." She wanted to curl herself in his arms right now. That seemed to be the only thing that would help.

"How's Jer?"

"Thanks to you he bolstered up enough courage to ask Cynthia Edgars to the dance."

"Good for him," said Dane, chuckling. "He's growing up, Tildie."

"He'll probably fall in love a dozen times." She smiled and swallowed. She only wanted to love this man, yet circumstances were still stacked against them. "I wanted to thank you for making Micki feel so brave and proud. She and Jer have both turned into mini-celebrities at school. Micki's so pleased."

"She saved the model," he said. "There will be a lot of kids very happy about that at Christmastime."

"She has so much confidence now she thinks she can take on the world." Tildie laughed, then let it fade. "She misses you very much. She's been asking when you're coming home, when she can see you...."

"I'm catching a flight for Boston in a few minutes," Dane said.

"Boston is a long way from Columbus." Tildie felt the blood drain from her cheeks.

"I'll be teaching design at Harvard," he explained.

"Teaching. Your father would have liked that."

He studied her features and leaned toward her slightly as though he might kiss her, but his gaze quickly flitted to the small group chatting by the door.

"May I walk you out?" he asked.

"Yes, please." After packing her last few notes in her briefcase, she snapped the latches shut. She slid naturally into the protective arm he held at the small of her back. The long deserted hall held only the lonely sound of her heels clacking on the hard floor. There would be so many things left unsaid. In Columbus they hadn't had time for a good-bye and now that was all they could say.

"How does your lawyer think the custody suit is shaping up?" Dane asked.

"It'll depend on what type of guidance the judge feels is important for a teenaged boy," Tildie said.

Dane breathed out heavily. "I have something that your attorney may be able to use to build a case against Paul," he said quickly, as though he'd made a decision and he wanted to say it before he changed his mind. "If you give me his address I'll send it to him."

"My attorney is a 'she'—Karyn—and I can give the information to her," Tildie said.

"Let her handle this," he cautioned. "It's not for you to see, okay?" His expression and voice asked for guarantees as he pulled a black video cassette from his pocket. "Paul evidently still likes challenges," he explained, his eyes narrowing. "It's all documented," he said, as he placed it in her hand. "It was more or less a parting gift from my government friends." Dane looked away from her an instant. "I may have mentioned the custody suit and Paul Moore to them a few times in the past couple of weeks." He felt tortured by being close to her and not being able to touch her, comfort her. Yet seeing her face gave him the serenity to tell her what needed to be said. "I know you can't afford anyone in your life right now, so I'll stay away." He swallowed. "I'm supposed to keep a low profile anyway." He'd decided not to ask her to consider Boston until the suit was settled.

"Good luck at Harvard. I know you'll be a wonderful teacher." Her eyes were round and dark. "You'll—"

"Don't, don't say any more," he whispered, leaning closer to her. His mouth brushed her lips. She reached to return his kiss, to tug gently on his lower lip with her teeth. His arms surrounded her and held her so sweetly she thought she would cry. He inhaled the fragrance of her silky hair and the lilac scent on her throat. "Goodbye, Tildie." His lips played over hers, tenderly, memorizing every nuance, every curve and sensation of softness. By the time she opened her eyes he had already turned and walked up the hall, his long shadow nearly reaching her feet. She tried to say goodbye but nothing came out as she fought back tears, which didn't flow until she sat beside a dark, rain-spattered window on the bus back to Columbus that night.

Dane's tears didn't come until a week later. They wetted his cheeks as he sat alone eating a peanut butter and jam sandwich, watching a shamelessly sentimental rerun of *Little House on the Prairie*. Half Pint crawled up onto Michael Landon's lap and curled against his chest seeking fatherly wisdom. "Sometimes things don't turn out the way we want," Pa said, "no matter how hard we wish for them."

JULY PASSED and most of August. Dane concentrated on his work, but even learning a new routine and helping brilliant students didn't occupy his mind and energy. Cambridge was a peaceful, storybook town and Harvard a society created for academic gymnastics, yet Dane Scott remained restless. For weeks he had taken his frustrations to the streets late at night, jogging for miles so he could fall into his empty bed exhausted. On some corners of the campus his lean, shadowy frame was referred to as the Cambridge phantom. But regardless of the miles and the exhaustion, Tildie haunted his nights. The memories of the smell of lilacs, the softness of her skin, and of her snappy retorts bewildered him and made him groan in the darkness. Like the man had said, there was only one cure. So when the break came between the summer session and the fall quarter, Dane Scott bought a plane ticket for Columbus.

He knew he was supposed to keep a low profile and he knew it was too early to see Tildie. There was still a month before the custody hearing, but he had to see her, talk with her, touch her. So after his last class of the summer he didn't leave his classroom until all his exams and projects were graded. He was finished at six in the morning and he couldn't wait any longer for his 9:00 a.m. flight. He rushed to his apartment, tossed a few things in a bag, pulled the Corwin Special out of storage and headed for Columbus. He knew that she wouldn't want to see him, that they would argue. But he was determined to make her see that they belonged together. He'd get her to promise that as soon as the custody case was over, they'd be together.

He anticipated every argument that the attorney could possibly have and formulated a solution. He didn't want to face the lonely consequences of her turning him down. In his quiet moments on campus his only thoughts had been of her, and at times during the day he had thought of things that he could do with the kids. He missed the family that he had nearly had. He wanted nothing more than to be with Tildie and Micki and Jer—and all the racket, bickering and love they would bring him.

He rang the bell of the Upper Arlington house at five in the afternoon. He didn't realize until that moment that he had traveled at record land speeds, and that he was still wearing the same clothes he'd worn the day before.

Tildie's eyes were darker and more vibrant than he remembered. Her lips parted in surprise and turned up slightly at the corners. She wore a long, bib-type denim apron over a soft rose blouse and a darker skirt.

"Hi," she managed almost casually. How many times had she dreamed that he would simply show up on her doorstep and she'd kiss him hello as though he'd just come home from a day's work.

"I know that it's before the court date," he started, "but I wanted to... say hello."

"So you drove over," she said, glancing at the heat waves shimmering on the red hood of the rocketlike Corwin Special. "Cambridge is a long way from Columbus. I heard it was quaint, but I also heard that they have modern conveniences, such as daily flights."

"Too slow," he said. His gaze traveled hungrily over her, soaking in details and sensations of sunshine and lilacs. "I was told to keep a very low profile for a few months," he answered, then, losing his patience, "but I couldn't stay away any longer." It took all his willpower not to gather her up in his arms. "I've been looking at this great old Victorian house in Cambridge—a real family place. I'd like for you to—see it." He rushed on. "It has a big backyard and a garden. It's in a terrific school district and the one Jer would go to needs a good rightfielder who can hit on the baseball team." He looked at her softly pursed lips. "I know what you're going to say. You haven't had your court date yet, you don't want to pack the kids up and move them across the country—"

"Dane—"

"I know you don't want to rush into anything. Me, too," he said, raking his hand through his hair. "I mean, I'm a staid college professor now," he said.

Tildie thought he looked like a very sexy, tortured soul, with his rough unshaven cheeks that she longed to feel against her skin. He looked as though he had stayed up all night. He wore tan slacks that had wrinkled at his hips from too many hours behind a steering wheel and a vanilla-colored dress shirt with the sleeves folded back and a striped tie with the knot pulled down, away from his throat. Seeing him so bewildered and vulnerable nearly made up for her lonely, sleepless nights over the past two months. She loved this man. There was no doubt in her mind.

"I thought a nice proper courtship of several months would be nice," he said, breathing out heavily. "I've always been partial to Christmas weddings. The kids would be off school. We could move..." He didn't want her frown to be accompanied by words, so he rushed on, "Anyway, you have to come to Cambridge because you're already a member of the Greater Boston chapter of the Caucus of Children's Rights. I signed you up for a year."

"That's appropriate, since I'm representing the CCR now," she said with a nod.

"That's great. I knew you'd get the job once they met you." He smiled. "So you could move to Cambridge and represent the group from there," he said. "So will you—"

A squeal of excitement interrupted his question and soon Micki streaked out the front door and launched herself from the front steps. Dane caught the little girl and spun her around in his arms as she wrapped her legs around his middle and hugged his neck.

"Oh, hey, that's what I needed," he said, rubbing Micki's back. "I've really missed you, Micki." He gave her a giant hug. "How's my girl?"

"Are you here to stay? Please say you're here to stay. Are you going back to work at Fun Design?" Micki could hardly get the questions out fast enough.

"Honey, Dane is teaching at Harvard now. We've talked about this before," Tildie cautioned the little girl.

"I have a group of incredibly talented students," Dane said, looking up at Tildie. He missed not having her to talk to. "It's amazing what they know at their age. I'm really not sure what I can teach them."

"Oh, I believe you can pass along some interesting tidbits about space exploration and the world." She tilted her head. "And possibly teach some old-fashioned ethics about those machines circling around up there," she said with certainty. "You'll do great, Professor Scott."

He loved the way she could make him feel so good about himself.

"Since you're a teacher, do you give tests and everything?" Micki piped up.

"Everything," said Dane, smiling. "As a matter of fact I had a stack of exams and projects to grade last night and as soon as I was done this morning, I said to myself, it's time to see Micki." He waited for her giggle. "I've really missed you and Jer."

"And mom, too?" Micki asked.

"Yeah." He lifted his gaze to take in Matilda Moore, and he hoped more than anything that she had missed him, too. But her expression was unrevealing. "Where's Jer?"

"At baseball practice," Dane and Micki answered at the same time and laughed.

"He should be home any minute," Tildie said, trying to keep happy tears from her eyes.

"Did mom tell you about Jer?" Micki asked.

"No, what?" He looked up, concerned.

"My attorney sent Paul a copy of...some evidence that she had received, and after seeing it he agreed to drop the custody suit before it reached court," Tildie explained.

"That's great!" He nodded. "I'm really happy...it worked out."

"Me, too." She had her son and there wasn't anything stopping her from loving her own rocket scientist.

"What's going on?" Jer asked as he walked up the drive. "You must have raced all the way from Cambridge," Jer said, touching the sizzling hood of the red car.

"Dane was in a hurry to ask us something," Tildie said.

"Oh, yeah? Really?" both of the children said at once.

"He would like us—"

"I'd like your mom to marry me."

"And for us to live in Cambridge?" Micki asked.

"Yes." The moment of silence nearly killed him. "You'll like it there, it's pretty and the Red Sox are looking real good for the pennant race this fall," he said to Jer.

"Dane thinks a December wedding would be nice," Tildie added.

"That's four months away!"

"School's going to start in a couple of weeks."

Dane nearly panicked. He didn't know if he could stay in Cambridge if they refused to come. He didn't want to be without them.

"You can make new friends there," he said.

"Transferring in the middle of the year would be the pits." Jer shook his head.

"It's better to get a good start." Tildie nodded wisely.

Dane swallowed hard.

"Moving at Christmastime." Micki made a face.

"Yeah, Micki's new teachers would need more time to get used to her," Jer teased.

"It seems it's unanimous," Tildie said, meeting Dane's bewildered eyes.

"Yeah, we should definitely move before school starts," Jer agreed.

"I want a pink bedroom," Micki put in.

Dane looked from one smiling face to the next and he began to sense a wonderful conspiracy.

"Eloise is coming back home in a couple of weeks, so we'll need a new place to live, anyway." Tildie shrugged, then met his eye. "Is that family-sized Victorian available now?"

"Do you really want to come?"

"Do you really want a houseful of people in a couple of weeks?" Tildie asked. She gave him one last chance to get out of loving her for a lifetime.

"Absolutely." He grinned. "It's much too quiet in Cambridge. I need the three of you."

"Can we eat while we make plans?" Jer asked.

"Sure," Tildie said, laughing.

"I'm going to have the best dad in the whole world," Micki squealed as she tugged on Dane's hand.

Tildie slid easily into Dane's protective, loving arm.

"Don't look so surprised. Did you really think I'd let you get away again without us?" She smiled.

"I hoped not," he said, nuzzling her hair and throat. "You smell wonderful." He breathed in deeply as she circled an arm around his back.

Tildie laughed. "I smell like fried chicken."

"Yeah." He spoke in a sexy tone and growled in her ear. "Delicious."

"Come on in, you two," Micki said, hurrying them along. "We've got plans to make."

"And dinner to eat," Jer said.

"Tell us about Cambridge!"

"Are there any neat girls there?"

The happy quartet set the table and enjoyed a noisy, happy meal, then planned their future together....

EPILOGUE

Merry Christmas Captain Starblazer,
On our first Christmas together we wanted to tell you that we love you very much and we're very glad that we're all together in our new home. We hope that you like what we got you for Christmas. In case you haven't guessed we think you are a real hero.

You were right. The Christmas wedding was wonderful, especially Grandpa Cabe getting lost in traffic after the wedding.

It was very nice meeting Aunt Annie, Uncle Joe and Channa. It's not everyone who brings a chimpanzee to a marriage ceremony. Remember that they invited us to visit their house next summer so we could meet their lion. Merry Christmas.

Love always,
Tildie, Micki and Jer

P.S. I like the baseball spikes very much, dad, I think they would go great with a Carl Yastrzemski bat.

P.P.S. I love my new Star Fleet commandship, dad. You are the best dad and the best toymaker in the world.

ATTRACTIVE, SPACE SAVING BOOK RACK

Display your most prized novels on this handsome and sturdy book rack. The hand-rubbed walnut finish will blend into your library decor with quiet elegance, providing a practical organizer for your favorite hard-or soft-covered books.

Only $9.95

Approximately 16" x 8" when assembled

Assembles in seconds!

To order, rush your name, address and zip code, along with a check or money order for $10.70* ($9.95 plus 75¢ postage and handling) payable to *Harlequin Reader Service*:

Harlequin Reader Service
Book Rack Offer
901 Fuhrmann Blvd.
P.O. Box 1396
Buffalo, NY 14269-1396

Offer not available in Canada.

BKR-1A

*New York and Iowa residents add appropriate sales tax.

Six exciting series for you every month... from Harlequin

Harlequin Romance·
The series that started it all

Tender, captivating and heartwarming...
love stories that sweep you off to faraway places
and delight you with the magic of love.

◆

Harlequin Presents·
Powerful contemporary love stories...as individual as the women who read them

The No. 1 romance series...
exciting love stories for you, the woman of today...
a rare blend of passion and dramatic realism.

◆

Harlequin Superromance®
It's more than romance... it's Harlequin Superromance

A sophisticated, contemporary romance-fiction
series, providing you with a longer,
more involving read...a richer mix of complex plots,
realism and adventure.

Harlequin American Romance™
Harlequin celebrates the American woman...

...by offering you romance stories written about American women, by American women for American women. This series offers you contemporary romances uniquely North American in flavor and appeal.

◆

Harlequin Temptation™
Passionate stories for today's woman

An exciting series of sensual, mature stories of love...dilemmas, choices, resolutions... all contemporary issues dealt with in a true-to-life fashion by some of your favorite authors.

◆

Harlequin Intrigue
Because romance can be quite an adventure

Harlequin Intrigue, an innovative series that blends the romance you expect... with the unexpected. Each story has an added element of intrigue that provides a new twist to the Harlequin tradition of romance excellence.

Harlequin Books·

**For the millions who can't read
Give the Gift of Literacy**

One out of five adults in North America
cannot read or write well enough
to fill out a job application
or understand the directions on a bottle of medicine.

**You can change all this by joining the fight
against illiteracy.**

For more information write to:
Contact, Box 81826, Lincoln, Neb. 68501
In the United States, call toll free: 1-800-228-8813

**The only degree you need
is a degree of caring**

LIT-A-1R